RNICKEL FIERCE VIOLET
BELIEVE
Kalamazoo Magn
ULOUS Popsicle BEL
Everlasting SNICKERDOODLE S
able
Dragonfly HOPE Wonder Zippity
Secret Apple Fritter KALEIDOSCOPE
PLENDIFEROUS Crunch HOPE
FACTOFABULOUS HICC
VIOLET Enchanting Plumb Ador
WHIMSY FIERCE
Sunrise SNICKERDOODLE HOPE
EROUS Dragonfly BITTERSWEET VIOLET
ICCUP Secret
Magical Plumb Adorable SPINDIDD
BELIEVE Wonder Crunch Rebel I L
OODLE STONEBERRY Everlasting SPLEN
Secret I LOVE YOU Magnolia Apple Frit
HOPE Enchanting SERENDIPITY
bel HICCUP SPIN

FEROUS Dragon KEEPER Rebel
Popsicle
PUMPERNICKEL Secret KALEIDOSCOPE PU
Magical KEEPER Magnolia
amazoo BELIEVE Rebel Kalamazoo FAC
RDOODLE STONEBERRY WHIMSY Plumb
E Zippity I LOVE YOU Magnolia KALEIDOS
nch HOPE Enchanting Wonder Zip
JLOUS HICCUP SERENDIPITY
SPINDIDDLY Plumb Ad
Plumb Adorable
inous BISCUIT Apple Fritter SPLE
WHIMSY Secret Everlasti
Crunch Zippity
UMPERNICKEL Magnolia FIERCE VIOLET
RY HOPE I LOVE YOU Enchanting Popsi
Wonder Kalamazoo BITTERSWEET SNI
KALEIDOSCOPE WHIMSY Magical Wonder
BELIEVE Crunch SNICKERDOODLE KALEIDO
ity
YOU Enchanting Secret Plumb Adora

a
SNICKER
of
MAGIC

by NATALIE LLOYD

Scholastic Press / New York

Copyright © 2014 by Natalie Lloyd
Illustrations by Gilbert Ford

Library of Congress Cataloging-in-Publication Data

Lloyd, Natalie, author.
A snicker of magic / by Natalie Lloyd. — First edition.
pages cm
Summary: The Pickles are new to Midnight Gulch,
Tennessee, a town which legend says was once magic —
but Felicity is convinced the magic is still there, and with
the help of her new friend Jonah the Beedle she hopes to
bring the magic back.
ISBN 978-0-545-55270-7 — ISBN 0-545-55270-2 1. Magic —
Juvenile fiction. 2. Single-parent families — Tennessee —
Juvenile fiction. 3. Mothers and daughters — Juvenile
fiction. 4. Friendship — Juvenile fiction. 5. Tennessee —
Juvenile fiction. [1. Magic — Fiction. 2. Family life —
Fiction. 3. Mothers and daughters — Fiction.
4. Friendship — Fiction. 5. Tennessee — Fiction.] I. Title.
PZ7.L7784Sn 2014
813.6 — dc23
2013027779

10 9 8 7 6 5 4   14 15 16 17 18
Printed in the U.S.A.   23
First edition, March 2014
The text was set in Sabon MT.
Book design by Nina Goffi

FOR MOM, DAD,
BRIDGETT, AND CHASE
I LOVE YOU MORE
THAN ALL THE WORDS
IN THE WORLD.

"They say all the magic is gone up out of this place," said Mama.

She looked straight ahead as she drove, past the white beam of our headlights, deep into the night, like she could see exactly what was up ahead of us. I couldn't see anything, though: not a house, not a store, not even an old barking dog. A big fat moon, pale white and lonesome-looking, was our only streetlight. I watched the way the moonlight painted her profile: the dark shadows under her cheekbones, the tight pull of her mouth. I didn't need to see her eyes to know how they'd look: sky blue and beautiful. Full of all the sadness in the world.

"Soooo . . ." I propped my feet up on the dashboard and wiggled my sock-striped toes. "Does that mean there *was* magic here to start with?"

The wind answered before Mama did; it swooshed through the van and flung her blond hair into a cloud of golden whirls and curls. Only my mama could shine like that when the rest of the world was so dark.

"That's what some people say," she told me. And then she stopped clutching the steering wheel so tight and her shoulders relaxed and I knew exactly why: She was about to settle into a good story.

"Midnight Gulch used to be a secret place," Mama said. "The mountain hid the town high-up-away from the rest of the world. And the river surrounded the mountain and kept it safe. And the forest stood up tall around the river and caught all of the town's secrets and songs in its branches." I relaxed into the sound of her voice. Her speaking voice is wonderful, but my mama's story voice is like nothing I've ever heard, like something between a summer breeze and a lullaby. "The town *had* to stay secret, you see, because the people who lived there had magic in their veins."

"Real magic?" I could barely even whisper the word. Just the thought of real magic sent shivers from my nose to my toes. This time it was my heart that answered, a steady drumbeat *yes* inside my chest.

Yes,

Yes,

Yes!

"That's the story they tell," Mama sighed. "They say some people could catch stars in Mason jars. And some people could sing up thunderstorms and some could dance up sunflowers. Some people could bake magic into a pie, make folks fall in love, or remember something good, or forget something bad. Some people had a magic for music. . . ."

Mama's fingers clutched knuckle-white around the steering wheel again. But she kept on telling:

"They could play a song and it would echo through the whole town, and everybody in town, no matter where they were, stood up and danced."

She cleared her throat. "They say some people glowed in the dark. And some people faded when they were sad — first they went colorless, then totally invisible. There are so many stories. . . ."

"And this magic town is the same town where you grew up?" I asked.

She nodded.

"Then why the hayseed would you ever leave a place like that?"

"All the magic was gone by the time I lived there. There was only a two-lane road and a traffic light that always stayed green. I figured that meant the magic had moved on out. Figured I had to move on, too, if I wanted to see any of it."

"Did you ever?"

"I see you." Mama smiled. "And I see Frannie Jo sleeping right behind me."

She glanced up in the rearview mirror at my little sister, who was snuggled up with our dog, Biscuit. Both of them were snoring sweetly, cuddled against all the clothes that we'd piled in the way-back seat. Frannie's nearly six, but people think she's even younger than that because she's so small. She blended in easy with the books and blankets and clothes.

"I got all the magic I ever need here with me," Mama sighed.

I smiled at her words. I wanted them to be true, but I knew Frannie and I didn't have the kind of magic necessary to get rid of Mama's sad. But maybe that kind of magic did exist somewhere. Maybe magic was just a few miles away.

My heart fluttered again. *Yes.*

Mama glanced up at the lonesome moon. The moon glowed down over her face like it was very happy to be noticed.

"I can't imagine anybody or anything lonelier than that midnight moon," said Mama. "That'd be awful — sitting up against ten thousand stars without arms to reach out and hold a single one."

For a time, we didn't say anything else. We just listened to the van *per-clunkity-clunk*, *per-clunkity-clunk* down the curvy road. And I listened to my heart, still singing *Yes, Yes, Yes* to all the questions I wasn't asking.

Suddenly, the *per-clunkity* gave way to a *boom-clackity* as we crossed over a long, narrow bridge. The crickets sang a little louder as we crossed that river. The moon shone a little bit brighter. The night air smelled like baking cookies. And my heart drummed steady: *Yes, Yes, Yes*. Good things happen when my heart says yes, especially if nobody else around me is saying much of anything at all.

Mama slowed the van and leaned her arm across me. "Take a look, June Bug. We're here."

She pointed to a sign that somebody'd painted up and shoved sideways into the hillside. A flickering spotlight shone up at the words:

MIDNIGHT GULCH, TENNESSEE
a proper place to call home

"Used to read different, before they painted over it," Mama said. "It used to say —"

"A *magical* place to call home," I whispered. I didn't need her to tell me. I could already see the word *magical* shining as bright as sunshine letters, even through all those layers of paint. I could see other words, too.

The stars above us spelled out:

Summer

Wonder

Homespun

And the yellow lines caught in our headlights curved into these words:

Stay

Listen

See

I heard a poem tangled up inside a rush of the midnight songs the crickets were whistling:

Finally,

At last,

Forever, and now,
Here you are.

I didn't say another word to Mama that night, but I could feel something good even then: the *YES* in my heart, the swirling-around in my belly, the prickly tingling all the way from the freckle on my finger to the tip of my pinky toe. That much wonderful could only mean one thing:

There was *still* magic in Midnight Gulch.

This is how I turned it loose. . . .

Mama liked to say that us Pickles were nomads. Sweet gypsies. Adventure seekers. But as we zoomed toward our first day of school at Stoneberry Elementary, I didn't feel adventurous at all. Traveling around so much had us all tired out. Mama most of all, even though she didn't realize it.

I saw the proof when she glanced at me in the rearview mirror. Her eyes used to be as bright blue as a summer sky, but now they looked like jeans faded from too many tumbles through a washing machine. "Are you nervous about today, girls?"

"A little," I sighed.

"A little," Frannie Jo mumbled. She clutched her small blue suitcase tighter against her chest and leaned against me. Since we never knew when Mama might wake us in the middle of night ready to bolt out of town, Frannie liked to keep a suitcase packed full of all her worldly treasures, the special stuff she didn't want left behind.

"Well, I have a good feeling about today." Mama nodded. "Anything can happen in a town like this."

"Does that mean we're going to stay a while?" I asked. I heard Frannie Jo's breath catch. Maybe people can't grow roots the same as trees do, but we both needed a place to dig in and grow some good memories. And so did Mama.

She only managed a shadow of a smile as she softly answered, "We'll see."

At exactly that moment, I saw my first word of the day:

Believe

The letters were made of melted sunshine. They dripped down the window glass, warm and tingly against our faces. *Believe* is a powerful word to see and to say. But that morning, I felt it. And feeling it was the best of all. I knew something wonderful was about to happen to me. I didn't know what, or why, or how. But I believed.

Frannie Jo and I stood on the sidewalk of Stoneberry Elementary School, waving to Mama as she drove off in the Pickled Jalapeño. We named our van the Jalapeño because it was green-brown and dented up and droopy-looking, kind of like a rotten pepper. And since it's just us Pickles driving around in it, the Pickled Jalapeño is what it became.

The Pickled Jalapeño made a *per-clunkity-clunk, per-clunkity-clunk* noise as it disappeared down the foggy road. I squinted my eyes at the cloud of exhaust billowing out the tailpipe and saw three smoke-colored words:

Spunkter
Sumpter
Siffle-miffle

Words that hover around cars or trains or boats or planes never make much sense. At least they don't make much sense to *me*. I'm not sure if that's how it works for other people. I know I can't be the only word collector in the whole world, but I've never met anybody else who has the knack.

As Frannie slipped her hand in mine, I felt something scratch against me. When I looked down, I realized she had a bunch of neon-colored Band-Aids stuck down the inside of her arm. That's why we keep Band-Aids hidden from Frannie Jo; she uses them like stickers.

"Hey." I squeezed her hand. "You ready for a new adventure?"

Frannie shrugged a shoulder.

I concentrated on the words shimmering around Frannie's blond ponytail:

Biscuit

Dump truck

Apple fritter

Frannie Jo was concentrating on her most favorite things: the name of our dog and the vehicle she aspires to drive when she grows up and also her most favorite food. That's her trick to keep tears from spilling out.

Sure enough, Frannie's chin started trembling. She nuzzled against my arm and blinked up at me with watery blue eyes. "Will you carry me?"

I sighed and hugged her close to my side. "You're too old

for people to still be carrying you around so much. Want me to catch a poem for you?"

Frannie nodded quickly. She sniffled, but she didn't cry. Frannie's a brave little Pickle. She leaned in closer to my side as we walked through the doors of the schoolhouse. I kept my arm locked tight around her shoulder. The world's got to be a scary place when you're no bigger than a bean sprout.

You'd think we were both invisible the way the big kids kept bumping into us. But I knew we weren't, because I could hear our sneakers singing squeaky songs across the tile floors. My sneakers were covered with the words I didn't have room for in my blue book. Those same sneakers had walked over the sand and grass and gravel of six different states. Moving around so much had us all tuckered out, and that's a fact. But at least the world is full of words to hold and see and keep. Frannie likes hearing words as much as I like finding them.

"Hurry!" Frannie squealed.

I made a big show of catching invisible words in my hands and putting them in my mouth and chewing on them. I knew my word-catching charade wasn't the best way to make a fast friend at Stoneberry Elementary School. But it was the only way I could think of to make my sister feel better. And I think if you're lucky, a sister is the same as a friend, but better. A sister is like a super-forever-infinity friend.

"Sticky as gumballs," I said, working my jaws up and down. Frannie smiled at me. I cleared my throat and declared:

"Per-clunkity-clunk, per-clunkity-clunk,
The Pickled Jalapeño keeps its heart in its trunk!"

Two girls in line at the pencil machine swiveled around to stare as we passed by. Any shimmer of confidence I'd stored up began to fizzle at exactly that moment. First impressions aren't my specialty, even in the best of times. And yelling crazy poem words in the hallway when you're the new girl in a new school is definitely not the best of times. But I soldiered on, lowering my voice just barely:

"Tipple-tap, tipple-tee, tipple-top, tipple-tat,
The old man keeps his heart in the brim of his hat.
Ratta-tat, ratta-tat, ratta-tat, ratta-tee,
Frannie Jo wears her heart on the edge of her sleeve."

Frannie swung my hand back and forth and shook her hips in rhythm to my words. She'd worn a yellow tutu over her jeans, part of last year's Halloween costume. The glitter on the skirt sparkled and sparked under the fluorescent lights as we tromped down the hallway.

We stopped in front of a first-grade classroom that smelled like crayons and peanut butter sandwiches.

I thought Frannie'd skippity-jump on into the classroom right away, but she hesitated. She chewed on her lip and fluttered her eyelashes in such a way that I thought she might be tearful again. But I didn't see sadness when she looked up at me. I saw determination. "I'm tired of first days," she declared.

I nodded. "Me, too. But people say this town used to be something magical. Maybe it'll be magical for us, too; Mama will like it here and so will we."

Frannie's eyes sparkled. "This is home?"

"Maybe," I sighed, and I nudged her through the doorway. Frannie pranced into the room with her chin high and her ponytail swinging. The words swirling around her head were all spunky words now:

Popsicle

Paper star

Poppy-seed muffin

Those were good words, bright and tasty. So I didn't feel so bad about leaving her.

I walked down the hall, concentrating on my squish-popping shoes. Thousands of words swirled through the hallways of Stoneberry Elementary, so I didn't look up. I didn't have time for word collecting just then because I had to save every last speck of my energy for class.

I'd been in enough new schools to know what would happen next. A teacher would probably ask me to stand up and say my name and where I was from. And I *would* stand up, but instead of saying anything, I would most likely just keep right on standing and staring. My mouth would stay wide open, but the words would never come.

Here's the thing: I see words everywhere, all around me, all the time. I collect them. I think about them. I say them fine if I'm talking to Mama or Frannie Jo or my aunt Cleo. But words are a mess when I try to say them to more than one person at a time. They melt on my tongue like snowflakes. They disappear right off the edge of my lips, and I end up standing there blinking, openmouthed, like the Queen of Dorkville.

That's how it had always happened before, at least. But Midnight Gulch used to be a magical place, so maybe this first day would be different. I stared down at my wordy-sneakers and practiced: "My name is Felicity Juniper Pickle. I'm from here and there and all across the world."

Because that sounded better than the truth: I'm Felicity Juniper Pickle and I'm from Nowhere in Particular. I sighed. Moving around so much should have made me bold and happy and free, I guess. Strange how I only ever felt lost.

I didn't know that the Beedle was watching me even then. I would find out soon enough, though. In Midnight Gulch, the Beedle was always watching.

My introduction to the sixth-grade class at Stoneberry Elementary went every bit as horrifically as I'd expected. As soon as I opened my mouth to speak, I saw these words shoot up like rockets from bookshelves in the back of the classroom:

Dork

Lonely

Loser

Clutzerdoodle

I tried to blink the words away, but they only ballooned up bigger. After two painful minutes of silence, I managed to mumble, "My name is Flea . . ." And the same girls I'd seen earlier at the pencil machine, who were now sitting in the front row of my classroom, giggled. So much for a new beginning.

As I stared down at my wordy-sneakers and took a stumbling step toward my seat, two hands pressed gently against my shoulders, freezing me in place.

I looked up into the smiling face of my new homeroom

teacher, Miss Divinity Lawson. Miss Lawson was most assuredly the youngest teacher I'd ever had. She was the prettiest, too. Her hair tumbled down her shoulders in long, loopy curls. Put a crown on Divinity Lawson's head, and she'd look just like a storybook princess. "May I have the honor of introducing you to the class, Felicity?" she asked. I managed to nod.

Miss Lawson kept her hands on my shoulders while she talked about me. She even made me sound almost interesting.

"Felicity has been on some marvelous adventures. She's lived in six different states with her family!"

I was nearly smiling by the time I settled into the empty seat in the front row, right beside a boy doodling chickens on his notebook. There hadn't been enough magic in the room to stop my stutters, or to make me feel confident in front of a room full of people. But I was *smiling*, just barely. Which meant Midnight Gulch was already different from all the other places I'd been.

Miss Lawson walked to the chalkboard and scrawled out a familiar word:

Stoneberry

Which didn't make much sense. Even I knew the name of the school, and it was only my first day. Everybody else had already been in class a few weeks, so surely they knew the name of their own educational institution. Next, Miss Lawson took a stick of yellow chalk and cut a squeaky line down the center of the word, making it two:

And that got me to thinking about the spider egg that Mama found in the way-back seat of the Pickled Jalapeño. None of us knew anything about spiders or their eggs, and while we didn't have anything against them, Mama didn't want them crawling through the van or nesting in her hair. So she squashed the egg with her rhinestone flip-flop and we soon discovered that's probably the worst thing she could have done. Because about a million baby spiders exploded out of the egg and scampered across the backseat. Mama screamed and whopped at them with her flip-flop, but I think most of them got away. If they're still in the van, we don't see them very often. Spiders don't make much fuss.

When Miss Lawson made two words out of *Stoneberry*, it became a spider word to me. Suddenly, those two words split apart and new words creep-crawled out of them, across the walls and under the door and out into the hallway:

Ton

TurboBoy

Note

Ruby

Ruby's the only word I wanted to keep. I pulled my shoe up in my lap and scrawled R-U-B-Y across the toe. I hoped somebody out in the hall snatched up *TurboBoy*. *TurboBoy* wasn't a real word, as far as I knew. But it sure did sound good.

"Here's the truth of it!" Miss Lawson hollered, spinning around to face us all. Her sudden burst of energy surprised me so much that I jumped. But nobody else seemed to notice. I guess they'd had a few weeks to get used to Miss Lawson's energy. Even though she stood tall and smiled, I could see:

Jitters

Impressions

Impressionable souls . . .

STEP LIVELY

All those words were blooming up like flowers out of her glossy black hair.

Miss Lawson said, "Every person you will ever meet, and every place you will ever go, and every building you set your foot in — has a story to tell."

"In fact!" she exclaimed. "One of my most favorite stories happened in *this exact place*." Miss Lawson's eyes sparkled in such a pretty way when she spoke. I wished I could put words together as easy as she could. Everything about her seemed bright, even her clothes. She wore a polka-dot sweater and a green skirt that swirled like a lily pad when she spun toward us.

She walked across the front of the classroom while she talked, her purple heels *click-clack*ing against the tiles. "As I'm sure you know, Midnight Gulch, Tennessee, is famous for two things: The first is Dr. Zook's Famous Ice Cream Factory. For those of you who are new to town" — Miss Lawson winked down at me — "you'll be happy to know there are forty-five marvelous and mysterious flavors of ice cream for you to try. Cake flavored, bacon flavored. You name it, Dr. Zook's makes it."

I might have been in Midnight Gulch for less than twenty-four hours, but I already knew about Dr. Zook's Ice Cream. I knew because Aunt Cleo's freezer was packed full of it. Cleo's partial to the Chocolate Chip Pork Rind flavor.

"But!" Miss Lawson clapped her hands. "Midnight Gulch isn't only famous for ice cream. Midnight Gulch is famous because it used to be a magical place. And the most magical people who lived here, the most famous duo ever to call Midnight Gulch their home, were the Brothers Threadbare."

Yes,

      Yes,

           Yes!

I pressed my hand hard against my ribs so my drumbeat-yes heart might calm down enough for me to hear the story. But it wasn't just my heart screaming *Yes!* this time. Even though I was certain I'd never heard anything about those magical brothers before, my ears tingled as though I'd been told some wonderful secret.

I saw one word appear across the wall of the classroom, the letters even taller than Miss Divinity Lawson, stretching all the way from the floor to the ceiling:

THREADBARE

I heard a steady chorus of yawns and sighs, most likely coming from people who'd heard the story once or twice or ten thousand times. But somehow I knew, before I even heard a single word, that this story would matter to me.

"Many years ago," Miss Lawson continued, "this schoolhouse didn't exist and this land was only an empty hillside. And on this very hillside" — she stomped her high-heeled shoe on the tiles to make sure we understood — "on September 15, 1910, the Brothers Threadbare had their famous duel.

"Like most people in Midnight Gulch, the Brothers Threadbare were simple, easygoing folks . . . who just so happened to have a little magic in their veins." She grinned. "Their real names were Stone and Berry Weatherly. The Weatherlys were farm boys, the same as some of you."

Miss Lawson crossed her arms over her chest. I wondered if her heart was pounding as loud as mine.

"Every family in Midnight Gulch had a different kind of magic. The Weatherly Magic was a particularly wonderful kind, though, because their magic had to do with music. Whenever Stone and Berry played their songs, the whole world seemed to dance. At the first strum of Berry Weatherly's banjo, the wind would roar over the valleys. The wildflowers would wave from the hillsides. The trees would shake their limbs and clap their leaves. When Stone played his guitar, the clouds swirled into a thousand different shapes: cloud lions, cloud tigers, thunderheads that ran like wild horses across the sky."

Desks squeaked and popped as people leaned up in their seats, trying to get as close as they could to the story Miss Lawson was telling. If the right person tells a story, I guess it doesn't matter how many times you've heard it. Your

19

heart still hears it brand-new. And Miss Lawson was an A+ storyteller.

"And the townspeople!" She clasped her hands together. "They *all* took to dancing whenever the Weatherly boys played music; their wicked, wonderful, magical music.

"Even when the Brothers Threadbare were out of town, doing shows in other cities, you could hear their music in Midnight Gulch. The music got caught in the trees and echoed all through town and through the woods. People danced down Main Street all day, every day, back then. They couldn't help it. They say that Midnight Gulch was the happiest place in the world, back when the magic was still here. Back before the Brothers Threadbare left town and never came back."

One of the pencil-machine girls tucked a swirly-twirl of blond hair behind her ear and asked, "Where'd they go?"

"Excellent question." Miss Lawson clapped excitedly. "At first, the Weatherlys left town together, on a tour. They traveled from the country to the city, hoping they could make enough money from their music to send back to the farm. They always started their concerts with a few magic tricks. Anybody with magic in their veins can do simple magic tricks, so that was easy enough. But soon, the brothers realized people were more interested in their magic tricks than in their singing. So they focused on the magic: They charmed mountain lions and made fire puppets. They flung handfuls of coal dust into the air and watched the ashes turn to butterflies. They were young and handsome and talented. People couldn't get enough of them. But sadly," Miss Lawson sighed, "their fame and fortune became a dividing line between them."

She tapped the line on the chalkboard again. "The brothers became jealous of one another. They got so jealous, in fact, that they finally decided to have a duel. Whoever won, they decided, could keep all the money and fame and fortune they'd earned. But the loser would be cursed forever with a wandering heart. The loser would leave town, never return, never settle down. And *never* do another magic trick."

The room felt especially icy all of a sudden, like somebody had turned the air conditioner to "freeze out." Miss Lawson felt it, too; she leaned against her desk and rubbed her arms.

"The brothers met right on this hillside," she sighed. "Newspapers from seven different states sent reporters to cover the event. At nine fifteen in the morning, on September fifteenth, the Brothers Threadbare began their duel. Their magic was wild and powerful by then. So they dueled for three whole days: sweating, shouting, always trying to outdo the other. Finally, it was Berry who cast the winning spell.

"And poor Stone Weatherly." She circled his name on the board. "He left town, cursed forever with a wandering heart. Nobody knows what became of him.

"Soon after he left, Berry discovered that, without his brother, his magic didn't work anyhow. Eventually, he disappeared from town, too. After that, people got restless and sad. They said Midnight Gulch used to be their favorite secret, their favorite place . . . but Midnight Gulch didn't feel like home anymore. People started leaving, breaking apart from their families and heading out in search of what they'd lost."

By this time, I had the fabric of my T-shirt all bunched up in my fist. I was even trembling, just a little bit. Because I knew what it felt like to have a family broken apart. And I knew what it was like to always be searching for a home.

"There were no more songs caught in the trees," Miss Lawson continued. "No more people dancing down Main Street. Even folks with other types of magic started using it less and less and less. And before people knew it, the magic was gone completely. And Midnight Gulch became the same as any other town."

I closed my eyes and tried to picture the kind of town Miss Lawson described — a place where people stayed in one place. Where families stayed together. I'd give anything to find a magic like that.

"And so," Miss Lawson said, "when the town built this school, they named it after both of the brothers — Stoneberry. I think it's time we had a special event to commemorate our tragic namesakes."

Miss Lawson spun around and pulled a white chart down over the word she'd hacked apart. She turned on a projector that whirred as loud as a helicopter.

These were the words lit up on the screen:

THE STONEBERRY DUEL
SEPTEMBER 15 AT 9:15AM
in the front-end auditorium (not the back-end auditorium)
(because that one is still flooded)
FREE Ice Cream!   FREE Funnel Cakes!
FREE Cotton Candy!

"Except we won't duel with magic tricks. The Weatherlys took all the magic with them when they left town. We still have the Beedle of course." She winked at us. "Which is just as wonderful, if you ask me."

Before I could ask her what in the world was a beedle, Miss Lawson said: "Our duel will be a talent show. You can sing, play a musical instrument, share an art project, shoot free throws —"

The blond pencil-machine girl gasped and waved her hand in the air. "I can turn fourteen cartwheels in a row!"

Of course she could.

"That's the spirit!" Miss Lawson clapped. And then she tilted her head and looked down at me, at the blue book on my desk. "Maybe some of you write poems, or stories. You are welcome to share those, too. Your words are pure magic, after all. Your words are necessary enchantments."

My heart agreed with her and so did the rest of me: from the tip of my ponytail to the inked-up toe of my sneaker. Plus, I liked the sound of free cotton candy. I thought of how that might look, if words spun up out of a candy machine:

Sugar-flossed

Pink and sweet

Love was the only word I'd ever found with a flavor to it; *love* tasted as sweet as cotton candy when I said it. When I thought about love and cotton candy, I thought about Mama and Frannie Jo and Biscuit and my aunt Cleo, too, who was most likely sitting at home watching soap operas and smoking a cigarette. She claims this is how she solves the world's problems. I love her for that reason and a thousand more besides. *Love* is too heavy a word, though, which is exactly why I don't like to say it.

"Any questions?" Miss Lawson asked.

The boy on my other side spoke up for the first time. He asked, "Why'd they call themselves the Brothers Threadbare?" His voice crackled like an old set of radio speakers. Or maybe like a thundercloud that rumbled and mumbled but couldn't quite work itself into a full-blown storm. If I had a voice that sounded as cool as that, I'd never shut up.

"That's a fabulous question, Toast." Miss Lawson grinned. "But I want you guys to figure out the answer on your own." She turned off the projector. "Sign-up sheet for the Duel is on the door. Step lively!"

Nobody moved.

Miss Lawson sighed. "Did I mention the winner gets one hundred dollars cash-money and a year's supply of Dr. Zook's?"

A wild stampede of students stormed past my desk and penciled their names on the sheet.

Miss Lawson clapped her hands and bounced up on her toes. "We'll duel all afternoon and make Stone and Berry very proud indeed."

Realizing this could very well be my opportunity to make my first friend in Midnight Gulch, I smiled at Toast and said, "That's a fancy robo-chicken you drew."

He sighed, and pushed his glasses up on his nose. But he never looked back at me. "It's a *space llama*," he thunder-mumbled. "Not a *chicken*." And then he moped up to the sign-up sheet, scribbled something down, and wandered out into the hallway.

This is a fact I know to be true, thanks to all my world-weary travels: Making new friends, in a new place, when you're the new girl, is harder than fractions.

The bell *bing-a-ling*ed through the speakers, and kids ran down the hall so fast you'd think the school was on fire. I stood up slowly, held my blue book against my chest, and walked to the list on the door. So many names, all smudged and spar-kling. Here's the crazy part: My heart told me to sign my name. But my head told me that I'd only make an idiot out of myself. Sometimes I daydreamed about sharing my words with people; I wanted to string them together until they became poems. I wanted to stir them into stories. But I'd learned the hard way that the words I caught were for me, and nobody else. My words would come out a mess if I tried to say them.

At my last school, in Kentucky, I tried. I wrote a paper called "Great Farm Artists of Kentucky" and my teacher enjoyed it so much that she asked me to read in front of the whole school at our weekly assembly. I managed to say my name fine, but in my introduction, I accidentally said "Great Arm Fartists of Kentucky" on account of being so nervous.

And you'd think *fartists* was the funniest word that had ever been spoken, because people started laughing so hard that the bleachers in the gym shook. Suddenly, the skin above my mouth got cold and sweaty. My nose hairs started tingling. My vision blurred around the edges. One of the eighth-grade girls sitting in the front row pointed to my face and laughed, probably because she saw my mustache of sweat.

That was possibly the worst three minutes and twenty-four seconds of my life. For six weeks after that, right up until the day we moved to Tennessee, people made fart noises when I walked down the hall. When I finally told Mama about it, her solution was the same as every other time I'd had a problem at school: She said it was time for a new beginning. So we packed up the Jalapeño and zoomed out of town. And while leaving all your problems behind and starting over sounds like a fine solution, it never really worked for me. My heart's a lot like Frannie Jo's blue suitcase: I can't seem to help packing up all the bad memories and taking them with me no matter where I go.

So I would never, nohow, no way, share my words again.

As I pushed my way out into the hall, a wad of paper whopped me in the forehead.

I might have walked off and left it there if I hadn't looked down and seen so many words spinning around the paper, thin as wire rings around a clay planet. The paper had a noise to it, too. Most words don't sound until they hit the air. But the paper hummed like an electric wire, right up until the second I touched it. I fanned it open and read:

Dear Flea,

I sighed and shook my head. I might as well have stood up and introduced myself by saying, "Hello, my name is Dog Tick."

Meet me at the yellow picnic table in the back of the playground.
Not the yellow table covered in bird poop but the other one.
Code word: PUMPERNICKEL
Your time has come, Felicity Juniper Pickle.

Sincerest regards,
The Beedle

LONELY

LONELY

The word slithered across the cafeteria table, which didn't surprise me at all. *Lonely* had followed me around for as long as I could remember. I never caught that stupid word in my blue book, but it kept showing up anyway. I knew it didn't make much sense to see *lonely* in a place like the Stoneberry cafeteria, because there was a constant clatter of noise: forks and spoons clanging, lunch trays smacking down against the tables, and people yelling things at each other like "Save me a seat." There were hundreds of people in there, or at least fifty, so I shouldn't have been lonely.

But there it was. I'm fairly certain *lonely*'s most natural habitat is a school cafeteria.

I tried to ignore it. I settled into the last seat at a corner table and took a tiny bite of my apple slice. Just as I figured, the apple wasn't sweet. Some words have a taste, and *lonely* is one of them. It doesn't matter if you're eating apples or

28

chicken fingers or peanut butter cookies — once you see *lonely*, everything tastes like sand.

I pushed the tray away and pulled my blue book out of my backpack. I caught some of the other words I saw skittering across the room:

Pocket

Bubble

Cage

Confine

Isolate

"Felicity!"

I stopped writing. I could have sworn I heard somebody yell my name. I knew my ears must have made it up, though. Nobody in that school remembered my name, probably. Except for Frannie Jo and Miss Lawson.

And some character called the Beedle.

I slipped the Beedle's note from the pocket of my hoodie and flattened it out over the table.

When the note first whopped me in the forehead, I figured somebody was playing a joke on me. Had to be. What if the Beedle was fake, and once I ran outside and found the bird-poopless table, all I really found was a bunch of kids standing in a circle laughing at my idiot stupidity? But even Miss Lawson had said the Beedle was the most magical thing in Midnight Gulch. I needed magic like that, the kind that made people want to stay in one place. The kind that made people want to stay together.

My shoulders slumped as I thought about Mama and what she might be doing right then. Her shift didn't start until late in the afternoon, which meant she had all day to roam around in the Pickled Jalapeño. That's exactly what she'd be doing, too, just roaming. That's all she ever wanted to do. She couldn't stop.

I tried not to think about what I'd do if she up and decided to go without me.

"Felicity!"

I did a quick glance around the room. Nobody was looking in my direction.

LONELY crawled out from underneath my tray.

I slammed my hand down fast and hard against it, as if it were some pesky bug I could smash. The sound was so loud that the kids at the table beside me stopped chattering and looked over at me. I didn't look back at them, but my cheeks felt warm under the weight of their stares. I pulled my hood up over my head and pretended not to notice.

Fact: I'd give away every word I'd ever collected to have a friend. Just one. Maybe it's impossible to make a friend unless you stay in a place long enough to memorize somebody's name. I doubted I'd ever get to find out. It'd take a miracle to make a bunch of gypsy Pickles finally settle down. A big miracle.

Or a little bit of magic.

Before I knew it, the day was over and I was on my way to the playground to find a mysterious someone called a Beedle. As I rounded the swing set and made my way toward the tables circled around the edge of the field, the part of me that wasn't half afraid was half excited. Until I found the bird-poopless table.

And then all of me was confused.

"Uh . . . the Beedle?" I asked. And then I immediately felt stupid for asking, because nothing about this kid looked like a Beedle. I hoped a character called the Beedle would at least have a cape and a mask and a mustache that twirled into curlicues at the edges. I expected a dastardly villain of some sort.

But the boy sitting at the bird-poopless table looked . . . normal. He was reading the newspaper and twirling a red pen in his fingers. He had narrow shoulders and a head full of messy-spiky blond hair that reminded me of a crown. He didn't look at me.

"Pumpernickel?" I whispered.

The boy glanced up then. His eyes were the greenest green I'd ever seen, like somebody had taken a neon marker and colored them in just before I walked up to him and called him a Beedle.

He sighed. "I can't believe I'm about to do this."

I glanced around nervously. "Do what?"

He folded his newspaper and smiled at me. My heart kicked *YES!* as strong as a mule kick. My heart had never said yes over a smile before.

"Most folks call me Jonah Pickett," he said. "That's what you should call me, too, from here on out."

He lowered his voice to a whisper. "But I'm the Beedle, too, sometimes, to those who need me. You definitely need the Beedle, Flea. You got time to talk?"

"Not exactly." I shuffled the heavy backpack strap around my shoulder. I wished I had time to talk, though. My heart seemed to like Jonah Pickett an awful lot. I wanted to find out why. But I did *not* want to be left behind at Stoneberry Elementary School. Mama's shift at the ice-cream factory wasn't over until midnight and Aunt Cleo drove like she'd just spilled hot coffee in her lap.

"I don't want to miss my bus," I said, surprised by how easy my words came out. "And my sister will start screech-ing something awful if I'm not on the bus before she is."

"Which bus?" The Beedle cocked his head at me.

"Bus 5548 — Day —"

"Grissom!" Jonah hollered. "Day Grissom's my bus driver, too. Since you're new here, I'll lead the way."

Instead of standing up as I expected, Jonah Pickett backed out from underneath the table in a motorized wheelchair. He clicked a button on the armrest, then clutched a handheld gear and sped forward, bumping across the playground so fast that I had to take extra-long steps to keep up with him. When we got to Bus 5548, Jonah zoomed around to the back of the vehicle and knocked his fist twice on the side of the bus. A metal lift lowered, clanging as it hit the sidewalk.

"Hop on," Jonah said to me. And then he knocked twice on the side of the bus again and yelled, "There's two of us, Day! Beam us up!"

"*Yeeeee-up!*" somebody hollered back.

The lift whirred as it lifted us off the ground. Once I stepped into the aisle behind Jonah, the lift folded up into the bus with a:

Clang

Boom

Pffff

"Thanks, Day." Jonah waved toward the front of the bus.

Our bus driver, Day Grissom, looked the way I would imagine Santa Claus looked if Santa forgot to trim his beard and got real skinny and started wearing plaid shirts and overalls. Day Grissom saluted us in the rearview mirror. Then he turned up the radio and bopped his shaggy head to the rhythm of the song playing: a feisty tune full of banjos and guitars that had a dancing beat to it. Bluegrass music, Aunt Cleo's favorite.

As I slid onto the seat, I saw Frannie Jo climb on the bus. The little girl holding Frannie's hand chattered as fast as a songbird, but I could tell Frannie wasn't listening. Her eyes darted frantically around the bus until she saw me waving. She smiled at me and waved back and settled into the seat beside her new friend. The words swirling around their hands were snappy:

Snickerdoodle

Dump truck

Alphabet soup

I let out a happy sigh of sweet relief. Frannie was already making friends in Midnight Gulch. Maybe the magic was working fine, for one of us. "Your sister looks like you," Jonah said. "Different hair color is all."

"Frannie has Mama's hair color. I have my dad's red hair." My throat got tight, but this time it wasn't my nervousness. My throat always closes up that way when I talk about Roger Pickle, so I changed the subject.

"So," I said. "You gonna tell me why the hayseed you call yourself a Beedle and what that has to do with me?"

"Shhh," Jonah said as the bus rocked us side to side. "Most people don't know I'm the Beedle. That's my business moniker, and it *has* to stay secret."

I liked *moniker*. The word dangled monkeylike down from the ceiling.

Jonah said, "I figured, considering what I need to tell you, it was best to go ahead and mention . . . pumpernickel.

But only like four people in the whole world know about my alias. You've got to keep it all secret. Okay?"

There were approximately fifty-seven questions sitting on the tip of my tongue about the Beedle, but the one I asked was: "Why would you tell me an important secret if you don't know me?"

Jonah shrugged. "Maybe because I know what we got in common. My family's busted all to pieces right now, too."

My throat felt tight again. "My family's . . . busted?"

"My dad's not here, either, not right now. He's a soldier. He's been deployed for eleven months and fourteen days."

"All we have in common is the 'not here' part," I said. "My dad isn't deployed. He's just gone for a while. Work stuff." My voice broke a little bit over the words. I cleared my throat and said, "He'll catch up with us eventually, though."

"Do you miss him?" Jonah asked.

I nodded.

"Then we have that in common, too. And I've moved around a bunch, same as you. We've been in Midnight Gulch for a few years. My dad grew up here. But before that, I lived all over the place."

I narrowed my eyes at Jonah the Beedle. "How do you know so much about me? My family just moved here yesterday."

"My mom does your aunt Cleo's hair," Jonah said, taking special notice of the too-long bangs hanging down over my eyes. "She does everybody's hair in Midnight Gulch.

People tell her all sorts of things. Mom says you'd be amazed what people tell you when you know how to give a proper shampoo. She'll snip those bangs for you."

"Maybe," I said. But maybe not. I felt hidden behind my bangs and I liked the feeling.

"Mom told me to search you out when you showed up at Stoneberry. But even if she hadn't, I would have tracked you down the minute I saw you staring at the sign-up sheet on Miss Lawson's door. Because my know-how kicked in."

And then he smiled as if he'd just handed me a Christmas present. As if the words he said made perfect sense. "What's a . . . *know-how*?" I asked.

Jonah leaned in close to me and said, "It's not easy to explain . . . but I got this *way* about me. I know how to fix what's ailing people. My granny's the one who first called it my know-how. I see something wrong. I know how to make it right. Before Granny passed on over, she made me promise I'd never waste my know-how."

"I'm sorry she . . . passed on over." I clutched my blue book close to my heart. "I'm sorry she died."

"Died?" Jonah laughed. "She didn't die. Granny Effie's a bounty hunter. She passed on over the state line to track down some rascal who stole money from Trixie's Tanning Salon. She'll be back soon enough. But what matters now is *you* — something big is bothering you. And lucky for you, I know how to make it right."

Jonah's face was so close to mine that I could count the small cluster of freckles across his nose. Ten freckles, that's all. Just a small constellation. His eyes looked even greener up close.

First thought: I hope I don't have anything crusty dangling from my nose.

Second thought: Jonah the Beedle might be the only person I've ever met who's as weird as me.

"Okay, then." I scooted back in the seat just a little bit. "What's your *know-how* over me?"

Jonah smiled triumphantly. "It's the Duel. That's when the know-how first stirred up, when you were staring at the sign-up sheet on Miss Lawson's door. Felicity Pickle, I'm going to help you win the talent show."

I gripped the seat in front of me. "That is a spectacularly bad idea."

"It is?" Jonah's smile faded. He raked his fingers through his blond hair. "Are you sure?"

I nodded. "I appreciate your . . . know-how. But did you hear me today when I tried to introduce myself to Miss Lawson's classroom? I got so nervous I nearly upchucked. Besides that, I have no talent."

"Everybody has talent." Jonah gave me a searching look.

I shook my head. "There's not much I'm talented at. Except climbing trees. And I can drink a milk shake real fast and not get brain freeze."

I lowered my voice to a whisper and said, "And I like words; I collect them. I like poems, songs, stories . . . everything. But words never sound right when I try to string them together and say them out loud. They're just for me to keep."

Jonah's forehead crinkled. "Explain."

Since Jonah'd told me his secret, I figured it was okay to tell him mine. "I've always seen words," I said. "I see them as clearly as I see you. Sometimes they have wings and sometimes tap shoes and sometimes zebra stripes."

That sounded ridiculous when I said it, so I hushed. But Jonah didn't laugh at me. "Keep going," he said.

"Sometimes I see words hovering around people," I told him. "Most people, anyway. The more interesting the person, the more fantastic the words. Words come in all sorts of shapes: stars, spaceships, pretzel words. Some words glow and some words dance. Sometimes I think I see words people are thinking about, or the words they want. The words that circle around my aunt Cleo's head are usually words I'm not allowed to say."

Jonah laughed at that. Making somebody laugh, without them laughing at me, felt a little bit amazing. So I kept going. "Most of the time, I figure I see the words that a person's mind doesn't have enough room to keep. I keep them, though. I collect them. You know how some people collect rocks or hedgehogs or belly-button lint?"

Jonah's forehead wrinkled. "Who collects hedgehogs?"

"Aunt Cleo." I nodded. "Not real ones. Plastic ones and porcelain ones and wax ones and stuff. I collect words, is the point. I keep them in my blue book."

I handed the book over to Jonah. It only occurred to me after he'd reached for it that I'd never let anybody touch that book before. My ears burned and my fingers prickled, but my heart said *YES*. So I didn't snatch it back.

"Mama calls me her poem catcher," I said. "I know how to catch words and keep them. But I can't get them to come out of my mouth exactly right."

"But you will." Jonah smiled. He didn't open my book, but he handed it back to me as gently as if it were a newborn kitten. "Obviously, your talent has to do with words."

"Words aren't a talent on their own," I added quickly.

Jonah tapped his forehead. "My know-hows are never wrong, Flea. You see the best words floating around crazy people, right?"

"Interesting people," I clarified.

"Same thing." Jonah chuckled. "Midnight Gulch is full of . . . *interesting* people. I'm friends with pretty much everybody. . . ."

That didn't surprise me.

"I'll introduce you to the most interesting people I know. You'll collect their words, and then you'll be so excited that you'll be jumping to share them at the Duel."

Before I could thank him politely and tell him *nohow, no way* would I do the Duel, Jonah spoke up again. "When Miss Lawson was talking about the Brothers Threadbare, you seemed really interested. . . ."

"Wait . . . you were in that class?"

He nodded. "I have lunch the same time as you, too. Did you hear me yelling your name? Probably not, since it gets so loud in there. Anyway, you seemed interested in the Threadbare boys. Am I right?"

As soon as Jonah said their name, the same wondrous feelings came rushing up inside me: the kick-thump of my heart and the catch of my breath. I tried to rub away the tingly sensations rolling up and down my arms. It seemed as if the air all around me was full of static electricity. I nodded. "Do you know much about them?"

Jonah smiled. "I know people who do. And when we start asking questions about the Brothers Threadbare, you'll definitely see awesome words." He leaned in close again and whispered, "I know how to help you, Felicity. I'd like to be your friend, too."

When Jonah Pickett called me his friend, my heart might have grown legs and crawled up into my throat. The word *friend* looked buggy, too, when it wriggled through the air — *FRIEND* grew six sets of legs and six sets of arms, and all the letters danced together, then kicked, then danced, then kicked again.

Jonah must have misunderstood the look on my face, because he said, "Is it okay . . . if we're friends?"

"Better than okay." I smiled, watching the friend-word squeeze out of the open window and flutter toward the sky. Fact: I had absolutely no intention whatsoever of participating in the Stoneberry Duel. But I could explain my dueling woes to Jonah some other time. Spending more time with him seemed too spindiddly an offer to pass up.

"Cool." Jonah smiled back. "And by the way, if you're interested in the Brothers Threadbare, you should also ask Cleo about them. That woman knows everything about everybody in Midnight Gulch."

When the bus screeched to a stop in front of the Sandcut Apartments complex, I stood up and said, "You never told me why you called yourself a Beedle."

"SHHH!" Jonah cautioned. "You can't go telling people you met the Beedle!"

"Right." I nodded.

"We'll talk about pumpernickel on Monday," Jonah said. *Monday.* Nothing good had ever happened to me on a Monday, magical or otherwise. But Jonah said *Monday* so easy, like we could handle ten thousand Mondays because we'd be friends through all of them.

"See you Monday, then," I said.

Day Grissom said my name as I stepped off the bus, except he said it this way: "Fliss-tee."

I looked back at him. "Yes, sir?"

"You kin to Cleo Harness?" he asked.

I nodded. "She's my aunt."

Day rubbed his fingers down the length of his scraggly beard. "Will you tell her . . ." He sighed. He chewed on his lip. He sighed one more time. "Will you tell her . . . that I said . . . *hi*?"

"Sure." I answered.

Halfway up the hill, I caught up to Frannie Jo. She was swinging her hips and bopping her head.

"I like this music!" Frannie hollered.

"What music?" I asked. Because all I heard was the good-bye-summer breeze pushing its way through the woods.

"This music!" Frannie Jo swung her hips side to side, the yellow tutu sparkling all around her.

Just as I was about to say something else, I saw a familiar word flickering up ahead. I stopped walking so fast both of us nearly toppled over.

THREADBARE

This time it was ripple-sparkling, hovering across a window on the third floor of the building: Aunt Cleo's apartment.

"Spindiddly," I mumbled.

"Do you hear the music?" Frannie asked.

"Nope," I said. But at the sight of that word, I heard something else loud and clear:

Yes,

    Yes,

        Yes!

I poured myself a glass of milk.

Swig

Swallow

Gulp

I watched the words come splashing out of the milk carton and dissolve down in my glass.

The crickets were singing twilight songs outside Aunt Cleo's window. The moon had bloomed starry white in the autumn sky. Dinner was over. Mama was working a late shift at the ice-cream factory.

"Aunt Cleo, do you know anything about the Brothers Threadbare?"

Cleo coughed and sputtered her tea. Her sewing scissors hit the floor, and her hands stilled. She pushed her glasses up on her nose and stared at me, as if she suddenly needed to study me especially carefully. "Why do you want to know about those boys?"

"Miss Lawson was talking about them in class." I

poured a second glass of milk for Frannie Jo, then nudged the refrigerator door shut with my hip.

"Your teacher told you about . . ."

"The Brothers Threadbare." I nodded. I could have sworn I saw Cleo's hands tremble as she reached for her scissors. "So do you know much about them?"

"Only a little bit," Cleo mumbled. She drummed her long red fingernails against the table, collecting all her thoughts about the Weatherly brothers. "But I don't know if we oughta talk about those boys." Her hand was trembling for sure when she lit her cigarette. Just the fact that Cleo was so suddenly nervous over dead-and-gone magician farmers made me want to talk about them even more. Apparently, I wasn't the only person who shivered just at the sound of their name.

"I need to know for school," I said, which was a little bit true. But the full-blown truth was this: I needed to know for me. I needed to know why my heart kicked every time I heard their name. I needed to know why the magic left when they did.

Cleo tapped her cigarette against the ashtray. The ashes spelled out:

Lucky

Cursive

Keeper

A fog of smoke escaped Cleo's lips when she spoke. "Threadbare was a stage name; the brothers were really just farm boys called Stone and Berry Weatherly."

"I know that part already. I'd like to know more about

the Duel." I sat down across from Cleo and she pushed a bowl of Doritos toward me. Frannie Jo lay on the couch, watching cartoons. Biscuit sat on the floor, staring up at us, waiting for the chips Cleo sometimes pretended to drop on the floor.

"Well." Cleo cleared her throat. "Stone played guitar and Berry played the banjo. Some people think the magic came from the musical instruments, not the men. And most people think there was nothing special about them at all, of course. Those stories are probably just old mountain fairy tales."

"Is that what you believe?" I asked.

Cleo didn't answer my question. But she coughed out a cloud of smoke and words:

Secret

Sorrowful

Holly

Holly is my mother's name.

Cleo didn't answer my question. "According to the stories," Cleo wheezed, "Stone lost the Duel because he couldn't roar like a lion. They were going back and forth making animal noises — Berry screamed like a panther and challenged Stone to roar like a lion, but no sound came out of that poor man's mouth. The storm cloud hovering up above him morphed into the shape of a lion, which is a much snazzier trick, if you ask me. But they didn't ask me. Because I wasn't born back then. And bets are bets and Stone lost. Biscuit won."

Biscuit sat up and raised one floppy ear.

"You mean Berry won," I said.

"Berry!" Cleo hollered. "Sorry, Biscuit." She tossed my dog a sympathy Dorito.

"Anything else?" I asked.

"The Brothers Threadbare were real artsy types. Music might have been their magic, but they were good at everything they put their hand to. Berry could sew. And Stone," she sighed, "was an artist."

"Like Mama!" I said. Part of our gypsy lifestyle had to do with Mama's job. She was a traveling artist. She painted murals all over the South. She used to, anyway. "She hasn't painted at all since before we left Kentucky."

"Don't I know it." Cleo nodded. "I doubt Stone was as good at it as your mama, but he was something. He was the first man ever hired to paint the Gallery."

"The what?"

Cleo accidentally tapped her cigarette ashes into the bowl of Doritos. I figured it'd be best not to mention it. "Stone painted the side of the drugstore; you know that first wall you see when you cross the bridge into Midnight Gulch? We call that wall the Gallery. Since Stone had magic in his veins, the picture he painted on the Gallery changed every day. They say he walked right into the painting every now and again. Sometimes, he did it to be funny. But sometimes, if he got mad over something his brother did, he'd go hide out in the painting and pout. That was some magic those boys had."

"Some magic," I mumbled. I thought about how it would feel to hide out in a picture, to have bones made of paint, able to stretch across a blank canvas any way I wanted.

46

"Of course, people's painted a hundred years' worth of graffiti all over the Gallery now," Cleo said. "You can't even tell what it looked like back then. The picture stopped changing, anyway, after Stone and Berry left."

"Because Stone was cursed with a wandering heart," I said sadly.

"Don't I know it." She stared at the grooves in the table and sighed.

"Do you think they regretted dueling once they'd done it?"

"Surely so." Cleo stood with a grunt. She tossed a stack of tabloid magazines off of the table and onto a chair. She pulled out a pile of quilt squares hidden underneath. "I figure they were too proud to say they were sorry. Pride sure does a number on people."

"One more question before I go to bed?" I asked.

Cleo took up her needle and began sewing plaid star patches onto the squares. "Sure, I reckon."

"Tell me about Roger Pickle?" I blurted the words out before I could change my mind.

Aunt Cleo's hands stilled. She looked up at me through pink-tinted glasses and I could see a world of sad in her eyes. A bunch of words zoomed out of the quilt, all star shaped:

Sorrow
Scandal
Holly
Frannie
Felicity

"Mama won't know," I begged. "She won't be home for hours."

I glanced over to see Frannie Jo, arms propped on the back of the couch. She wanted to know more about Roger Pickle, too. We wanted to know a thousand things, but we would settle for one more thing at a time.

"Okay," Cleo said softly. She laid her patches gently in her lap.

Patch it

Mend it

Stitch it back together

Those words were threads around her gray-blond hair, binding together in the shape of a star, then a drawbridge, then a full-bloomed flower.

"For one thing" — Cleo ran her hands over the quilt patches as she spoke — "Roger Pickle liked to dance. He'd turn up the radio and take your mama's hand and pull her out to the middle of the room. He'd spin her around and hold her tight and soon she'd laugh and forget that she didn't know the steps."

Frannie Jo closed her eyes.

Cinderella

Snow White

Sleeping Beauty

The words glittered in an invisible crown around her head. That was the only dancing Frannie knew, the kind she'd seen in movies. She'd never seen how Mama used to dance, when she'd shake her hips and fling her hair around and laugh. Wild dancing. Free dancing. I want to dance that way someday: free as a mountain girl, not bound up like a princess.

Cleo cleared her throat. "He could play a guitar, too. Played in a rock band over in Knoxville sometimes, but he mostly played for your mama. She said he could sing down the stars."

"Anything else?" I asked.

"He named you Felicity because he said it meant 'intense happiness.' And that's exactly how he felt when he held you in his arms for the very first time."

I could hear my heart again, speaking *yes* but in a gentler way than it usually did. *Yes*, this is truer than true and you can believe it. *Yes*, this is worth remembering no matter what else you figure out.

"And *you*." Cleo stood up and swooped Frannie Jo up into her arms. "He called you Francis Josephine after both your grandmothers. They were wild and wonderful and unique people. And he wanted you to be like them."

"And!" She held out her hand to me. "He loves you both, a heap and a bunch and more than you know. No matter where he is, what he's doing now, or what's happening between him and your mama, he loves you."

"He might come back," I said. I knew Mama hoped the same thing. She still carried a picture of him in her purse. In the photo, Roger Pickle wore a black T-shirt and blue jeans and a beard every bit as red as his hair. And so that's always how I pictured him, wearing those same clothes, looking that same way. I worried that most of the memories I had were the made-up kind. I could remember how I felt when he picked me up in his arms and I rested my head on his shoulder. I remember it because that's the safest I've ever felt. But I don't remember much else.

"He might," Cleo said. She didn't sound very convinced. She kissed Frannie Jo on the forehead. "But he loves you, no matter what."

"One more thing?" I asked as Cleo tucked us in. Frannie and I shared an inflatable mattress in our room, which had formerly been Aunt Cleo's craft room until we surprised her and moved in.

Cleo sighed. "One more."

I looked up at the picture situated on Aunt Cleo's wall: a black-and-white photograph of a man standing beside a hot air balloon. I saw the word again, *THREADBARE*, stretched across the balloon's canvas.

"What's *threadbare* mean?" I asked.

"Shabby-looking," Cleo said. And I saw the other words, too:

Old
Thinned out
Roughed up
Well loved

She wheezed a laugh. "Threadbare's what I am, I guess. Will you do me a favor, Felicity? Don't tell your mama that we talked about those boys. She doesn't like that story."

I opened my mouth to ask why, but Cleo pressed her finger against my lips and said, "No more questions. Y'all are making my brain tired." She walked over to the tiny window in our room and raised it up just barely. I heard crickets singing their good-night songs to one another. And I *smelled* something glorious, like warm cookies just pulled out of an oven.

"I call that the sugar wind," Cleo said. I could hear a smile in her voice. "It's the smell of the waffle cones they bake down at the ice-cream factory." I think we were both comforted to know Mama was working in a place that smelled so wonderful.

Cleo left the door cracked open for us so we'd have light if we woke up, so we wouldn't stumble through the dark. Frannie snuggled up close to my one side, and Biscuit snuggled up close to the other.

"Catch me a poem?" Frannie asked.

I whispered:

"Frannie Jo lives in a house of stars.
She has a cloud for a pillow
And a comet for a car.
She smiles like a sunrise,
Cries a rainbow when she's hurt.
She'll dance across the sky tonight,
Then shake the stardust from her skirt."

Frannie snored softly, but I knew she'd heard my words. I saw them still shining above her, each letter rippling with her easy breaths:

Comet
Cloud
Ballerina

I wished I could fall asleep as fast as Frannie Jo, but I knew I wouldn't be able to until I heard Mama come back. I tried not to think about what might happen if she left work, got in the Pickled Jalapeño . . . and kept on driving. Left town, just disappeared. Like Roger Pickle.

Like the Brothers Threadbare.

THREADBARE

I closed my eyes and thought of those magical brothers playing music while the clouds swirled into new shapes above them. I thought about Roger Pickle playing guitar while my mama danced, her skirt swirling all around her as she stomped and jumped and kicked her legs. If I had magic in my veins, like the Threadbares did, I'd make a home for all of us. And then I'd use my home magic to help Roger Pickle find us. I'd fill up a flare gun with blinking stars and shoot them into the universe. They'd spell out:

We're home.

Or maybe: *We're* your *home.*

He would follow the stars and find us. I'd see his favorite words spinning around his head: *Holly. Felicity. Frannie Jo.* I'd hug his neck and we'd dance on home, wherever home is. Because home is where shabby hearts like ours belong.

The one stipulation Aunt Cleo had given us when we showed up at the Sandcut Apartments complex with a dog and three grocery bags full of dirty clothes was this: We had to go to church with her.

I could see in Mama's eyes that she wanted to take our hands and holler for Biscuit and stomp right back to the Pickled Jalapeño, but something convinced her otherwise. I saw the words *French fry* floating through the hallway, and it's not because we craved them but because we'd been eating French fries and service-station nachos for weeks. The Pickled Jalapeño needed a rest and so did we.

So Mama said, "Fine." I'm sure she hoped God and Aunt Cleo would forget about our arrangement. But neither of them did.

Cleo shuffled toward the Pickled Jalapeño that Sunday morning wearing a silky dress in a bold print of blue flowers and hummingbirds. The hummingbird wings looked like they were fluttering when the warm wind blew around us.

But Cleo's hair didn't budge. Her hair was poufed up high onto her head, into a stiff gray-blond haystack heap.

"The way you wear your hair makes you look old, Cleo," Mama said. And she added, "It ages you." Because I guess she figured Cleo didn't understand what *old* meant. Cleo didn't seem to care. Maybe because she *was* older than Mama. Cleo was almost twenty years older than Mama.

Mama's hair was golden blond, the way Cleo's probably used to be, but Mama still wore her hair long and wavy. Before we lived in Kentucky, Mama braided feathers into her hair. She always had paint in her hair, too, and she kept paintbrushes in the pockets of her jeans. She painted the ocean. She painted people's faces. But she hadn't painted anything in a long time.

Mama's pretty blue dress tried to cling to the frame of her body but couldn't find anything much to hold. Frannie Jo was better at clinging. Mama kept Frannie perched high up on her bony hip.

"Hey, Cleo." Mama shifted Frannie Jo to her other side. "Why don't we wait and go next week?"

"If you could walk as fast as you talk, we'd be at the van by now," Cleo wheezed. She lit a cigarette and took a deep drawl. "Toss me the keys. I'm driving."

"Why're we taking my van?" Mama asked. "Church was your idea, remember? Because you think I'm a way-ward soul."

"All of us can fit in your van!" Cleo hollered. "We won't

fit inside the Beast of Burden." The Beast of Burden is what Aunt Cleo called her Nissan sedan.

I didn't much think we fit anywhere: us Pickles or my aunt Cleo, who tied a leopard-print scarf around her neck before we pulled out of the complex.

Cleo swerved the Pickled Jalapeño into the parking lot of the Friendship Community Church and turned off the ignition. She was already standing in the parking lot when she realized she forgot to put the van in park, so she had to open the door again, and hop backward through the parking lot on one leg, trying to jump back in the driver's seat. We stood there and watched while the van rolled backward and Cleo hollered, "Stop! Stop! Stop! STOP!"

The Pickled Jalapeño finally did as it was told. Aunt Cleo left the van where it stopped, right in the middle of the lot. She slammed the door, yelled out an unsavory word, and leaned over, clutching both knees to steady her breathing.

"You just gonna leave it parked there?" Mama asked.

"They know me here," Cleo heaved. She threw down her cigarette, which she'd kept clutched firmly between her teeth the entire time. "They don't care where I park."

"Hope they don't mind how we look, either," said Mama. She brushed my bangs out of my face and said she'd get them cut next time she got paid, and she fussed over Frannie's yellow tutu, which Frannie'd insisted on wearing over her dress.

"Nobody cares how you look," Cleo said, heaving as she climbed the stairs. "And I said you had a *wandering heart*, Holly. Not a wayward soul."

✳ ◇ ☀ ✳ ◇ ☀ ✳ ◇ ✳

There were hundreds of words spinning through the church house, but they were so clear that I didn't see them at first. Then the light streamed golden and blue and red through the stained-glass windows and I saw the words plain: They shimmered like water. We had an entire ocean of words above us. Old words from the hymnals spun closest to me:

Yonder

Wayfarer

Everlasting

Everlasting had a sound to it, ocean water splashing over rocks. I whispered the word. I shivered because I liked the sound of it so much.

"Shhh," Mama said. But she smiled down at me even then. She liked the way I cherished words.

When the woman sitting in front of us tucked her gray hair behind her ear, I saw a single word escape from her ear:

T i r e d

So small I nearly missed it. Bold letters, though. The preacher at the pulpit wiped his forehead, and I saw a word leave his mouth that he never said out loud:

Lonely

". . . if only we could be more like the Beedle," the preacher was saying.

I sat up straighter in my seat. It's not that I'd forgotten Jonah's pumpernickel secret, but hearing the word *beedle* come out of somebody else's mouth made me realize how special that secret was. And anyhow, I only knew the Beedle's identity, not exactly what he did or why he called himself the Beedle.

The preacher said, "We need to follow the Beedle's example, do good things for people without expecting anything in return."

So Jonah's know-how was anonymous. He did a bunch of good for people, but he didn't want them to know who did it. That sounded ten different kinds of ridiculous to me. My heart was right about my first friend: He was weirdly wonderful.

"Let's close in prayer," the preacher said. I wondered if he knew how many prayer words had been circling through the room the whole time, even before he told us to pray:

Help me
Hold me
Hear me
Please

I looked down at my blue book, hoping from far off it might look like my eyes were shut. I wrote down some of the words I'd seen. I didn't hear much of what the preacher prayed until he said, "I pray that you know today how deeply you are loved. And I hope you take the time to pray for the ones you love. Tell them how much they mean to you this week. Your words don't have to be fancy, just sincere."

So I gave my words to God without closing my eyes and without speaking a single one of them. Silent words, the kind a person's heart speaks. Turns out my heart had a bunch to say. I prayed for the Beedle first. Then I prayed Mama might get inspired to paint something again. Next up was Aunt Cleo. I nudged her with my elbow and whispered, "What do you pray to God for?"

"A man," she whispered. But then her whisper turned into a snort, and then a snicker. And then she got so tickled at her own joke that the pew vibrated with the laughter she was trying to hold back. I didn't understand what was so funny.

"You two," Mama whispered. "Hush. You're supposed to be praying."

So I prayed for a man for Aunt Cleo, since that's what she said she wanted.

I prayed for Frannie Jo and for Biscuit. I prayed we could make a home here in Midnight Gulch. That Mama would settle into this place instead of driving us back out.

I prayed for Roger Pickle. I prayed he'd write a song about me, maybe sing my name tonight when he sang down the stars. Maybe I would see my name spelled in galaxy dust and I would know he remembered me.

And then the pastor said:

"Felicity . . ."

I gasped and my mama glared at me, nostrils flared, thinking I was causing some silent ruckus, no doubt. But the pastor wasn't looking at me. His eyes were still closed tightly. His hands clutched the podium so hard his knuckles were pale.

"Felicity," he said, "means 'intense happiness.' The world is a sorrowful place. And we know there are kinds of happiness that don't last, that fade off, that leave us feeling wrung out and fickle —"

"Pickle!" Frannie Jo gasped. "They're kicking us out!"

Mama clamped her hand over Frannie's mouth and pulled her into her lap.

"But there are true, intense kinds of happiness," the preacher continued. "Felicity is a particular kind of joy . . . a wondrous joy. This week, I dare you to choose joy."

And then the preacher said, "*Amen.*"

"*Amen.*" Cleo nodded.

"Amen!" Frannie echoed. And then she nudged me with her elbow and said, "Will you watch me do a backflip off the pew?"

"No way," Mama answered for me. She grabbed our hands and hauled us toward the door, smiling sweetly at folks. The only thing Mama disliked more than church was pointless small talk. But we'd barely even stepped out of the pew when somebody reached for her arm.

"Holly? Is that you?"

Mama nodded curtly and didn't object when the woman threw her arms around her and squeezed tight, like they were long-lost best friends. I thought she might scoop me and Frannie up into a hug, too, but she didn't. She just smiled down at us. I liked the way her red lipstick hugged her gap-toothed grin.

Made from scratch
Ready to rise

Those were her words.

"Girls." Mama rested her hands on my shoulder. "This is Ponder Waller. She owns the pie shop on Main Street. We went to school together —"

Before Frannie or I could say hello, Ponder spoke up again. "I never met an artist more talented than your mama. I always said she was a star — I knew Holly Harness was gonna go places. Cleo's told us all about some of the murals you painted —"

"Cleo exaggerates." Mama grinned, and prodded us on ahead of her out the door. "But thank you for the compliment. We gotta get going."

"You and the girls come by for some pie one day!" Ponder said as we bumped our way through the crowd. "My treat!"

Mama never looked back. But I did. As she hauled us out the door, I saw my name, *Felicity*, shimmering across the stained-glass window. I'd never seen my own name before. I'd never thought about how pretty it would look with the light shining through it.

* ◇ ✳ * ◇ ✳ * ◇ *

"Tell you who's found their wondrous joy," said Aunt Cleo. The Pickled Jalapeño rocked us down the road while we dined on French fries and chicken nuggets.

"The Beedle!" she hollered, when none of us said anything.

I stopped mid-chew. "What about the Beedle?"

"Don't talk with your mouth full, June Bug," Mama said.

Aunt Cleo took an extra-big bite and said, with her mouth especially full, "The Beedle is a local hero, a do-gooder. He or She or It leaves notes on people's doors, flowers in mailboxes, extra change in that one space downtown that has the meter. The Beedle is always watching. Always doing what needs to be done. Has been for fifty years now."

"Fifty years!" I nearly choked on my French fry. "That's impossible!"

"That's magic!" Cleo reached for some of Mama's French fries, but Mama slapped her hand away.

And now I was more confused than I'd ever been. Because I knew the Beedle wasn't magic. The Beedle was that spikey-haired Jonah Pickett. And I couldn't figure out how the hayseed a twelve-year-old spikey-haired do-gooder had been in business for fifty years. . . .

"The Beedle puts flowers on Abigail Honeycutt's grave," Cleo said.

She nodded back toward the direction we'd come from, toward the church. "The Honeycutts have all been gone for so many years now. I guess most of us had forgotten their story. Or we'd decided not to remember it, which is very different but every bit as bad. The Beedle was the one who reminded us. One day the weeds were pulled up and the kudzu was cut back and there was a bundle of red roses settled against Abigail Honeycutt's grave."

"I didn't think Abigail Honeycutt had a grave," Mama said sadly.

"Her memorial, then," Cleo clarified. Then she looked back at me. "That's too sad a story. We'll talk about that some other day."

We let the sad quiet linger in the van for a time. Finally, Mama sighed and said, "I can't believe the Beedle is still doing those things. That doesn't make any sense. That's impractical. The Beedle can't last forever."

"That's magic, I guess," Cleo said. She glanced up at me in the rearview mirror. "What's got you looking so perplexed, Felicity Juniper?"

Of course, I couldn't tell them the Beedle was my first honest-to-goodness friend and he was only twelve. So instead of answering Cleo's question, I said, "Day Grissom told me to tell you hello."

Mama let out a low whistle at exactly the same time Cleo said, "Lord help us all."

"Is he still sweet on you, Cleo?" Mama asked.

"Was he sweet on you *ever*?" I asked.

Cleo didn't answer either one of us. She pushed her big round sunglasses up on her nose and said, "Somebody pass me my cigarettes."

And that was the end of it. Cleo didn't say another word until we got home, but Mama laughed. "Day Grissom. Some things never change."

Mama's laughter sounds prettier than any word I've ever heard.

Frannie was the first one to see the surprise waiting for us at Cleo's. Propped against the door was a box of dog treats, a coloring book, and a giant carton of Dr. Zook's called Hannah Banana Coconut. All three presents were tied up with a red ribbon.

Mama read the note out loud:

Dear World-Traveling Pickles,
Welcome home to Midnight Gulch.

Sincerest regards,
The Beedle

"God bless the Beedle," Cleo laughed.

Mama didn't say anything, but the smile on her face reminded me of the smile she used to have: her painting smile, her dancing smile. *Magic.*

She picked up the box and carried it inside.

There in the hallway, I said another prayer with my eyes open and without speaking any words at all. I thanked God for Jonah, because somehow he'd managed to make Mama smile without even knowing her. I prayed I could give him something in return, too: something as good as that smile and as pretty as the red silk ribbon he'd tied around the dog treats.

I wished I could give him the word *red*. *Red* is a blooming word. I watched it rise up in front of me and sprout leaves and vines that stretched all across the apartment complex. Mama and Cleo and Frannie didn't see it, of course. But I did. I picked an invisible flower and I tucked it in my hair.

"Shannon Buchanan, don't you cry for me! I come from down in Ducktown with a *ban*-jer on my knee!"

Day Grissom slapped the knee of his worn-out jeans as he sang. He kept his other hand squeezed tight around the big fat steering wheel of the bus, thank goodness. Midnight Gulch was full of fog and rain, and even though the fog looked pretty billowing out of the mountains and over the roads, driving through that mess can make a person nervous. Especially if you're being driven by a Grissom.

Day's radio was broken, he said, so he'd decided to serenade us. His voice crackled as loud as old radio speakers when he sang, and I kinda liked the sound.

"I like how some people say it ban-*jer* instead of ban-*jo*," Jonah said. "Makes it sound more special."

I pinched Jonah hard on the wrist.

"Um . . . *ow!*" he said. And he pinched me hard right back.

"I thought maybe you were a ghost," I said. "I figured that's maybe how you've been in business for fifty years."

Jonah sighed. "I can't explain stuff about pumpernickel here on the bus. I'll tell you later."

"When later?"

"Soon as we get off this bus later."

"Everybody sing!" hollered Day Grissom.

We sang along as the bus circled around the mountain roads of Midnight Gulch, then down into the valley, then past the Sandcut Apartments toward downtown.

The bus zoomed past the Gallery that Aunt Cleo told me about. I squinted real close trying to see magical pictures underneath all the layers of paint. But my eyes weren't attuned to pictures, only words. And the only words I saw on that wall were the ones somebody'd spray-painted there. They trembled and shivered against the bricks. They didn't belong.

"They should let somebody repaint the Gallery," Jonah said when he saw where I was looking. "But I don't know if anybody in Midnight Gulch has the knack."

"My mama has the knack," I said. And I remembered the summer when she always had paintbrushes in her pocket and paint freckles in her hair. I couldn't understand how somebody who liked to paint as much as Mama could just up and stop. Put the brushes away and quit, completely. I wondered if she'd ever start again. I wondered if she even wanted to. I sighed, "She used to have the knack, anyway."

"You worry about her a lot, don't you?"

I nodded, remembering what I'd seen last night. I'd waited up like always, until I finally heard the soft click of

Mama's key in the door lock. I rolled off the inflatable mattress and crawled to look down the hallway. Mama sat on the edge of Cleo's couch with her head braced between her hands. I held my breath, afraid she was crying. But I didn't hear any sobs. Didn't see any tears. I didn't see any words, either, but I'd never seen words floating near Mama.

After a time, she stood up and walked to the window and leaned her forehead against the glass. And I knew. Somewhere out there, beneath the stars and shadows, the road was calling out to her already. She was itching to go again, and we'd only been there a day. Before long, we'd set out. We'd load up the Jalapeño and leave another town, never to return. Just like the Brothers Threadbare.

"She's always looking for a reason to leave." I swallowed. "No matter where we go."

Jonah nodded but didn't say anything. At first, I was afraid talking about Mama made him uncomfortable. But when I glanced over at him, I realized his forehead was crinkled again, like he was thinking up some tremendously great idea. "Maybe that's why you have to do the Duel."

So much for great ideas. "How you figure that?"

"Maybe if your mama sees you competing in the talent show, sharing your words . . . If she sees how happy you are here in Midnight Gulch, then she'll want to stay for a while."

"I wish it was that easy," I groaned.

"Maybe it is," Jonah said. And then he leveled me with one of his deep-dimpled grins, the kind that made me feel like butterflies were tap-dancing inside my chest. If Jonah didn't grow up to be a professional do-gooder, he should be a politician. With a smile like that, he could convince anybody to do anything. Someday I might work up enough nerve to tell him about his marvelous smile, but not yet. Instead, I turned my red face toward the window and concentrated on the foggy mountains surrounding Midnight Gulch.

"I haven't been to this part of town," I told Jonah. Mama first said no when I asked if I could spend the afternoon with him, but then Aunt Cleo said she'd take Frannie for the afternoon and they'd have a big time together. So there I was.

"You'll get to see plenty of the town today," Jonah said. "We're one of the last stops. I'm taking you to meet Interesting Person Number One. He knows all about pumpernickel." Jonah grinned. "Even better, he has *inside* information about the Threadbares."

"How?" I whispered.

"You'll find out." Jonah smiled. "Tell me more about the way you see words. Can you poke them? Can you kick at them? Can you hold them in your hand?"

"Sort of," I laughed. "But no more than you can hold a soap bubble in your hand. Words are pretty while they last, though. They never look the same. Sometimes words are blinky bright. Firefly bright. Sometimes words are shadows. I collect them on my shoe if I run out of room in the blue book."

"Show me!" Jonah's green eyes sparkled.

I pulled off my sneaker and hoped to heaven that my striped purple sock didn't stink like a dead skunk.

Jonah inspected the words I'd inked along my shoe.

"Sometimes words cluster together. They're cloudy." I pointed to the heel. "Takes a while to pull the words apart and decide which ones I want to keep. Some words have thin wings when I see them. Others hum; they make an electric sound, like they'd light up if I plugged them in. The words that hum and buzz are the ones that can't stand to not be said, I figure."

I pointed to the white stripe over the toe of my shoe. "*Kaleidoscope*: That one sparkled and it had a sound. Popped like Coke fizz until I wrote it down."

"What's *ardwolf*?" Jonah tapped the heel.

"It's a hyena that stays up all night and eats termites."

"Excellent." He nodded. "I already know what *paradigm* is." He traced his finger across the inky-purple spikes of the letters. *Paradigm* was a fun word to collect; it copied along the ceiling of the Pickled Jalapeño over and over. Same word, but it spun out at least a hundred different ways before it finally dissolved.

"Did this word dance when you found it?" Jonah pointed to *pirouette*.

"Spun through the air," I said, and nodded. "It reminded me of a purple ribbon."

Jonah raised his eyebrow. "Spindiddly?"

"I saw it on a carousel at the fair. I don't think it's a real word, so I gave it a meaning: *Spindiddly* means 'better than awesome.'"

"Did you see *sailboat* bobbing along on the ocean?"

"Nope. Vehicles and motorized things have words around them, but they never make much sense. They're fun to say but not much for keeping. I saw *sailboat* in a rinky-dink antique shop near Myrtle Beach, hovering around a fake sailboat, one of those little bitty boats they keep in glass bottles. Dreaming of what it could never be, I'd guess."

"What's this?" Jonah asked.

"*Needler*," I said. "That's what Aunt Cleo calls a person who won't mind their own business. Like when I try to eavesdrop on Cleo's conversations with Mama, she'll say, 'Felicity, stop needlin' in.'"

Jonah nodded. "My mom's a needler."

"That's mean!"

"She wouldn't be offended. She'd say the same of herself. She says her first job is styling hair and fixing carburetors but her favorite job is sorting out other people's business."

Jonah and I both laughed.

"Will I meet your mom today?" I asked.

"Probably not today. But definitely soon." Jonah split apart a granola bar wrapper.

Crunch
Cluster
Cram

Those words shot out into the air first, but then he pulled the granola free and broke it in half to share with me. He gave me the bigger half.

"Felicity . . . can't you picture yourself at the Duel, sharing your words? Just a little bit?"

Truth be told, I could picture it easy. And as I pictured it, my heart dropped somewhere in the vicinity of my belly button. I thought of standing on a stage with shaky hands and tingling ears and sweaty lips. I thought of how my words came out twisted when I tried to say them in front of all those people. My words were a mess to everybody but my family.

And Jonah.

"Uh-oh," Jonah said. "You look like you're about to puke."

I sighed. "That's a possibility."

"Day!" Jonah yelled toward the front. "Pass back Le Barfbucket!"

Once Le Barfbucket made its way back to our seat, Jonah held it toward me. "Okay," he said. "Launch!" And he turned his face away.

"I'm fine now," I said. And I smiled in spite of all my nervousness. "I've never had a friend willing to catch vomit for me."

Jonah seemed relieved that he wouldn't have to be that friend, either. He tucked the barf bucket under the seat and said, "What's the word you see most often, Felicity?"

"*Lonely*," I said. "I see it all the time, mostly in school and in church and in malls and driving down the road. Always the places where the most people are. Isn't that weird?"

"Probably not," he said. "Probably not at all. Do you see a word close to me right now?"

I nodded. And I nearly laughed out loud again. "It's a word I've never seen out and about before, not on any other person ever. *Splendiferous*. That's your word. It's yellow with six legs and it's crawling up your arm."

"Splendiferous, huh?" Jonah glanced down at his arm, even though he couldn't see anything. "I like that. Tell it to stay for a while, okay?"

But when he said that last part, he looked right at *me*, at the freckles on my face and the laugh on my lips and the sad in my stare. If his green eyes had been lasers, they would have zapped right through me.

He smiled as he reached for my wrist, and I thought he might pinch me again the way I'd pinched him. But instead, he grabbed the red pen he kept clipped to his newspaper and he wrote that word:

splendiferous

Right on my hand, in the messiest letters I'd ever seen.

"There." He smiled. "That's the first word I ever collected. Keep it safe for me?"

I felt my face heat up, so I looked at my lap instead of his face. I realized I still held half of his granola bar. My hands were sticky and my wrist was inky. My heart pounded out the happiest melody — *yes* — I'd heard in a long time.

✳ ◇ ✴ ✳ ◇ ✴ ✳ ◇ ✳

Bus 5548 dropped Jonah and me off in front of a swirly, spiraled gate. The rain was only dribbling by then. A thick river of fog rolled around my ankles. Maybe it was the fog that made the mansion behind the gate look extra creepy. Or maybe, I decided, the house doesn't just *look* creepy. Maybe that house was so spindiddly creepy I shouldn't be walking toward it.

I thought about pinching Jonah one more time to see if he was a ghost, but then I noticed something else. . . .

Jonah must have seen the surprise in my eyes, because he said, "Decent size house, huh?"

But I wasn't even looking at the house anymore. I saw a single word threading through the rusty gate:

THREADBARE

Jonah wheeled up to the speaker situated on the gate and pushed a button. When the speaker buzzed, Jonah sat up tall in his wheelchair and yelled, "Pumpernickel!"

The gate startled me when it swung open. I sure noticed the house then: all three stories of it. The mansion was made of pale gray stone. Maybe. It was hard to tell because the stone didn't show much through all the ivy dripping down from the gabled rooftops. Red flowers bloomed bright as needle pricks out of all the green. Raindrops clung so tightly to the petals that every flower looked covered in diamond dust.

"Oliver owns Dr. Zook's Ice Cream Company," Jonah explained.

"People sure must love ice cream," I said.

"It's not just the ice cream," Jonah said. "Oliver created a special formula that makes the ice cream stay cold for at least twenty-four hours even if it isn't in a freezer. His invention revolutionized the world of frozen novelties."

I pictured Oliver as a cantankerous old millionaire sitting in a dark office in the farthest corner of that expensive stone house. He'd probably be wearing a black suit. He'd probably have a pinched face and wiry glasses and a beard. Definitely a beard. He probably never looked up from his desk.

Jonah's wheelchair made a steady *zrrrrrr* as he led me down the foggy walkway to Oliver's mansion. The yard was bordered by fancy hedges trimmed into animal shapes: a bear, an elephant, an anteater, a lion. The tallest hedge, so tall it could have been a tree, was cut into the shape of a hot air balloon. We passed by two tall columns with stone gargoyles situated on top of them. Both gargoyles had a pair of sunglasses positioned over their eyes.

Beside the steps leading up to the porch, somebody'd built a sturdy-looking wheelchair ramp. Before we could get there, the front doors squeaked open.

An elderly lady stood in the doorway — she was plump the way grannies sometimes are, pillowy and huggable-looking. She kept her white hair tied back behind her head

74

in a poufy bun. She grinned at us and clapped her hands and ran down the ramp, squealing.

"Should I be afraid?" I asked.

"Charlie Sue Hancock is Oliver's assistant. She gets excited over company."

Charlie Sue ran at us full speed, both arms straight out like she might take off and fly.

"Should I duck?"

But I didn't have time to duck. Instead I *OOFED!* as Charlie Sue swooped in and flung her arms around me and Jonah both. She smelled like coffee and expensive perfume.

"Welcome to Midnight Gulch, Felicity Pickle!" she hollered, pushing me back to take a good look at me.

"*Laaaaaaws*, Jonah," she said. "You were telling the truth. Felicity is *plumb* adorable."

Plumb adorable.

Plumb *ADORABLE?!*

My face burned bright red. Prickly red. I'd never been called plumb *anything* before. I didn't glance at Jonah to see if his face was prickly red, too, but I had a feeling it wasn't. Jonah never seemed embarrassed over his words. Not that those *were* his words. I was certain Charlie Sue Hancock was elaborating. Mega elaborating. Elaborating to the ten-thousandth degree of elaboration.

"Oliver said he'd meet you both in the boardroom," said Charlie Sue. "He's been on the phone all day with some clients up north. They're wanting a shipment of Blackberry

Sunrise and Oliver's been telling them *NO, SIR, NO WAY* all day long. You *know* how he feels about *that one*."

"That's his most popular flavor," Jonah told me. "But Oliver won't let them sell it anywhere besides Midnight Gulch."

"Why's that?" I followed Jonah and Charlie Sue into Oliver's mansion.

" 'Cause that stuff's got a little secret ingredient." Charlie Sue winked at Jonah. "We call it M-A-G-I-C."

* ◇ ✳ * ◇ ✳ * ◇ *

Oliver's boardroom was actually a library. A good library. A library where books looked worn-out and well read and loved on. The library was two stories tall with a balcony that wrapped around the top level. The big window on the top floor was propped half open. A rebel beam of sunlight pushed through the clouds, shining through the rain beads stuck to the screen and glass. And then that strange, golden rain light shone warm and pretty over Oliver's books. I wondered if the sun had missed the books, had waited as long as it possibly could to shine over those spines again. I knew how that felt, to love a story so much you didn't just want to read it, you wanted to feel it.

And Jonah was right about Oliver's mansion being good for word collecting. I wasn't really participating in the Duel, of course. But if I were, Oliver's house was the perfect place to collect. I saw them everywhere:

So.

Many.

Hundreds and billions and trillions
of words.

Woven across the ceiling. Shining as soft as the September sun. I was surrounded by words and stories and dust-speckled light. That's a pretty perfect way to be.

In the center of Oliver's library was a round table. Jonah pulled a chair out and wheeled underneath the tabletop. While he prepared for his meeting, I explored the first level of Oliver's library. The walls were mostly covered by book-shelves, but one wall was full of maps and photographs.

There was a map of Midnight Gulch and another map of the state of Tennessee. Tennessee was poked full of so many stickpins that it looked like one of Cleo's stuffed hedgehogs.

Pictures were propped against the books on the shelves — black-and-white photos of people, mostly.

Jonah pointed to a colored picture in a frame made of aluminum can lids. "See that one right there? That's how I first met Oliver."

The photograph showed a little white building. A line of smiling kids stood in front of it, grinning toothy-big. They looked Frannie Jo's age.

"Can you keep another secret?" Jonah asked.

"Yes," I said. Which was mostly true. I knew as soon as I got home I would tell Biscuit. I tell her everything, but as far as I know, she doesn't go blabbing to anybody else.

Jonah said, "I started saving up Coke cans a few summers ago. I took them to the recycling center and saved up all the change and eventually I had enough money to build a little school for some kids in Haiti. My uncle is a missionary there and he's always sending me letters about the dreams he's working on. One day I read his letter and my know-how kicked in. So I started saving."

I looked at the picture. I looked back at Jonah. "How many cans did that take?"

"Thousands," Jonah said. "But it didn't take all that long. Mom and the guys at the shop all helped me; they all saved up Coke cans and sent them my way."

"You built a *school*?"

His cheeks burned bright red. "It was a little school."

"With *Coke cans*?"

The red on his face crept quickly from his cheeks all the way to his hairline. He nodded and unfolded his newspaper and started concentrating on the stories there. "Keep it a secret, okay?"

"No problem. I sure wouldn't want people knowing I built a whole entire school. Out of Coke cans. That's definitely the kind of secret you don't want getting out."

"It feels better when it's secret," Jonah said. "Oliver heard about what I'd done, even though I did my best to keep it quiet, and one thing led to another and he appointed me the new Beedle."

"The *new* Beedle?" I asked. "What happened to the old Beedle? Why even call it a Beedle?"

"You'll see," Jonah said. He pointed to the air all around us. "See any words worth keeping?"

"I see a sky full of words." I scribbled furiously in my blue book:

Becoming
Halcyon
Ravel
Serendipity
Summer

"Ice cream!" Charlie Sue hollered as she pushed a silver cart through the library door.

She set down tall glass ice-cream dishes in front of me and Jonah. Then she spread a towel across the center of the table and set out six cartons of ice cream. I still wasn't sold on Dr. Zook's Ice Cream being the best thing to come out of Midnight Gulch. But that's because I'd only tasted Aunt Cleo's carton of Chocolate Chip Pork Rind, and I'd gagged four times. The flavors Charlie Sue set out looked a whole lot more intriguing:

Orangie's Caramel Apple Pie

Virgil's Get-Outta-My-Face Fudge Ripple

Andy's Snickerdoodle Sucker Punch

Jim's Just-Vanilla's-All-I-Want

Day's Chocolate Orange Switcheroo

Marsh-Mallory Mocha Delight

"I'm partial to Aunt Lillie's Lavender Rosewater," said Charlie Sue.

"Are they all named after people?" I asked.

"Not all of them." Jonah reached for the Chocolate Orange Switcheroo flavor. "People in Midnight Gulch like to send in their ideas, though. If it's any good, Oliver gives them credit."

Jonah plopped a spoonful of Chocolate Orange Switcheroo into my glass. "Try this one."

I took a small bite to start with. The ice cream melted against my tongue, sweet and fruity and smooth. Then came the switcheroo part — a chocolate fudgy flavor that caused the corners of my jaws to tingle with happiness.

Bittersweet

Tangy

Citrus

Crazy good!

I watched the words freeze against my ice-cream glass. I stopped to write them down, and that's when I noticed a very familiar word drifting across the table:

Stoneberry

"Stoneberry," I mumbled.

"Makes sense." Jonah nodded. "Like I said, Oliver has done all sorts of research on the Weatherly brothers."

"Didn't need to go far for research," said a man in the doorway.

Even though I knew that man had to be the mysterious millionaire Oliver, I was still a little surprised. Because

Oliver did not *look* like a millionaire. He looked like a farmer or a cowboy, maybe. But mostly he just looked like somebody's grandpa.

Oliver was shorter than I figured he'd be. He had a shiny bald head and a fuzzy white mustache. He wore faded jeans, and a flannel shirt rolled up to the elbows.

"Hey-yo!" Oliver grinned at me. "And good morning and welcome!" He didn't talk like a millionaire, either.

When he reached to shake my hand, I noticed a dark tattoo on his forearm. But I couldn't make out what it was just yet.

"Hey-yo and thanks," I said.

Oliver glanced at Jonah and raised one fuzzy eyebrow. "Pumpernickel?"

Jonah nodded. "Felicity's the one I told you about. Remember? She's cool."

"All righty, then." Oliver nodded. "Jonah says you're interested in the Weatherly brothers, Miss Felicity?"

Yes!

     Yes!

          Yes!

"Yep," I answered.

Oliver pulled a picture frame off one of the bookshelves and handed it to me.

The photograph was old, black-and-white, and faded. But I could tell that the man in the picture was young. His dark, shaggy hair fell down over one eye. He wore overalls sized a bit too short for his long, lanky frame, and he held a banjo high up, right across his chest. I could tell he wasn't playing that banjo, though; his hand clutched too tightly around the neck. I wondered if he was in a habit of holding his banjo over his chest to protect his heart. Maybe that banjo was a shield to him. Maybe he felt safe behind it.

Oliver tapped the picture frame. "Berry Weatherly. He was a famous magician, but you've heard that already, I reckon?"

I nodded.

"Well," Oliver sighed. "There is always more to the story than what you've heard. Here's what most people don't know about Berry: He liked cold weather and hot coffee. He loved to sew. And he loved to tell stories. Stories were his best magic. And" — Oliver's fuzzy mustache turned up at the edges when he smiled — "Berry Weatherly was my grandfather. I'd be happy to tell you more about him. The *truth* about him."

Yes. Yes. Yes, my heart pounded over Oliver's words. My heart always pounded out a *YES* when people were fixing to tell me a good story.

"Felicity," Jonah finally said, "in case you haven't figured it out yet, this is Oliver Weatherly . . . the original Beedle of Midnight Gulch."

"Charlie Sue!" hollered Oliver. "Could you bring me a —"

Before he could finish, Charlie Sue bumped the door open with her hip. She set down another glass ice-cream dish and a new carton of ice cream on the table.

Blackberry Sunrise

"You're a wonder!" Oliver said to her.

"And don't you forget it!" Charlie Sue said with a nod. She pulled the door closed when she left.

"Jonah says that's your most popular flavor," I said, pointing to the pale purple carton.

"Hey-yo! You better believe it," Oliver answered. "People buy it by the gallon because it helps them remember. The problem is that you don't know what *kind* of memory this ice cream's going to dredge up. We make every carton out of the blackberries that grow wild down by Snapdragon Pond. If you take a bite" — he tapped the carton with his spoon — "and the blackberries taste sweet, you remember something good. But if you take a bite and the blackberries are sour, well . . . that means you're about to have a sad memory. Remembering is still important, though, no matter if it's good or bad. You want to try it?"

"I'd better not." I shook my head. Because there was one memory in particular I'd worked too hard to forget.

Oliver nodded. "Jonah says you'd like to know about the Beedle."

"And the Brothers Threadbare," I said, trying to sound casual.

"I know plenty about both," Oliver said, ". . . as long as I have some Blackberry Sunrise to help me along."

Oliver's shoulders slumped as he took his first bite. I wondered how good a memory could possibly be if it weighted so heavy against him.

Oliver began, "I was a rotten kid, Miss Felicity. Spoiled, self-centered, and careless. Honest truth: I used to sit up in that very window and shoot ever' dove that flew past here. Just for meanness' sake.

"My mama said that was an awful offense, to shoot a dove. I told her people did it and they've been doing it forever. She said one thousand people doing a thing didn't make it right. She said doves were sweet birds. They're small and gentle and they only wanna sing. She said that whenever you see a dove, that means hope's coming down. Where's the sport, my mother asked, in shooting a creature so sweet?"

Oliver sighed. "Her words stuck to me, even though I pretended they didn't. 'Cause I wasn't just mean to doves. I was mean to people, too."

"But all of that changed!" Jonah interrupted. He pushed away his empty ice-cream glass. "You *always* spend too much time on the before parts, Oliver. Tell Felicity about the good. Tell her about the woman preacher who changed the course of your days."

A sad smile stretched over Oliver's face. "Her name was Eldee Mae Cotton and she was, indeed, a traveling preacher. She drove a red pickup truck from Knoxville, Tennessee, all up through the Appalachian Mountains. When she came here, to Midnight Gulch, some folks got real backward over it. *Law sakes* — they said. *A woman preacher! It ain't right!*"

"What's wrong with being a woman preacher?" I said. "I think that's awesome."

"So did I." Oliver grinned. "Eventually." He ate another spoonful of Blackberry Sunrise. "But honestly, the reason I first drove out to the fairgrounds to listen to her speak was to see if the crowd might start heckling and hollering and teasing her. And if they did, I figured I'd jump right in. Just to have something to do."

"But then," Jonah butted in, rushing Oliver along.

"But then I got flabbergasted when I saw her," Oliver admitted, "and I couldn't say a word. Firstly, I liked the way she talked — gentle as a songbird. But mostly, I got tongue-tied 'cause she was the prettiest thing I'd ever seen."

Mama would have loved to paint the look on Oliver's face right then. His eyes sparkled, sad and blue. His cheeks wrinkled up into a lonesome smile. If the midnight moon could smile, it would look just the same as Oliver's. Two words arched over his shiny head:

Eldee Mae

Her name looked as pretty as writing in a storybook. I watched the letters of her name curve and stretch, taking up all the space in the room before they faded away.

"Sweet Eldee Mae," Oliver sighed.

The way he said her name made my heart cramp. In all my years of word collecting, I've learned this to be a tried and true fact: I can very often tell how much a person loves another person by the way they say their name. I think that's one of the best feelings in the world, when you know your name is safe in another person's mouth. When you know they'll never shout it out like a cuss word, but say it or whisper it like a once-upon-a-time.

Oliver sighed again and said, "I stood there and listened to Eldee Mae talk about heaven and hope and love. I'd never cared much for that sort of talk in a church house, but I could have listened to her for hours. I got so caught up in what she was saying that I didn't even realize she'd come to stand right in front of me. She was a tiny thing. Probably no taller than you, Felicity, no bigger than a dove. I saw a feisty-spark in her eyes and I thought — *This is it. This crazy preacher lady's about to tell me what's what. . . .*"

"Did she?" I asked.

"No, ma'am," said Oliver. He leaned up on his forearms. I could see his tattoo clearly now: a dove with ink-black wings.

"Eldee Mae reached out for me" — he tapped his chest — "pressed her hand right over my heart. And she said to me, '*God ain't forgotten about you, Oliver Weatherly. He doesn't forget anybody. Hope's coming down.*'"

"What'd you say back?" I sighed.

"I laughed in her face," Oliver admitted. "But she didn't look offended. She went back to preaching and I drove home as fast as I could.

"I fell asleep underneath that very window." Oliver pointed toward the second story again. "And when I woke up the next morning, that's when I saw the shadow" — Oliver fluttered his fingers in front of his face — "just weaving back and forth across the room. I glanced out the window and hey-yo! As sure as I live and breathe, there was a hot air balloon swooping back and forth across the sunrise. I staggered outside just in time to see it crash-land in my front yard, honest truth."

As Oliver spoke, my mind called up a peculiar memory.

. . . the picture on my aunt Cleo's wall.

. . . the sad man beside the hot air balloon.

"Who was in the balloon?" I whispered.

"An old man," Oliver said. "A very, very old man. He was a stout-looking fellow, though, despite his age. He tumbled out of the balloon basket and shook the dust out of his thick white hair, cussing up a firestorm of words until he looked at me. Then his eyes opened up wide, big as gumballs.

"That old man put his hand over his heart and blinked at me like I might disappear. And then he said . . . '*Berry?*'

"I said to him, '*Yes, sir?*' But then I corrected myself real quick. '*No, sir. Berry Weatherly was my grandfather. I'm Oliver Berry Weatherly, his grandson, named in his honor.*'

"Hey-*yo*," Oliver sighed, taking another bite of Blackberry Sunrise. "That man looked like he might fall over dead when I told him that. He kept his hand pressed against his heart when he said, '*What do you mean . . . was your grandfather?*'

"And I told him that I'd never actually seen Berry Weatherly. He took off long before I was even born and never came back to town."

Oliver shook his head sadly. "Those words barely left my mouth before the balloon man started crying. I'll never forget the big tears rolling down his face. '*You look so much like Berry,*' he said to me."

I reached over and patted Oliver's tattooed arm. "What'd you say back?"

Oliver sighed. "I got feisty with him, I admit. I asked

him how the heck he knew my grandpa Berry. And where the heck he came from. And why the heck he'd crashed a balloon into my yard.

"That old man looked me right in the eye and said, '*I come from everywhere now. But before that, I came from this town. I landed my balloon here because I have words worth saying. And I knew your grandfather . . . I know your grandfather . . . because he's my brother.*'"

I put down the carton of Chocolate Orange Switcheroo with a thud. "So that means . . ." My eyebrows raised so high I thought they might float off my forehead. "That man was . . ."

Oliver settled back into his chair. "You remember how I told you there's always more to the story than what you hear? Well, this is exactly what I was talking about. Most people in this town only know the story of the Duel."

Oliver looked up toward the second-story window with a sad sparkle in his eyes. "They don't know about the day Stone Weatherly came back to Midnight Gulch."

"Oliver Weatherly!" Charlie Sue peeped back in the door. A pair of thin purple glasses were balanced on the tip of her nose. "Don't hold this meeting too long. The weatherman says a bad storm is headed this way."

Oliver rolled his eyes. "Virgil Duncan is not a weatherman. He's a meddling old farmer with a transmitter in his barn."

"Does it always rain here?" I asked.

Charlie Sue nodded. "Most of the time, yes. You should get Oliver to tell you his theory about why, but not today. Y'all don't wanna be stuck here in a storm, and Virgil says it's going to be one of the worst of the year."

Storm or not, the light in Oliver's library was fading fast. That meant that the sun was sinking on into the mountains for the night. If the sun was nearly tucked in for the night, that meant the birds were finishing up their daytime songs and that meant that the crickets were tuning up their string legs for twilight symphonies. And all of that put together meant that I needed to go home pretty soon or I would be in a heap-load of trouble.

But my heart was telling me to stay put just a little bit longer. Listening to my heart usually turned out to be the right thing, even if it got me grounded for life.

"I'm almost done talking," Oliver said.

Charlie Sue rolled her eyes and shut the door and mumbled something about Oliver never, ever being done talking.

"Stone Weatherly didn't stay here long," Oliver said. "He was cursed with a wandering heart and had to keep moving along. He was such a lonely man."

"I'll bet so," I said. "Especially if he flew around in a hot air balloon. There's nobody to talk to up in the sky." Nobody except the midnight moon. And the moon only knows how to shine.

"That's a fact," Oliver agreed. "Stone Weatherly stayed for a day and told me stories. He told me about his wife. They met in a hot air balloon race, he said. He told me about his family." Oliver's eyes twinkled. "And then he told me the *real* story of the Brothers Threadbare and why they quarreled . . . or *who* they quarreled over, I guess I should say."

Oliver leaned closer to us and whispered, "He told me what *really* happened that day at the Duel."

Jonah glanced at me and I glanced back at him and I knew, the way only friends can figure out silent signals between each other, that Jonah was every bit as fascinated by the magicians in Midnight Gulch as I was.

"Before Stone climbed back in his balloon," Oliver said, "he gave me his guitar."

"The guitar he played to make the clouds change shapes?" I asked.

"The same one exactly!" Oliver smiled. "Stone told me there was still magic in those strings. He hadn't played it since he left town, since he'd vowed never to do magic again. But he told me it wouldn't have mattered if he could. He didn't want to play his guitar without his brother there. He said all the magic was meaningless without Berry around. He told me to give the guitar to Berry, if I ever saw him again, and, if not, just to find a good home for it."

"Which he did." Jonah smiled.

"Hey-yo, did I ever," Oliver said with a grin.

"And he gave you some good advice . . ." Jonah said. I could tell what Jonah was doing: trying to ease Oliver through the sad parts of the story. Trying to speed him up toward the good.

"That's right," Oliver said. He didn't need Blackberry Sunrise for this part. I could tell he was remembering it as clearly as the day it happened.

"Before Stone climbed into the balloon, he told me to stop wasting my time and try to do some good with my life. '*Your words matter more than you know*' is what he told me. And then he climbed back into that balloon and flew away. Just like a dream."

Oliver turned his face to the fading light. "Eldee Mae

was right. Hope came down." Oliver laughed. "Crashed right into my yard, I'd reckon!"

"What happened with Eldee Mae?" I asked.

"Ah!" Oliver grinned. "Later that same night, somebody knocked on my door. Lo and behold, there stood Eldee Mae Cotton. Her truck broke down near here, and she asked if I could help her fix it up."

"Did you?" I asked.

He grinned again. "Eventually. But first I took Stone Weatherly's advice. I said the only words that mattered. I told her that I loved her."

Oliver chuckled, probably remembering the look on Eldee Mae's face. "Took me some time to convince her she loved me, too. We got married the next summer. She was tired of being on the circuit, tired of talking about hereafters. Lots of right-now passing her by, she said. So we figured out ways to do good for people, to help them find joy in the here-today."

"So they bought the ice-cream factory," Jonah said, smiling. "The Honeycutts used to own it, but they'd all passed away and the factory was going under. Eldee said they should buy it and spruce it up again."

"Every good idea was Eldee's idea," Oliver agreed. "After I bought the factory, we started leaving free cartons of ice cream for people. And that was a fine idea. Eldee said we could do better than that. We'd started reading local papers and listening to the news and planning anonymous good deeds for people. Always in secret, if we could. It's better that way."

Oliver reached for a pad of paper on the table and wrote:

The Beedle

And then he wrote *Beedle* backward:

Eldeeb

And then he cut it down the middle and made a spider word of it:

Eldee / b

"That's my wife's name, of course. And the *b*, that's my middle initial. The Beedle became our giving name. We'd always leave a note behind, with a red ribbon tied around it. Red was Eldee's favorite color."

Oliver's chin trembled, just barely. "We had plenty of good years together. Hope came down for me, many more times than I ever deserved."

"And now the Beedle is my job!" Jonah said proudly. "But Oliver is still the CEO."

Our conversation was rudely interrupted by the loudest thump of thunder punching the sky that I'd ever heard. Rain pelted the upstairs window again, and new words dripped down the glass:

Tremble

Quake

Secret

Curse

My hand shook as I jotted down the words in the blue

book. "I really should go home soon. But I wonder — did you ever hear from Stone Weatherly again?"

"No, ma'am." Oliver shook his head. "I have a feeling they both spent the rest of their time trying to find each other, trying to break that dang curse. Most people don't know about that part, either. The curse was very specific, you see:

"Cursed to wander through the night,
Till cords align, and all's made right.
Where sweet amends are made and spoken,
Shadows dance, the curse is broken."

My heart thumped *yes* so loudly that I could hear it echoing in my ears.

I wrote Oliver's words in my blue book: *Cords align. And all's made right.*

Oliver said, "I don't know what that means — cords aligning. But I like to think the Weatherly brothers tried to figure it out. They tried to make things right. So many squabbles seem stupid and silly as you get older."

As Charlie Sue loaded the ice-cream glasses and empty cartons back onto the silver tray, I asked, "Why do you think they called themselves the Brothers Threadbare?"

Oliver scratched his bristly mustache. "One of the big-city papers called them the Brothers Threadbare on account of how shabby their clothes were. The reporter joked about their accents and their style of music. Said they were nothing but redneck farm boys. The paper called them homespun, shabby, and threadbare.

"But!" Oliver smiled. "Instead of getting mad over it, Berry and Stone decided to embrace it. They liked the name so much that it became their stage name: The Brothers Threadbare. Folks loved it, too. Because folks loved *them*. Those dancing clouds and dancing crowds never cared about shabby clothes. They were so grateful for a dancing day."

"My aunt Cleo thinks *threadbare* means 'well loved,'" I said.

"Cleo Harness?" Uncle Oliver's smile widened. "I didn't realize she was your kin."

I nodded. "My mama's sister."

"Huh." Oliver looked down at the grains of the table, the same way Cleo looked off when she had finished talking about a particular topic.

He finally said, "She's a smart woman, Cleo Harness. She's right, too. Threadbare's what we all get to be, if we're lucky. Will you do me a favor, Miss Felicity?" Oliver propped his arms on the table and leaned toward Jonah and me. "Make sure you always find out *both* sides of a story before you decide what's true. All righty?"

"Sure thing," I said. I might have pondered how weird his words were if it weren't for the much bigger weirdness I realized:

Oliver's dove tattoo, the tattoo I was one hundred percent

positive I'd seen on his arm not even an hour before, had disappeared.

"Where'd the . . ." Before I could get my question out, thunder growled across the sky again. Oliver shot up out of his seat. "Charlie Sue's bringing the van around to take y'all home. I guess that idiot weatherman was right. He said September seventh would be the rainiest day of the year."

Jonah said something, but I couldn't hear him over the ringing in my ears. September 7. And a storm was coming. I felt like somebody'd dumped ice water down my back. "You're sure that today's . . . the seventh?"

Jonah nodded. "You okay?"

"No." I rocketed out of my seat. The chair flipped backward against the shiny hardwood floors with a solid thunk. At the exact same time the chair hit the ground, thunder cracked the sky again. "I have to go home now. *Right* now!"

Jonah wheeled over to me. "Are you scared of storms?"

"Storms and sevens." I tried to breathe deep, but my chest couldn't suck in enough air. "I'm not afraid of them, but Mama's superstitious about them. Every time we've ever left a town, it's always been on the seventh, or during a bad storm. When both things combine" — I shivered — "Mama always leaves. Always."

✳ ◇ ✴ ✳ ◇ ✴ ✳ ◇ ✳

Rain blew sideways into my face as I ran up the stairs toward Cleo's apartment. Flashes of purple lightning illuminated the entryway as I pushed off the ground and flung myself through the door.

Just as I feared, Cleo's apartment was a full-on ruckus.

Biscuit was half hidden underneath Cleo's couch, trembling at every clap of thunder. Frannie sat on top of her little blue suitcase, which she'd dragged out to the middle of the living room floor. Before I even said her name, she flew at me and latched on so tight I nearly lost my breath.

"Is Mama still here?" I gulped.

"She's packing our things." Frannie's words were muffled against my jacket.

And then I heard them, Mama and Cleo bickering as they stomped down the hallway. I didn't know if they were trying to talk louder than each other or just louder than the storm. Mama carried a plastic laundry basket full of our clothes and books and the very few earthly possessions we'd packed along with us. She smiled when she saw me in the doorway.

"Good news, June Bug! You remember my crazy friend Babette from Virginia? She knows somebody who knows somebody who got me a job in Seattle. Can you believe it?"

My throat felt scratchy and dry when I tried to swallow. "That's big news, all right."

Cleo propped her hands on her hips. "Holly, you can't possibly be thinking about driving off in this mess. . . ."

And back to arguing they went.

The room was too loud and too full of thunder, lightning, and yelling. Frannie Jo hugged me tighter, like I was the only thing in the world she had to hold on to. Words floated up out of Mama's laundry basket and burst apart, until the ceiling was made of lightning-bolt letters that never reconnected.

"I don't want to leave." Frannie Jo blinked up at me. "Do something. Please."

"We can't go," I yelled, so suddenly and so loud that I scared myself.

Before I could talk myself out of it, I blurted out, "We can't leave, because I'm in the talent show."

I looked up at Mama and Cleo's shocked faces. "I'm a contestant in the Stoneberry Duel. It's a big deal; the whole town's going to be there. And I can't leave now that I've promised to participate. I told Miss Lawson I'd read some of my poems." I hadn't actually done that yet, but it sounded like a fairly believable lie.

Cleo cocked her head sideways. Mama's eyes narrowed, but not in a mean way. She looked like she was trying to figure out what the heck I was up to. "You hate public speaking."

"But I want to try again anyway." That was lie number two. "Cleo says the only way to overcome a fear is to tackle it head-on. So that's what I'm doing." Cleo hadn't actually said that about me. She said it about the characters on her favorite soap opera. But I hoped it still counted.

I watched Mama's face. I waited . . .

Finally, I saw the shadow of her smile. "You're in the talent show? I'm so . . ."

I held my breath.

"Proud." Her smile bloomed beautiful across her face. "The Duel's only a couple of weeks away, right? I guess we can wait until after that to leave." Mama planted a quick kiss on my forehead and said, "I'm so proud of you, June Bug."

I forced a smile, even though all I wanted to do was crawl under the couch, like my dog, and hide until the Duel and the storm and every other bad thing in the world had blown away.

* ◇ ✳ ✳ ◇ ✳ ✳ ◇ ✳

That night I propped my elbows on the windowsill and stared up at the star-patched sky. If I looked down, I could see the rusty roof of the Pickled Jalapeño parked crooked in the lot. If I looked straight ahead, I could see lights scattered through the dark mountains. They were porch lights, probably. But I imagined they were sleeping stars. I made a wish on every single one of them. Jonah'd be thrilled about me dueling. But I couldn't summon up even a teaspoonful of happiness. In fact, I had a strange, sinking feeling that I'd just made everything worse.

"I need a miracle, Frannie Jo."

"Amen!" Frannie yelled. She was bouncing on the inflatable mattress like it was a trampoline. "A big miracle."

"Exactly," I groaned. "Pray for a BIG miracle. And pray it turns up lickety-split quick."

Here's what I've learned about miracles: Sometimes they turn up quick, and sometimes they take their sweet time getting to you. It's hard to tell either way because a miracle never looks exactly how you think it should. Some miracles are big and flashy, and others are sweet and simple. Some miracles make you want to shout, and others make you want to sing.

And some miracles, the very best miracles of all, show up wearing cowboy boots.

Jonah the Secret School-Building Beedle Do-Gooder had to help out in his mama's shop the next afternoon. I offered to help, too, but Jonah told me to go straight to Cleo's and start picking out some important words I might be able to use in the Duel.

"You told your mom you'd write a poem, right? That's perfect. That's a spindiddly talent, Flea. You better write a few of them, though. Miss Lawson says everybody's talent has to last at least three minutes."

Jonah must have seen the fear in my eyes, because he quickly added, "Something good will happen at the Duel. Trust me."

So I sat beside Frannie Jo on the bus ride home, flipping through the blue book in search of awesome words. But thinking about words got me to thinking about standing in front of the entire school at the Duel. And I felt barfy again.

"Hey, Fliss-tee Pickle!" Day Grissom hollered from the front of the bus. "How's your aunt Cleo doing?"

"She's fine as frog hair," I said. "She's probably either sewing or solving the world's problems."

"Don't I know it!" Day grinned. "I never met a more talented woman in all my days."

As Day pulled up in front of the Sandcut Apartments, before I stepped off the bus, he said, "Fliss-tee?"

"Yes, sir?"

Day drummed his fingers against the steering wheel, trying to find some sort of rhythm for the words about to come out of his mouth.

Right then is when I realized Day Grissom had a chunk of a doughnut stuck in his beard. I figured it'd be rude to mention it, but I couldn't help but stare. A beard is a gnarly place for a pastry to reside.

Day must have noticed me staring, because he looked down and said, "Oh!"

And then he untangled the doughnut from his whiskers and started eating it.

"I wondered where that got to!" he said. Crumbs spewed out of his mouth as he spoke. "Will you tell Cleo I said . . . hi?"

"Sure thing." I didn't tell him that I'd delivered that same message, "*Day Grissom says hi*," five times already and the response was always the same. "*Pffft*," Cleo'd always say. Or "*Toss me that pack of cigarettes*."

Frannie Jo and I had no more than opened the door to Cleo's apartment when Cleo yelled my name.

"Felicity Juniper Pickle!"

"I'm right here!" I kicked the door shut with my heel.

Aunt Cleo's hands were propped on her hips . . . or at least the vicinity of the region her hips probably were under her long, flowing dress. Cleo's eyebrows were knit so close together that it looked as if somebody'd taken a Magic Marker and drawn a squiggly black line across her forehead.

Biscuit sat on the floor, staring up at Aunt Cleo, cocking her head from one side to the other, trying to figure out whether or not she was in trouble.

"Felicity," Cleo heaved. "You take this dog on a walk. A *long* walk. She's been chewing up my quilt squares, running circles on my carpet. She's stir-crazy today, and that's making *me* crazy. I gotta finish this wedding quilt for the Slavens and I can't have it smelling like puppy slobber. I'll never get another job if it does."

Cleo's real job, when she wasn't fixing the world's problems, was quilt making. Cleo says people used to ask her for nursery quilts — hedgehog patterns were her specialty. The hedgehog quilts were all the rage for a few years, but then people got tired of those.

So Cleo started making wedding quilts instead. Those were easy, she said, because people always wanted the same pattern: wedding rings.

The rings on Cleo's quilts are way prettier than real wedding rings, though. All the wedding rings I've seen are plain gold, boring and simple and round. But the rings on Cleo's quilts were shaped like gigantic onion rings. And they were packed full of colors, all the pieces and patches she'd saved up over the years. Cleo collects fabric the same as I collect words.

"Here." Cleo tossed me Biscuit's leash. "Go explore down around the picnic tables, but don't go any farther than that, understand? And take your sister walking with you."

"Yay!" Frannie squealed. "I'll go get my hat!" A few minutes later, she scampered back into the living room, wearing a paper pirate hat with ROWDY RANDY'S PANCAKE HOUSE stamped across the front. She was also wearing a baseball mitt over her hand.

"What's the mitt for?" I asked.

Frannie shrugged.

"Get on out!" Cleo waved us toward the door. "Go have fun!"

"Wait!" I hollered. "I nearly forgot to tell you! Day Grissom says hi."

Cleo sighed. "Toss me that pack of cigarettes before you head out."

✳ ◇ ✵ ✳ ◇ ✵ ✳ ◇ ✳

I probably should have clipped on Biscuit's leash as soon as we walked out the door so she could scamper around and stretch her legs. But I decided to carry her down the stairs instead. Sometimes I like to cuddle her as close to my heart as I can. Biscuit never seems to mind. She nuzzled her soft face against my cheek and licked me on the nose.

"Can I walk her now?" Frannie asked, as we reached the last flight of stairs.

I clipped the leash on to the dog collar, settled Biscuit on the ground, and then passed the leash to Frannie.

But Frannie tried to grab on to the leash with her baseball mitt instead of her hand. So the next thing I saw was a streak of white as my dog barked and took off in a speedy run.

Frannie screamed. Screaming is Frannie's involuntary reaction to most things. "Felicity! My dog!"

"Don't worry! I'll get her!" I was already chasing after Biscuit, jumping down the stairs three at a time. "Stay right there, Frannie Jo!"

I leaped from the last step and ran as hard as I could down the hillside, hollering for Biscuit every step of the way. My sneakers pounded dust-colored words out of the ground:

Zippity
Velocity
Dash-away
Boundless

"Biscuit!" I yelled. "What the hayseed are you running after?" But Biscuit never looked back. She sprinted past some picnic tables with her leash trailing along behind her.

I swung my arms and pumped my legs as hard as I could and then I jumped — arms straight out in front of me so I could grab on to Biscuit's leash.

I heard somebody yell, "I got her!" at exactly the same time that I slammed into the ground and yelled, "*OOMPF!*"

106

When I opened my eyes, the first thing I saw was the tip of a tan cowboy boot. As I glanced higher up, I could see jeans and a plaid shirt, too, the silhouette of a tall man standing against the sunlight. He was laughing while my dog climbed all over his shoulders, licking his face and his ears.

"You okay?" the man asked as he reached down to pull me up off the ground. "This is some guard dog you've got here."

Biscuit licked his face in agreement and he laughed again.

I dusted the grass and dirt off my pants and shielded my eyes and tried to get a better look at the dog saver. He was as thin as a zipper, with scruffy blond hair and stubble along his jawline. He was smiling big while he petted Biscuit, but the dark circles under his eyes made him look kinda tired. Kinda sad, too. I smiled up at him and thanked him for catching our dog.

He passed Biscuit back to me and chuckled. "I think your dog's the one who caught me."

That's when I realized he had a guitar case slung behind his back. As soon as he let my dog go, he clutched tightly to the strap across his chest. The way he held it reminded me of the picture of Oliver's grandfather. I thought about how Berry Weatherly held his banjo over his heart like it was a shield, the only protection he had between him and the world.

I nodded to the man and turned to wander off when I heard him yell, "Hey! I'm looking for Cleo Harness and I hear she lives in this apartment complex now. Do you know her?"

I spun around and narrowed my eyes to try and assess whether or not he had any criminal potential. He didn't *look* mean. He looked like a regular grown-up with sad, sky-colored eyes. He was handsome. But I wasn't stupid, and I didn't let that fool me. I figure the witch that took Hansel and Gretel probably looked like a prom queen. He was awfully sweet to my dog, though. And Biscuit's a good judge of character.

"What do you want with Cleo Harness?" I asked.

He looked down at the ground and dragged the tip of his boot back and forth across the grass. "I'm an old friend of hers. Just wanted to say hello."

I had two instincts building up inside me right then. The first was to say, *No, sir. You keep right on walking.* Because I didn't want this handsome grown-up to go rob Aunt Cleo blind, shove all her quilt patches and tabloid magazines and porcelain hedgehogs into his guitar case and dash out of town.

But my other instinct was *YES*. Because what if this man was the answer to my prayer? I'd prayed for a man for Cleo and now a man was standing in front of me. He looked a lot younger than Cleo, but maybe age doesn't matter as long as you're already old. Even the Beedle couldn't have put together an opportunity so fine.

So what I settled on saying was, "You wait *right* here, mister."

I tucked Biscuit underneath my arm again and ran for the apartment.

Almost no time had passed before me and Cleo were back down by the picnic tables. The man hadn't moved an inch. I saw words of cities shining all around him:

Nashville

Roanoke

Kalamazoo

Bakersfield

Burnside

Home again

Home again was the color of ashes.

The man with the guitar looked at Cleo. His mouth smiled, but his eyes stayed sad. "Good to see you, sister."

Sister?

Cleo said nothing. She kept her cigarette in her mouth and had Frannie Jo on her hip. I still had Biscuit perched on my hip. And we stared that man down like two outlaws in a Western cartoon about to have us a showdown.

Frannie Jo pointed to the man's case. "I like guitars," she said.

"It's a banjo, actually," the man said. But his voice wasn't as strong as when he first spoke to me. He looked at Cleo, hoping she'd give him some answers.

"Are you a famous musician or something?" I asked.

"No," he said. And his smile turned so sad that I wished I hadn't even asked.

"Ain't for lack of talent, though," Cleo spoke up. "Girls, this here is my brother, your uncle Boone."

"You're my uncle Boone?" I grinned ear to ear. "Mama told us about you! She says you have songs on the radio!"

Boone stared down at his shoes again. "I had one song on the radio. That was a long time ago. Nothing since then."

"What are you doing back in Midnight Gulch?" I asked.

Aunt Cleo was the one who answered me. "If I had to guess three reasons he's back in town, I'd say one, he's run out of money and two, he needs a place to stay and three, some floozy out in Nashville broke his heart again."

"And four" — Boone swallowed — "I'm so hungry I could eat a horse."

"All I got's potato chips and ice cream," Cleo said.

"We have an uncle!" Frannie squealed. Biscuit wiggled her tail.

Boone nodded. "Y'all are a lot bigger than I thought you'd be. I thought you were babies."

"People grow up," Cleo said. "People change." I could hear a rasp in her voice that I'd never heard before.

Boone kept staring at his boots. I'd never seen somebody stare at the ground so long. "I never really knew how to contact Holly. Is she here, too?"

"Cleo got her a job at the ice-cream factory," I answered, taking a step closer to him. "She'll be home tonight, though."

His eyes flickered up to meet mine. "She and I don't talk much these days."

"Holly probably don't know how to get in touch with you," Cleo said. "Since Boone *Harness* ain't appropriate for

110

Nashville. He goes by Boone *Taylor* out there, girls. Because he says Boone *Taylor* sounds better on a stage."

Boone didn't argue. He scraped the toe of his boot back and forth across the grass, making an invisible line.

Boone on one side. Cleo and the Pickles on the other. I didn't care for that at all.

"I don't care what you call yourself," I said softly. "I'm just glad to have an uncle."

One side of Boone's mouth tipped up in a grin. I'd seen that grin before. When that grin stretched out into a full-blown smile, it would be a dancing smile. A painting smile. Just the same as Mama's.

We all got real quiet then. Boone kept blinking at Cleo with those lonesome blue eyes and I could tell — by the way he was chewing on his lip and clutching that banjo strap — that he thought she would turn him away. But I knew Cleo wouldn't do that.

"C'mon, then, I reckon." Cleo sighed.

And while we followed her in, I kept glancing back at my uncle. I didn't know if Boone was magic or a miracle, or an answer to some prayer I didn't know I'd prayed. It didn't matter how he got there.

I believe a family's still a family no matter if you have two people or ten, no matter if you're raised by a mama or a grandpa. A family can look a hundred different ways, I knew that. But ever since I came to Cleo's, and from the first spindiddly second I knew Boone was my uncle, I felt like puzzle pieces that I didn't know were missing started snapping together against my heart. I didn't just want to belong to a place anymore. I wanted to belong to my family, and I wanted them to belong to me.

Boone's boots thudded heavy against the sidewalk. His heart was weighing him down, I could tell. The words above his head were long guitar strings. They trembled, as if some invisible hand strummed against them:

Failure

Failure

Failure

But Cleo's were the same as they always were:

Patch it

Mend it

Stitch it back together

My aunt and uncle both seemed so sad that I almost felt guilty for being happy. Not just happy, but the happiest I'd ever been.

I had Mama and Biscuit and Frannie Jo. And now I had an aunt and an uncle, too. I had a best friend named Jonah and I knew secrets about the Brothers Threadbare that nobody else knew. *Lonely* had followed me around for so long. That word was always perched somewhere close, always staring down at me, waiting to pounce out my joy. But I hadn't seen *lonely* near me in a while. And I hadn't seen it near the people I loved, either.

"I love this music!" Frannie Jo hollered. And she started grabbing fistfuls of silent, summer air.

Cleo sighed and kept walking and Boone nodded and

stared down at the pavement like he'd remembered, for the first time since coming here, that his family was a bunch of lunatics.

But suddenly, I stopped right on the sidewalk. I didn't hear music, but I did hear something, and at first it was so faint I thought it was just the wind or the birds in the woods. But the sound wasn't any of that. I heard the sound of wind chimes, far away but moving closer.

Boone and Cleo kept walking, like they didn't hear a thing.

I heard it, though. I looked across the parking lot and into the woods. As the sound of the wind chimes faded, I remembered something peculiar Oliver had said:

"And then he told me the real *story of the Brothers Threadbare and why they quarreled . . . or who* they quarreled over, I guess I should say."

"Well, that's got nothing to do with me," I said out loud to the creepy-chimey wind.

The wind didn't answer me, but my heart sure did.

Yes.

Yes.

Yes.

I realize it's not such an uncommon thing for people to have aunts and uncles, but I'd never met my family before we moved to Midnight Gulch. I'd talked to Cleo on the phone a few times, and Mama'd shown me pictures of Cleo visiting me when I was a baby. I'd never even seen a picture of Boone Harness. I always knew he was special, though, because of the way Mama said his name.

For the longest time, I thought she was calling him Boom. I finally asked her one day, "Is his name Boom, like a firework?"

"Not Boom," she'd laughed. Then she fluttered her hand against her chest. "His name is Boone, like a heartbeat."

And now Boone-like-a-heartbeat was sitting right in front of me in the Pickled Jalapeño.

Cleo was driving through town like a mad woman, swerving around street corners so fast that the tires squealed. Mama didn't seem to mind Cleo's crazy driving today. She was happy to have the day off from work, and I was happy to see her in regular clothes again, in her paint-stained jeans and a white T-shirt. She still hadn't painted anything, but I figured the fact that she was wearing her paint clothes was a good start. Mama sat in the front seat, angled around so she could catch up with my mysterious uncle.

All of us were fascinated by Boone, Frannie Jo especially. She sat right up against him in the middle seat, blinking her big blue eyes up at him like he was the King of the World.

Suddenly, the van lurched a hard left so fast that Frannie smooshed into Boone, and I smooshed into the window.

Mama shoved her sunglasses up into her hair and glared at Cleo. "Where you going? The creamery's downtown."

"You don't think I know how to get downtown? I *live* here. I decided to take the girls to Snapdragon Pond."

"Oh." Mama shrugged at the same time Boone slid down into the seat and asked, "Why?"

I rested my chin on the middle seat. "You don't like the pond, Boone?"

Boone shook his head. "I just . . . I didn't want to get out so soon. I don't mind riding in a car, but I don't want to be outside. I don't want to see anybody. I need a few days to . . . you know . . . *recover*."

Frannie rested her hand on his arm. Her fingernails were painted bubble-gum pink. "Are you sick somewhere?"

"Right here." Boone tapped his heart.

"Boone," Cleo groaned from the front seat. "There ain't nothing about sitting all by yourself all day, crying into a bucket of ice cream, that's gonna make that broken heart heal any faster. You need fresh air and sunshine. There's nobody at Snapdragon Pond this time of year anyway."

Boone let out a quick sigh of relief. "That's good to know."

Cleo grinned in the rearview mirror. "I was hoping maybe you could play some songs for us. The girls ain't ever heard you play. You bring your banjo?"

"Nope," Boone clipped. He chewed on his bottom lip, the same way Mama does when she's nervous. "Honestly, I don't know if I'll ever play that banjo again. Every good love song I played came to me because of *her*. Now they're all ruined."

Mama turned around and patted Boone's knee. "I'm sorry, sweetie." She said it the same way she talks to us when we're hurt or sick or sad.

Aunt Cleo wasn't quite as comforting as Mama.

"Boone!" Cleo hollered. "Stop being so dramatic. Holly, don't baby him. If he's a real musician, then he'll find a new song. A better song. It's time to face the world again! Ain't that right, girls?"

"Cleo's right," I said quietly. I patted his shoulder. "You'll find a better song."

Frannie Jo lifted her arms up toward heaven, like she was about to shout "Hallelujah." "Felicity can help you! She catches poems for me! She sees words on people sometimes."

I shook my head at Frannie Jo and tapped my finger against my lips. *Shhhh*. I didn't want Boone to know about

116

my word-collecting ability because I didn't want him to think I was a freak.

"Is that right?" Boone turned around to look at me. I felt my cheeks go red, every freckle on the bridge of my nose tingling like a little lava drop.

Boone smiled. "Do you see any words hovering around me right now?"

I nodded. I definitely saw some words:

Regret

Has-Been

Idiot

Deadbeat

"Well?" Boone blinked at me. "What words do you see? Can I use them in a new song?" Boone had the same blue eyes as Mama and Frannie and Cleo. My eyes are a different color from theirs. I wonder if my eyes look as sad as theirs, though. I wonder if I see things the same as they do.

I know I see words they can't see.

I wonder if I can see other things they can't. Jonah can read a sad story in the newspaper and find a way to help somebody. I'd like to do that, too, see things better than they are.

"New beginning," my voice crackled. "Those are your words: *new beginning*." I didn't make eye contact with Mama. She'd know it was a fib. And anyhow, I wasn't lying, not *exactly*. I might not have seen those exact words sitting on my uncle's shoulders, but they were still true words. They *could* be, at least.

"Yeah?" Boone's cheek dimpled like he was about to smile at me. "New beginning?"

I nodded. "Your words are shaped like sparrows. They're perched right on your shoulders."

"Ain't that something," Boone said softly, like he was amazed by my skills.

Frannie Jo smiled back at me as if I was the coolest girl who ever lived. Someday she'll probably stop looking at me that way, but I hope it's not for a long time. Mama wasn't looking at me. She had her face turned toward the light of the window. The sun was doing its best to shine on her, to warm up all the cold places down in her heart.

Aunt Cleo caught my eye in the rearview mirror, though. She winked at me. I winked back.

"New beginning," Cleo drawled. "You heard it, Boone. Today's your day for starting over."

A smile stretched full and easy across Boone's face. He sat up taller in his seat and nodded, just once. Affirmative. He believed me.

Craziest thing happened then:

Regret, Has-Been, Idiot, Deadbeat . . .

I watched every last one of those words pop like bath bubbles and disappear.

My heart kicked hard against me: *Yes. Yes. Yes.*

Maybe sometimes the words I say are as magical as the words I see.

"I used to be that way," Boone said. He looked out the window, at Midnight Gulch blurring past us. But I knew he was talking to me. "When I was a kid, I could see things, too. Not words, like you see. But when somebody played a piano, I saw the notes like colors. It's a hard thing to explain. But if somebody played C-sharp, I'd see purple. They'd play A-flat and I'd see yellow, and on and on. Same thing happened when I heard somebody play a guitar or a violin. Or a banjo." He grinned. "Music notes looked like colors to me. That's why I started playing, because it was like painting with no paintbrush. I learned to paint songs. Seemed as cool as any magic I'd heard of in Midnight Gulch."

I propped my arms on the middle seat and rested my chin on my wrist. "Do you still see colors when you play?"

I've wondered if words will be harder to collect as I get older. I wonder if, someday, they'll just become flat letters in books. I'd like to keep seeing words the way I do now, if I can, but there's a chance they could disappear someday. There's a chance they could disappear tomorrow.

"Sometimes I still see colors." Boone glanced back at me. "When I'm playing my best, I still see colors."

I sat back and smiled. Maybe I'd see my words forever, too. Maybe I could paint pictures with my stories someday. And if not, maybe an even better magic would find me.

That's a wonderful word: *maybe*. I watched *maybe* stretch out, long and starry. The letter *y* looked as fiery as the tail of a comet; it looped around our shoulders, connecting us all together.

* ◇ ＊ * ◇ ＊ * ◇ *

"Welcome to Snapdragon Pond, girls!" Cleo swerved the van into a gravel parking lot and stomped the brakes so hard I heard all of our seat belts catch. There were no other cars in the lot. As far as I could see, there was no water, either.

"Aunt Cleo," I asked, "is Snapdragon Pond . . . made of rocks?"

Boone chuckled. "Pretty much."

"Pond's a short walk that way." Cleo pointed to a path swirling into the woods. "Everybody grab a camping chair out of the back. Boone, you can carry the snack bag, too."

"Yes, ma'am." Boone saluted.

"Also," Cleo said, "I brought us a box of wings."

Frannie gasped.

Boone's whole body went still. "A box of *what*?"

"Wings," Cleo said louder. "Frannie Jo wanted to play fairy kingdom, so I made everybody their own pair of wings. Y'all strap on a pair of wings, grab a camping chair, and then we'll walk to the pond."

Frannie Jo was so excited that she started bouncing in the seat, fluttering her hands together.

Boone remained perfectly still. He seemed to be pondering the situation carefully. "Think I'll wait here in the van."

"Boone! It won't kill you to have fun!" Cleo's holler was persuasive. But it wasn't Cleo's hollering that melted Boone's broken heart. It was my little sister.

"Boone." Frannie said his name like a heartbeat, the same way Mama did. She twisted her hands together and shrugged her shoulders. "Is it a stupid game? Is that why you won't play?"

"No! It's not stupid!" Boone tried to smile at Frannie, but I could see the panic in his eyes. "Fairy kingdom . . ." he sighed. "It's . . . an *awesome* game."

Frannie stared at her lap and smoothed the fluffs of her yellow tutu. "But you won't play?"

Mama raised an eyebrow at Boone, an I-dare-you smile pulling at the corners of her mouth. Cleo slid out of the van and heaved open Boone's door, holding out a pair of grown-up-size wings. The wings were made of wire and gauzy camouflage. I didn't even know gauzy camouflage existed, but it looked so tough and pretty. I hoped Cleo made mine the same way.

Frannie Jo tapped Boone's leg and smiled up at him. "I have a fake sword in my suitcase. You can be the fairy prince! I'll be the princess."

Boone nodded toward my aunt. "Is Cleo the wicked witch?"

Cleo narrowed her eyes. "I'm the Boss Fairy."

"Obviously," Boone sighed. He zipped his hoodie with one quick *zrrrrrp*. He reached for his wings. "Lead the way, Boss Fairy."

* ◇ ☀ * ◇ ☀ * ◇ *

I sat on the banks of Snapdragon Pond and freewrote. The grass was cool and prickly against my legs. The shadow of my gauzy-camouflage wings made pretty patterns on the page of my blue book.

Important Facts about Snapdragon Pond

1. Snapdragon Pond looks bigger than a pond, more like a lake. It's surrounded by tall pine trees, and I can see the mountains rising up all around us. Cleo says Snapdragon Pond is so shallow that people put their camping chairs in the middle of the water and sit there all day during the summer. That sounds boring to me, but I guess it'd be fun if you were sitting with people you liked.

2. The water looks like a mirror. I can see pine trees and blue sky and clouds reflected in the water, like somebody flipped the world. Maybe there's an upside-down universe hidden in Snapdragon Pond. Or maybe that's the real universe and we're all just living upside down.

3. There are no fish in the water, but when I stand on the shore, I see a bunch of fish-shaped words. In case Jonah asks, so far I've seen: <u>depth</u>, <u>breadth</u>, <u>snorkel</u>, <u>submarine</u>, <u>subterfuge</u>, <u>slick</u>, <u>gilleyboom</u>. I'm not sure <u>gilleyboom</u> is a real word but

"There's my word collector." Mama kneeled down beside me and tugged at my wings. "I hate to interrupt, but will you come with me? There's a place near here I'd love to show you."

The way Mama's eyes sparkled gave me reason enough to tuck the book carefully into my backpack. Mama grabbed my hand and pulled me up tall.

"Hey, Boone," Mama said, as she slid her thin arms out of her wings. "I want to show Felicity something. Keep an eye on Frannie?"

Boone still had his wings on over his hoodie. He and Frannie looked like thieving fairies, rummaging through Cleo's snack bag. Cleo was asleep in one of the camping chairs, her feet propped up on a red cooler, her wings pressed sideways and flat behind her. Boone gave Mama a thumbs-up.

Mama helped me shrug out of my wings. Then she winked and said, "Follow me." She was using her story voice now. I'd follow that voice anywhere.

Mama clutched my hand tightly in hers and we took off in a run. We ran along the shore of Snapdragon Pond, down the hill, and into the woods. Mama didn't trip or stumble, not even when the ground was covered with moss and brambles. Because I was holding her hand, I didn't trip, either. Twigs made *pop-snip-snap* sounds underneath the weight of our shoes.

Patches of sunshine streamed down through the forest canopy, falling over us in sudden waterfalls of light. I watched leaves twirl down from the high places. Words came twirling toward us, too:

Becoming
Unfurling
Bloom up
Bright and fine

Mama pulled me along behind her. Occasionally, she'd glance back, her blond hair swinging across her face, and yell, "You okay, June Bug?"

I nodded. I was breathless and happy. I was better than okay.

Mama slowed down to help me navigate a steep incline. We both laughed when my sneaker made a funny *FWOP* sound as it came down in a clump of mud. Finally, we walked into the shady grove of the tall trees. The shady trees were different from the pine trees; they had long, tangly limbs and thick trunks. They were connected together by strong roots and long shadows. Mama pointed at the tallest tree, the extra-leafy one. "Feel like climbing?"

The truth is that I've never cared anything about sports. In PE, I do my best to get hit with the dodgeball on the first throw so I can sit out and read instead of play. I'd rather eat a hot dog at a baseball game than play baseball. I'd rather paint a soccer ball than kick one. I don't mind running, but only if I'm running toward something wonderful. I don't see the point in running away from anything, ever. But tree climbing is different. Tree climbing is natural and easy and I'm pretty sure I could climb for hours and never get tired.

Mama says it's the mountain girl in me. She says mountain girls climb trees and fences and anything else that gets us closer to the stars.

I reached up for the thick, low limb, gripping the scratchy bark tightly between my hands. Mama gave me a boost and I swung my legs up, too. I found my footing, easy. Soon, I heard her climbing up behind me. Together, we made our way up through the limbs.

"How far can I climb?" I breathed. Because with the mountain wind in my lungs and the sun shining down on me, I felt like I could climb to infinity. I could climb past the clouds, to the place where Jack found the giant's castle. I could climb to the prickliest star in the sky and scratch its back. I could climb past that even, all the way to heaven, and give God a high five for bringing my family together. I could climb to eternity. I could climb to forever.

"That's far enough," Mama said. She sounded like her breath was running out. When I looked back at her, her face was a pretty pink color. I steadied my feet and leaned back into the strong branches, reaching for Mama so she could take my hand and come up beside me. She nestled in against me, shoulder to shoulder. I was glad Mama had only brought me. Whenever Frannie Jo climbs a tree, she'll curl up like a cat on one of the branches and start screeching until I get her down.

"This is the forest that surrounds Midnight Gulch," Mama breathed. "Keeps the town secret from the rest of the world. Remember me telling you that story?"

I nodded.

"When I was a little girl, I used to play in these woods. This tree was my favorite place to climb. I'd climb as high in these branches as I could go, just so I could see *that* . . ."

Mama pointed to the tall mountains rippling against the sky, circling us.

"I like the mountains, too," I said. "From up here, I feel like they're hugging me."

Mama smiled. "I'm not talking about the mountains. I never loved them the way you do. I always felt like they hemmed me in."

Hemmed mountains made me think of Aunt Cleo's words:

Patch it

Mend it

Stitch it back together

"Look closer." Mama leaned her scrawny arm across me and pointed. The friendship bracelet I'd made her last summer was still tied to her wrist, barely a bundle of frays now. I'd made one for Frannie Jo, too, three strands for the three of us. "You see that little spark of silver out there on that mountain? If you keep watching, you'll see another flash of light soon. Look closely."

"I see it!" I saw *lots* of it, actually, flickers in a steady vertical line down the mountain.

"Those are cars." Mama smiled. "That's the interstate winding down the mountain. Isn't that exciting? When I was a girl, I used to sit up here and dream about where those people were going. Every flash of light up there is a

126

new adventure. I couldn't wait to have an adventure of my own."

My heart sank down into the vicinity of my sneakers. Mama was always thinking of going. Never staying put.

Stop settling in here, I told my heart. Because it didn't matter if I bought us two more weeks of time or another month, even. Having extra time here would only make it harder when we finally left. And Pickles always leave. Soon enough, there'd be a new town. A new first day of school. A new cafeteria where apples tasted like sand and *LONELY* creepy-crawled all across the tables and wedged itself in all my books.

I managed to whisper a question I'd been wondering about for a while. "Do you drive sometimes when I'm in school? During the day, before you go to your shift at work, do you go drive around that mountain?"

Mama nodded. "Sometimes. You know how I am."

I didn't want my next words to come out, but they did anyway. They were wild words. I couldn't control them. "You won't ever drive away without me, will you?"

"Felicity," Mama sighed. I cringed at the hurt in her voice. "I'd never do that. Look at me."

Her face was still beautiful, even blurred through the tears I was trying not to cry.

"I won't go anywhere without you," she promised.

I asked, "Why did you hate it here so much?"

"I don't hate it," Mama said, staring down at her brace-let again. She picked at one of the frays. That bracelet was

127

falling apart; it'd fall off her wrist someday and she wouldn't even realize it. "But sometimes I feel like I'll lose my mind if I don't keep moving."

I knew that already. I've always known it. When I was a baby, it was a car or a van rocking me to sleep at night, not a rocking chair. We stayed in towns a few months at a time, sometimes a whole year. When I was little bitty, Roger Pickle traveled with us, but I guess he got tired of always adventuring. Or maybe he just got tired of us.

Just thinking about Roger Pickle made my heart feel like somebody'd drop-kicked it. A whole stack of questions — mean questions — tried to work their way out of my mouth.

I wanted to ask Mama outright: *Why don't you ever talk about him?*

Why don't you paint anymore?

Why can't you try to stay here?

Why won't you try?

But I didn't say those things. Instead, I threaded my fingers through hers. She traced an invisible heart on the back of my hand, connected the freckle-dots. "Life's always an adventure for us, June Bug. We've got rambling hearts. We gotta keep moving, right?"

Mama had a rambling heart. But I wasn't so sure I did.

My heart wanted to bloom up bright and fine here in Midnight Gulch. I wanted Mama to love it here like I did. I wanted Cleo and Boone and Jonah and Miss Lawson's history lessons. I wanted a town that smelled like baking cookies all the time. I wanted mountains with magic caught up inside them. I wanted that stupid Duel about as much as I wanted chicken pox, but I'd do that even, if it meant I could stay.

"June Bug?" Mama sighed.

"We've got rambling hearts." I lied for the second time that day. Because the only thought worse than leaving Midnight Gulch was the thought of Mama leaving without me.

"That's my girl." Mama sounded relieved. She set her eyes on the sparkly interstate. I knew she was wishing us somewhere far away.

The words in the woods hung like fat apples from the branches:

Becoming
Unfurling
Bloom up
Bright and fine

I gathered those words in my heart. Then I set my eyes on the mountains and wished they'd never let us go. *Keep us safe. Keep us here. Hold us tight.*

Mama and I walked back out of the woods just in time to hear Frannie squeal, "I want to stay here forever!"

"Fine by me." Cleo smiled. She opened up her little red cooler and sloshed through the ice. She pulled out an orange soda bottle and passed it to my sister. "We can stay here all day, at least."

"Cleo Harness?" yelled a familiar, husky voice from the edge of the woods. "Is that you?"

"Pack up!" Cleo hollered. "We're leaving!" She kicked the cooler lid shut and stood up so fast that her camping chair stayed stuck to her behind.

Boone lifted his plastic sword toward the sky and waved his other hand in greeting. "Day Grissom?" he yelled. "I haven't seen you in forever!"

Aunt Cleo looped the cooler over her arm like a purse and said, "C'mon. We're leaving. Now."

Frannie's smile fell into a frown. "You said we'd stay forever."

"I changed my mind," Cleo yelled as she stomped toward the path.

I ruffled Frannie's hair and promised to catch her a poem on the way home and she sighed okay.

With our fairy wings secured, we grabbed our chairs, and Boone got the snack bag and we marched back toward the path.

"I can help y'all carry something," Day said as he walked up beside Cleo.

"Don't need help," Cleo mumbled. She never looked at Day, just stomped on past him. He didn't seem surprised.

"I'm telling the truth, Cleo," Day said, shoving his hands deep into his pockets. "You look just like an angel right now."

Cleo's wings were bent, turned sideways against her back. With her hair piled haystack-high on her head and

130

her black sunglasses covering half her face, she looked to me more like an angry bumblebee than an angel. Cleo didn't respond to Day's compliment. She kept on walking.

I waved at Day when we passed him. When he waved back, I thought I saw a sad smile hiding under his beard.

Boone stayed back to talk to him for a few minutes. When he caught up to us, he gave Cleo a playful punch on the shoulder and said, "What happened to all those new beginnings you were talking about?"

"Hush, Boone." Cleo tucked a cigarette into her teeth. "Mind your own business."

Mama chuckled. Boone winked down at me and started whistling. Frannie Jo slid her hand into mine and held on tight.

Someday, when I got brave enough to taste Blackberry Sunrise, I hoped that exact memory is the first one I'd think of: The sunset colors stretched across the sky. Tiny red leaves twirled down around us along the wooded path. I wanted to remember Boone's lonesome whistle and the way Cleo's cigarette smoke curled so elegantly, so gracefully up toward the sky. I wanted to remember the way Mama kept looking up toward the clouds, smiling at the birds swooping through the treetops. I never wanted to forget all the ways we were connected that day: By our shadows and sunlight. By pounding hearts and a starry maybe.

By the nearly silent flutter of our broken wings.

"Poets and paupers," Jonah said. He was glancing down at the words I'd just penciled in the blue book.

Day Grissom's bus had dropped us off on Main Street at Dr. Zook's Dreamery Creamery, the only ice-cream shop in the world that had all of Dr. Zook's 45 Mysterious Flavors. Jonah said Zook's was the most swankified place to get some work done. His Beedle work consisted of (1) scheming up nice things to do for people and (2) helping me plan for the Duel. Which he was still convinced was my key to convincing Mama we should stay in Midnight Gulch.

My work was to get inspired enough to write my poems for dueling day. Also, my work was figuring out how to deliver that talent without barfing all over the stage.

"That's why I brought you here," Jonah said. "Because ice cream is wholly inspirational."

But I thought he meant Holy Inspirational.

So I said, "Amen!"

And Jonah shrugged his shoulders and said, "Hallelujah!"

And he bought two pints for us to split.

"Poets and paupers." I nodded toward the window. I reached for the pint of Uncle Duane's Sublime Key Lime Pie. "Those are the words I see across the street at the pie shop."

"No way!" Jonah's green eyes glittered sparkly wild. "That's what that building used to be called. Way back before it was Ponder's Pie Shop, it was a pub called The Poet & Pauper. That's one of the oldest buildings in the whole state."

Jonah leaned across the table toward me. He had a secret-telling look on his face. So I leaned in real close to listen. I liked keeping his secrets.

"You've met Ponder, who owns the pie shop? Well, she's kin to the Smiths. And the Smith magic had to do with cooking."

"How so?" I took a last bite of key lime deliciousness and pushed the pint across the table to Jonah.

"Back during the Civil War," Jonah began, as he nudged his pint of Erin's Peach Pecan across the table to me, "Nancy Smith worked at that shop making spy pies. Soldiers would walk in there and tell Nancy certain secret information. And, somehow, Nancy Smith could bake that information into the pie. There were no slips of paper. No number codes. No tangible pieces of evidence. It was the secret she baked in. Soldiers could taste those pies and know all sorts of important things. The whole war might have turned out different if it hadn't been for Nancy Smith."

"Spindiddly!" I said.

Jonah grinned as he leaned back in his seat. "People claim Ponder's pies still have a snicker of magic."

"A snicker?"

"That's magic leftover," Jonah explained. "Not good for much, not as fancy as it used to be — but enough to make it special."

I leaned across the table and whispered, "Do you think your know-how is a snicker of magic?"

"Maybe." He shrugged. And then he cocked his head at me. "I think your word collecting is a snicker of magic."

"Word collecting's not magic," I argued. "It's just a quirk, just how I am."

Jonah twirled his pen through his fingers. "The Brothers Threadbare probably thought that way. Until the day they saw what their music did to people, how it made them dance. Made them happy."

"In case you've forgotten, the Brothers Threadbare wrecked this town."

"Not at first," Jonah countered.

Oliver's story of the Threadbare curse had stuck with me. I'd written the words in my blue book, but I might as well have written them inside my head and inside my heart and in the air all around me. Because I couldn't stop thinking about them. And I didn't know why.

The Brothers Threadbare were dead and gone.

They had nothing to do with me.

And anyway, the only magic I was interested in was the kind that would make Mama stay put. I'd give anything to find a snicker of magic like that. I looked back across the street at the words *poets and paupers* still fluttering over Ponder's door. "Is there a snicker of magic in Ponder's pies?"

Jonah shrugged his shoulders. "Maybe. She doesn't bake secret spy stuff anymore, of course. But they say her blackberry pie makes people fall in love. And her apple pie makes people feel brave. All I know for sure is that she makes pies that are spindiddly delicious."

"What does that guy do?" I pointed to the scrawny man dancing down the sidewalk across the street. Since Jonah and I had arrived at Dr. Zook's, I'd watched the man set up a huge radio near Ponder's Pie Shop. Then he plugged a microphone into the radio. And now he was singing so loud and hard his face was red. Explosive red. "Does he have a snicker of magic?"

"That's Elvis Phillips," Jonah said. "He stands on Main Street and sings songs by Elvis Presley. No magic there. He figures since his name is Elvis, he's got a similar calling as the King."

"Is he crazy?" I asked.

Elvis Phillips closed his eyes and leaned back. Then he clinched his fist, kicked his scrawny leg out, and howled the final lyric of "Jailhouse Rock."

"He's no crazier than anybody else in Midnight Gulch." Jonah smiled.

"This Duel's making *me* crazy." I looked down at the mostly empty page of my blue book. "I could use a slice of Brave Apple Pie. A gargantuan slice."

Jonah asked me exactly how many poems I'd written for the Duel, and I told him the truth, that I'd written exactly zero-zilch-nothing-nada.

"Flea!" Jonah hollered. "We have less than one week left!"

"Exactly," I said. "It'd be easier to break that stupid curse than compete in the Duel."

Jonah shook his head. "Something good is going to happen at the Duel."

"You said that already."

"Then start believing me!" He leaned closer to me and whispered, "Beedle intuition is always spot-on."

"No matter how many words I write, they're still just words. Words aren't the same as talent."

With a carton of ice cream in one hand and a spoon clutched tight in the other, Jonah looked as determined as I'd ever seen him. "Your words are talent. And I'm going to help you see it."

"I'm grateful for all the ways you're helping me," I sighed. "But when the Duel's over, it won't matter if I win or lose. It won't matter if I say something smart or stupid. In the end, I still have to leave."

Jonah must have seen the panic in my face, because his voice drifted back to peaceful-easy as he said, "Don't worry about your poems yet." He reached across the table and turned to a blank page in the blue book. "Just make a list of random facts. That'll get your pen moving and your imagination running."

Jonah opened his newspaper and started circling and plotting and planning good deeds. I glanced all around me, trying to find some inspiration. I saw an old couple with matching sun visors. They were eating ice-cream cones full of rainbow-colored scoops. I watched a girl with red hair hold a novel in one hand and a waffle cone in the other. She was mumbling the words of her story, so happy to be reading that she didn't notice the pink dollop of ice cream on her chin. I watched little kids stand on their tiptoes and stare at all the bright flavors kept safe behind the glass.

I wondered if any of those people had blue books, too. Did anybody else in the world see words the same way I did? Was word collecting a kind of magic, like singing at the clouds and baking spy pies? Maybe my words were only a snicker of magic. Maybe they were nothing. But they were still mine.

I concentrated on my blue book again. I decided I might as well write about myself.

The 5 Most Interesting Facts about Myself

1. I am Felicity Juniper Pickle. My first name stands for "wondrous joy." My second name stands for a coniferous plant. My third name is Pickle and it stands for all my people behind me and ahead of me.

2. I have a heart-shaped freckle under my right eye. Mama calls it a love bite.

3. I live in a town that used to be full of magic. I think there's still magic here. It's just been playing hide-and-seek for a very long time. This town is also full of sad stories and sweet people. I like it here. I want to stay forever.

4. My best friend's name is Jonah Pickett. He likes to split stuff with me. He splits granola bars and brownies and cans of Dr Pepper and cartons of Dr. Zook's Ice Cream. He always lets me have the bigger half.

I glanced across the table at Jonah. I looked back down at my book. I wrote:

He is splendiferous.

5. Because of Jonah Pickett, I signed up for the Duel. Even though:

5a. I would still rather floss with barbed wire than participate.

The only perk of my impending Dueldom was spending more time with Jonah. Hanging out with my family was fabulous, but my time with Jonah was a different kind of wonderful. Jonah Pickett was like snow days, field trips, candy stores, and Christmas Eve all blended into one big *swoosh* of a feeling.

"Felicity," Jonah drawled.

My face tingled red because I realized I'd been staring at him for way too long.

I shifted my eyes back to the blue book and cleared my throat. "Yep?"

"Is Boone staying at Cleo's apartment, too?"

I nodded. "Cleo says we're packed in tight as sardines. Me and Frannie Jo and Biscuit sleep in the craft room. Mama sleeps on the couch. Uncle Boone sleeps in a sleeping bag in front of the laundry closet.

"Last night, Aunt Cleo forgot he was there and she tripped and fell over him. And her lit cigarette caught the edge of his sleeping bag on fire. Cleo tried to beat out the fire with her house slipper while Boone tried to wriggle out of the sleeping bag, but the zipper was stuck. I don't know if it was the hollering or the smell of smoke that woke up Mama, but she got the fire extinguisher. Then she barreled down the hall, spraying the fire extinguisher like a wild woman. Ruined Cleo's carpet."

Jonah laughed. "We gotta figure out something really good to do for Cleo."

He scribbled a few notes in the corner of the newspaper. Then he reached down into his backpack.

"I picked these up for your uncle."

Jonah passed me a box of new banjo strings.

"Spindiddly!" I said. "But how are you going to get them to him? Boone barely leaves the apartment. He's too sad over the Nashville floozy."

Jonah pulled a roll of red ribbon from his backpack and tossed that across the table, too.

"I figured you could do it." He smiled at me. "Just write something clever on the box and sign it . . ." Jonah mouthed *the Beedle.*

My heart felt heavy in a good way, holding me steady in a moment I needed to be sure and remember.

I leaned across the table and whispered, "*I* get to be . . . pumpernickel?"

"Is that all right? I was thinking the other day, when Oliver talked about Eldee Mae helping him out all those years, that it'd be nice to have an accomplice. Only if you want to, of course."

"I want to!"

"Spindiddly." Jonah smiled. And we both looked out the window just in time to see Elvis Phillips do the split.

✳ ◇ ✳ ✳ ◇ ✳ ✳ ◇ ✳

The wind-chime wind chose that exact moment to make its way down Main Street. And this time, the wind brought a creepy-cold feeling along with it. At first, I pushed the ice-cream carton away from me because I figured the cold was a delayed case of brain freeze.

But then I heard the chimes: soft, quiet, caught in the wrinkles of the autumn air. I hated that sound.

140

Jonah sat up straighter at exactly that moment and I was about to ask him if he heard it, too, if he felt as bone-cold as I did.

But Jonah looked out the window and smiled. "Right on time," he said as he pushed away from the table.

"Pack up the blue book, Felicity!" said Jonah. "There's somebody I want you to meet."

The wind-chime wind had faded out by the time Jonah led me down Main Street.

I thought about Miss Divinity Lawson's words. "Every place has a story," she'd said. So I imagined how Main Street looked one hundred years ago when the Brothers Threadbare played here. Miss Lawson said that the music was so wonderful, so loud and wild and strange, that the trees caught the songs and wouldn't turn them loose. People could always hear the music, she'd said, *"even when the Brothers Threadbare were out of town."*

I thought about people dancing down that very same street I was walking down. Maybe the street looked different then. Maybe people dressed different back then. But I'll bet their hearts sang out *yes-yes-yes* when they danced up the dust of this road.

Nobody was dancing here now. Nobody except Elvis Phillips. And I was fairly certain that's not the sort of dancing Miss Lawson had in mind.

Elvis stopped howling long enough to say hello to Jonah

when we passed by. Next, we both said hello to Ponder Waller. She was busy sweeping the sidewalk around her storefront, a polka-dot apron cinched tight around her waist.

Made from scratch
Ready to rise

"Bring your mama and sister back and let me feed y'all!" she reminded me. And I promised I would. The door to her shop was propped open with an old book. Smells of sugar and caramel apples drifted into the street, enveloping us in a warm haze of pure delight.

"Bet that's what heaven smells like," Jonah said.

"Amen," I said.

"Hallelujah," Jonah agreed.

I pulled out my blue book to collect the words Ponder was sweeping up alongside all the dust and dirt and feathers around her door:

Whimsy
Wonder
Celebration
Sorrow

"We're turning here, Felicity," Jonah said. And it's a good thing he told me, because I was concentrating so hard on my words that I might have kept on going.

As we turned onto Second Street, I could hear the river gurgling somewhere close by. And if I could hear the river, that meant we were close to the bridge that brought me into Midnight Gulch.

"The Gallery's right up ahead," Jonah said. "Have you seen it up close yet?"

"No," I answered. My heart ached as we walked toward the old building. "But it looks even sadder up close than it did from far off."

The paint was mostly chipped off the Gallery wall, but not enough for me to tell what Stone Weatherly had painted there one hundred years ago. His painting was probably faded by now anyway. Time fades every picture, no matter how bright it is to start.

The spray-painted words on the Gallery still trembled and shivered, like they didn't belong there. But today, the words weren't the only thing that looked out of place.

A skinny woman sat on the sidewalk, her back against the Gallery wall. She kept her knees pulled up against her chest and her eyes cast down. She kept an old canvas bag slumped on the ground beside her.

I couldn't tell much about her face right then because all I could see was her hair: dark black and long, with yellow ribbons twisted through the braids closest to her face. She held a cigarette loosely between her skinny fingers. Smoke curled off the tip and rose up into the most extraordinary words:

Magnolia
Star root
Dragon

Luminous
Memory

The silver bracelets along her arm jingled pretty as she lifted the cigarette to her mouth. That's when I first saw her face; it was as strange and pretty as her words had been. She was spellbinding.

She must have noticed us right then, too. She smiled, starry white.

"Jonah Pickett," she rasped. "How'd you know I'd be out here, Honeybee?"

"Florentine calls me Honeybee because my hair is blond and prickly," Jonah said.

"And because you're so sweet!" said the woman, who looked about the same age as my mama. They were both too young to have so much sadness caught in their eyes. "How'd you know I was sitting here hoping for company?"

Jonah wheeled up beside Florentine. He pulled an icy pint of Blackberry Sunrise from his backpack. He grinned as he handed her the ice-cream carton and a plastic spoon. "The Beedle knows everything."

Florentine glanced at me. She glanced back at Jonah and raised an eyebrow. "Pumpernickel?" she asked.

Jonah nodded. "She knows."

"Does she now?" Florentine drawled. "This girl must be something special."

"Yes, ma'am." Jonah smiled at me. "She sure is."

The tips of my ears burned so hot I thought about running off to dunk my head in the river. Instead, I sat down on the sidewalk across from the starry-smiled stranger.

"You better tell me more about her, then," said Florentine. "Better tell me more about this pretty little girl you done told your pumpernickel secrets to."

"She's my best friend, Felicity Pickle," Jonah said.

Best friend. Not just a friend, a *best* friend. The *friend* word fluttered around between us, still squirmy and bug-legged. Now it had a set of golden wings.

Jonah said to me, "I wanted you to meet Florentine because she's a poet."

A poet. No wonder she was a strange and starry-smiled kind of pretty. No wonder she was beautiful. Poets always are.

"I've been many other things, too," Florentine said. "I've been a laundry folder and a bread baker. I worked at a fish market on the Georgia coast. I flicked scales off them fish for so long that I still see words that way, shiny as scales, brittle as bones. And somehow, someday, somewhere along the way" — she shrugged her shoulders — "I became a poet."

"Felicity's a poet, too," Jonah said softly.

"I'm not a poet." I gulped. I reached down to touch the fluffy crown of a dandelion blooming through a crack in the sidewalk. "I make up silly little rhymes for my sister sometimes. But I'm not a poet."

Jonah rolled his eyes. "She's got stories worth telling, Florentine. She just doesn't believe it yet."

"You will." Florentine starry-smiled at me. Then she chuckled. "Don't matter, anyway, if you do or if you don't. Stories aren't peaceful things. Stories don't care how shy you are. They don't care how insecure you are, either. Stories find their own way out eventually. All you gotta do is turn 'em loose."

I felt a chill twirl down my spine, all the way down to my toes, then back up to the tips of my ears. The same strange, cold feeling I had earlier pricked at my arms again. That stupid wind-chime wind followed soon after and I remembered Oliver's words as clearly as when he first spoke them:

And then he told me the real *story of the Brothers Threadbare and why they quarreled . . . or who* they *quarreled over, I guess I should say. . . .*

That's got nothing to do with me, my head said to my heart.

But my heart disagreed.

I shivered at the creepy wind-chime sound. Florentine cocked her head ever so slightly to the side, looking at me. She'd noticed.

And then she glanced down at the slouchy bag beside her.

Florentine gently rested her hand on top of her traveling bag. As soon as she did, the wind chimes stopped.

The cold feeling faded away, but I couldn't stop shivering. Thunder rolled, low and steady across the sky.

146

"Storm must be coming soon," Jonah said.

Florentine kept her eyes fixed on her traveling bag. Then she slowly looked back up at me. "Storm's coming indeed," she said softly.

I didn't say a word. I let my heart do all the talking. *Yes. Yes. Yes.*

"Better make yourself comfortable, Felicity Pickle," said Florentine. "I've got a story worth telling."

Silver-gray rain clouds crept slowly over the mountains and across the skies of Midnight Gulch. I had a feeling that, just like me and Jonah, the storm was scooting in close so it could hear Florentine's story.

Florentine crushed her cigarette down onto the pavement. She laced her fingers together over her knees. The knees of her jeans were worn out, barely held together by thin white frays. She wrapped the threads around her finger as she spoke.

"I was born down in south Georgia," she said. "I grew up at the end of a red-dirt road, in a farmhouse that some folks claimed was magic. And after the tornadoes blew through . . ." Florentine shook her head. "That's when I knew those folks were exactly right. I'll never forget the night the storms came. We had seven twisters total, all before the sun came up.

"Those storms pulled hundred-year-old trees out of the ground." Florentine said. "Pulled houses right off their foundations. Even the courthouse was nothing but a pile of bricks and stones and broken glass. But the farmhouse where I lived with my granny Opal stood tall; not even a shingle was blown off our roof.

"I asked my granny Opal why we came out so fine. She looked over at the cupboard in our kitchen, the one she always kept locked up tight, and then looked back at me and said, 'A little bit of magic goes a long way.'

"And I said to her, 'So you do have something magic locked up in that cupboard?'

"She said, 'I got nothing but burdens in that cupboard, child. That's what keeps us safe. And that's what keeps us heavyhearted. Strange magic is what it is. Dark magic. You never, ever open that door. Understand?'"

Florentine popped open the carton of Blackberry Sunrise. She savored a big spoonful. I could tell the ice cream was doing its job, helping her taste old memories and remember the details.

"My granny Opal was the only family I had," Florentine continued. "My only friend, too. My speech was twisted when I was a girl; words got stuck in my mouth when I tried to speak 'em out. Granny Opal didn't mind, but everybody else sure made fun of me for it."

Florentine passed the Blackberry Sunrise back to Jonah. I could tell these memories didn't taste good.

"The only place I wanted to be was up in my tree. I'd take my granny's books and climb up to my favorite branch and read myself a good story. The story words were the only things that steadied my soul. Those words weren't twisted. They didn't break apart. They took me out of this world. Some books are magic that way. Your body stays right here, hiding in a tree, tucked away in a closet, sitting up against a crumbling old building." Florentine grinned. "But good stories take your heart someplace else. My body'd never been out of south Georgia. But my heart lived everywhere. I'd lived a hundred lives without ever leaving my tree."

"I know that feeling." I smiled.

"Every word collector sure knows that feeling, whether you've been catching songs or poems or stories. You've been caught in that magic." Florentine sighed. "I read other people's stories. But I kept my own words hidden."

"But you talk so pretty now," I said.

"I wish Granny Opal could have heard me find my voice again," Florentine said. "She told me that it was fine that I steadied my heart against the pages of a book. *'But that ain't no way to live,'* she told me, *'getting so caught up in other people's stories you never have one of your own.'*"

Jonah passed the ice cream back to Florentine again. She savored another bite.

The way the two of them kept passing the ice cream back and forth reminded me of the money plate passed around at the church. I considered how that would be the neatest idea, if the deacons passed around bowls of ice cream instead of bowls of cash-money.

Offering
Sacred

150

Everlasting

. . . Words that belonged in a sanctuary filled up the spaces between the three of us. But those words looked as fine there as they'd ever looked in a church, and I wondered if there was something sacred, something everlasting, about melted ice cream and summer days and good stories. "Florentine," Jonah said, "tell Felicity about the day you set out to find your own story."

She nodded. "I still didn't see any point in talking to people. But I liked the idea of having my own story somewhere out in the big wide world. And I knew my story wasn't in that town. Or even in that old, magic house. So I took this old backpack and I filled it with books. And just as I was about to leave, I remembered the night the storms came, the night my granny pointed to the locked door and told me about the magic behind it. The magic that kept my family safe. That kept my family heavyhearted . . .

"So I found the key." Florentine swallowed hard. "And I pulled those burdens out of that cupboard. And I put them in here, too." Florentine patted her traveling bag.

"I hitched my bag around my shoulders — it was so heavy, heavier than I thought it would be. As I pushed the screen door open, I heard my granny say my name.

"'*Florentine*,' she called to me. She was standing in the kitchen. Her chin trembled and her eyes were so full of sorrow that I nearly fell backward at the sight of 'em. '*I know what you got in that bag*,' she said. '*Women in this family been carrying those burdens for years. They'll surely keep you safe, that I know. But they'll make you so heavyhearted that you won't even want to open your eyes some mornings. That's strange magic you're taking with you. Sad magic.'*

"But I took 'em anyhow," Florentine said. Her voice was pressed flat with regret. "For ten years now, I've been packing these burdens along."

"What are they?" I asked. I was hoping Florentine would open the bag up and show me. But she didn't.

"Those aren't stories worth troubling you with," Florentine said. "They're mine to carry. I figured since I had these burdens keeping me safe, I'd explore a little bit. So I set off to the ocean first. I lived on one of the little islands off the coast of Georgia. That's when I worked at the fish market. Wasn't worth it for the pay."

Florentine plucked one of the threads on her jeans and wrapped it around her ring finger. "But it was worth it for Waylon Cooper. He was a sailor most of the time, but he was a song catcher, too. I didn't say a word to him, but he didn't mind. He'd talk to me anyhow. He'd invite me out to hear him play his music. We didn't need my words between us.

"One day, me and Waylon pooled our money together and bought old bicycles from a tourist shop on the island. We bought a mermaid map, too. This old couple that owned the shop said there were hundreds of mermaids hidden near that island, that we'd be sure to see them if we knew where to look. So Waylon and I rode up and down the shores, looking for mermaids. We *never* found mermaids," Florentine laughed. "But I wrote poems in the sand and he sang songs about the setting sun.

"One day he told me I should stop writing poems in the sand. Told me I needed to be brave enough to put them down on paper. Brave enough to say what I felt. So I told him I loved him." Florentine smiled. "I said it without even thinking. It was as if my heart spoke without getting permission from my mind. Those were the first words I'd said in years — *I love you*."

Florentine rested her head back against the Gallery. "I always felt brave when he was with me. Waylon's the reason I started writing my own poems."

Jonah smiled proudly. "Florentine's famous."

"I ain't famous!" Florentine blushed. "I have a little bit of a following, I guess. That's all because of Waylon, too. On weekends we'd ride our bikes to new towns. He'd hang up flyers and I'd read my work. Those were good days."

The thunder let out a long, sad sigh across the sky.

"What happened to Waylon?" I asked.

Florentine shrugged her shoulders. "He's still fishing, I guess. Still making music, still singing about sunsets and starry nights. This kept getting in the way." She patted the traveling bag again. "Waylon shouldn't have to worry about this. So I left the beach and found my way here. I should have come here to start with. Somehow, I'm gonna leave these burdens here. Then I'll go back to the ocean."

"So . . . just leave the bag, then. Walk off and leave it." I looked at Jonah. He shook his head no. I suppose it should have occurred to me that Jonah had already tried to help Florentine get rid of those stupid burdens.

Florentine chuckled. "There's more to it than that. I have to find something first. And I don't even know what I'm looking for."

"Then let's start with the easy," Jonah said. "What *exactly* is in that bag?"

"I don't know exactly," Florentine said. "But I sure got an idea." She shivered the same as I did whenever the wind-chime wind blew.

Tiny dots of rain plinked down, making polka dots all around us on the sidewalk. The thunder rumbled louder. But I didn't want to leave Florentine. She told stories in such a way that I swear my heart heard them before my ears did. I wanted to wrap up in her stories, curl them around my shoulders like a quilt.

"We should head out soon, Felicity," Jonah whispered. He knocked the metal rims of his wheels. "I'm sitting on metal. If lightning strikes, my chair's gonna shoot off into space." He laughed nervously. "I'll be a Jonah Rocket instead of a Jonah Pickett."

"Florentine," I said as I stood up off the sidewalk. "If you don't know what you're looking for . . . how will you know when you've found it?"

"Maybe it'll find me before I find it," she said. "All I know to do is wait. I'll watch. I'll wait. Then I'll drift on down to the coast."

"I'm a drifter, too," I said. "My family's from here originally, but I've been all over the place."

"Who'd you say your people were?" Florentine asked.

The thunder rumbled above the mountains again.

"I'm part Pickle," I said. "The Pickles are from Kentucky. And I'm part Harness, too. And they're from here in Midnight Gulch."

"Harness . . ." Florentine stretched the word out long, ended it in a hiss.

She smiled and cocked her head at me. "Do you know any stories about your people, Felicity? Your people who lived years ago."

"Not really."

"You should," Florentine said. "Won't do you much good trying to find your own story if you don't know theirs. I don't know much, but I certainly know that."

Florentine glanced down at her slouchy bag of burdens like she could feel its weight even when it wasn't slung around her shoulders. "I know things about this town," she said. "I know stories about the people in it. About the people who *used* to be in it."

She looked me right in the eye when she said, "If your people are who I think they are . . . then you got a story worth telling, for sure. You got magic in your veins, Felicity Pickle."

"Florentine said I had magic in my veins — word for word, *that's what she said*!"

"Uh-huh." Aunt Cleo pulled a red plate out of the sink. She passed it off to me and I swirled the dish towel around it once before setting it off to dry.

"She says she knows things about this town," I said. "She knows things about people. She says our people might be magic."

Cleo didn't say anything. I looked to my uncle instead. "You hear me, Boone? We might have some family magic!"

Boone sat on the couch, fixing shiny new strings to his banjo.

New strings for new songs.

Sincerest regards,
The Beedle

I couldn't wait to tell Jonah what I'd written. I maybe shouldn't have drawn a tiny heart in place of the *o* in *songs*, but otherwise I think I did a fine job.

"We got magic in our veins," Boone sang softly as he turned the banjo pegs extra tight, then plinked a string.

Plink.

Zing.

Thrum-de-ding, thrum-de-thrum. Bing.

"That banjo's already making happier music." I grinned.

"Spindiddly!" Boone winked at me. "Mighty sweet of the Beedle." *Thrum-de-ding. Thrum-de-ding.* "This Florentine person's talking nonsense, Liss. If we had magic in our veins, we'd be a little luckier than we are. I don't know anybody with worse luck than a Harness."

"Pickles have bad luck, too," said Frannie Jo.

"Ugh," Cleo groaned and rested her arms on the sink. "I ain't having this conversation! I promised Holly that I wouldn't mention those stupid stories."

Boone and I said at the same time, "What stories?"

Cleo fumbled around in her apron pocket until she found her lighter. The flame on the tip trembled when she tried to touch it to the cigarette in her mouth. "Just silly old folktales," she mumbled.

But the way Aunt Cleo glanced at me right then told me the exact opposite. I could tell by the sad in her eyes that she didn't believe those stories were folktales at all.

"Tell me what you know," I said. "I can handle it. I'm in sixth grade."

Cleo sighed and set her dripping dish on the counter. Then she stomped out of the room.

When Cleo shuffled back into the kitchen, she was holding the framed picture that hung on the wall of her former craft room, my current bedroom: the picture of the man standing beside a hot air balloon.

"Started with him." Cleo passed the frame to me. "That man . . ."

"Is Stone Weatherly." I nodded. "He was one of the Brothers Threadbare."

"The magician?" Boone rocketed off the couch. His boots clomped across the kitchen tiles. He was still cradling the banjo in his arms.

I saw our faces reflected in the glass as we leaned in close to study the picture.

"That *magician*," Cleo said, "was also your no-good-lowdown-deadbeat-drifter great-great-grandfather."

"We're part Threadbare?" I nearly hollered out. "Then we do have magic in our veins. BIG magic!"

"I love magic!" Frannie Jo squealed.

Biscuit yipped and wiggled her tail.

"Y'all won't love this magic." Cleo shook her head. "We're kin to Stone Weatherly. *Stone*. You know the story, Felicity. Stone is the brother who *lost* that dadblamed duel."

Boone held the picture closer to his face. "So . . . what's that got to do with us?"

158

"Means it ain't magic we got in our veins now," said Cleo. "All we've got is the stupid curse that witch woman gave."

"Witch woman?" I mumbled. "I've never heard anything about a wi —"

Thunder cracked against the sky so loud that the dishes by the sink rattled and the lights flickered.

Frannie Jo ran for Cleo's arms. Biscuit crawled under the couch.

"We better get the flashlights out," Cleo said. "Just in case we lose power."

Boone and I followed Cleo so closely down the hall that we all slammed into each other when she stopped.

The closet door fell off its hinges when Cleo opened it, but she simply sighed and slung the door against the wall. "Before the Brothers Threadbare had their stupid duel, they called on some old witch woman to set a curse on the loser."

Cleo plopped a big orange shoe box labeled JUNK, ETC. into my arms. "And it was a humdinger of a curse: *Cursed to wander through the night, till cords align, and all's made right.*"

I shivered as Cleo repeated the words Oliver had already told me.

Boone tapped nervously against his banjo. "But that was a long time ago. That's got nothing to do with us, right?" His voice sounded shrill and crackly.

"Stone Weatherly *lost the duel*," Cleo repeated loudly, half of her body hidden in the closet, rummaging through boxes and quilts. She emerged holding a small wooden container, which she settled on top of the junk box. "And because he lost, he had to leave town and live out that curse for the rest of his days. He couldn't sit still. He'd sleep for a few hours, but then he'd wake up in the middle of the night, sleepwalking, sleep-running, sleep-dancing-a-jig. Stone became *restless*. He managed to marry, eventually. But he never had much of a life. Hardly ever saw his wife or his kids because he couldn't settle down. He couldn't set roots in any place. He was cursed with a restless soul."

"Like Mama." I gulped.

Cleo didn't answer. Neither did Boone. But I felt my heart whisper against my ribs: *Yes.*

I swallowed down the fear in my throat. "Why'd he fly a balloon?"

"Because that's the only way he felt any peace." Cleo scooped up a quilt with her free arm and tossed it into the hallway. "As long as Stone's body was moving, his heart could rest. He saw the whole world from the basket of that balloon. But the whole world's nothing compared to people you love. Stone didn't ever see his family."

"And we're cursed the same as him." I didn't ask it like a question. I said it in the for-sure affirmative. We were cursed. Cursed Pickles. Cursed Harnesses.

"S'only a story," Cleo murmured. She huffed as she reached farther back into the closet, pulling out extra pillows and another shoe box of flashlights and batteries. Then she propped the door back against the closet.

160

We piled all of our survival gear plus a bag of Cheetos into the hallway.

Boone didn't help us. He was still studying the picture of Stone Weatherly.

"Cleo." Boone narrowed his eyes at the picture. "Is that a banjo on his back?"

"Guitar," Cleo said. "Stone's brother, Berry, played the banjo. He played the very same one you're holding, in fact."

Boone's eyes glanced up slowly from the picture. "Come again?"

Cleo's nostrils flared as she looked away. She took a long draw of her cigarette. "I'm done telling these stories. I promised Holly I wouldn't mention them. Y'all are going to get me in a heap of trouble."

Boone's eyes sparkled mad-blue. He pulled the banjo off his shoulders and shook it at Cleo. "*Why* do I have a banjo that belonged to the Brothers Threadbare?"

Cleo heaved a sad sigh as she leaned back against the wall. The lights flickered again. Thunder pounded against the rooftop. Cleo narrowed her eyes up at the ceiling, took the cigarette out of her mouth, and hollered, "Hush!"

Cleo was the only woman I knew who was brave enough to yell at a storm.

"Cleo!" Boone clipped. He was the only man brave enough to yell at my aunt.

"Fine!" Cleo seethed. "Our mother's family lived way up in the backwoods of Virginia. One day when she was still a little bitty thing, she saw a fancy old car zooming

161

down the gravel road toward her house. Mother said an old man stepped out of the car; he was a scrawny feller with sad eyes and shaky hands. The man said he'd come there looking for Stone Weatherly. Well, Mother'd grown up hearing stories about her grandfather, of course, but she'd never met the man. Mother told the visitor all that. She told him about the day Stone Weatherly's balloon drifted off into the sunset and never came back. Nobody'd seen Stone Weatherly in years. Nobody ever saw him again, as far as I know."

I let out a shattered breath. Because I *knew* somebody had seen Stone Weatherly again. Oliver had seen him. Stone had gone looking for Berry, the same as Berry had gone looking for him. I opened my mouth to tell Aunt Cleo, but my heart kicked hard against my ribs: *WAIT*. And then again, *NOT YET*.

Cleo spoke softly, "Mama told the old visitor that Stone Weatherly was gone. She'd no more than said it when the old man sat down on the porch and cried a waterfall of tears. The visitor introduced himself as Berry Weatherly, and then he told her the *real* story of what happened to the Brothers Threadbare. He told her about that mean old witch woman who set the curse. Before Berry left, he gave mother the banjo that he'd played alongside his brother all those years ago. Said the banjo didn't sound good without his brother playing, too. He told her to give the banjo to Stone if she ever saw him again. If not, he told her to find a good place for it. Mother gave the banjo to me. I passed it on along to you. And there was something else, too —"

162

Cleo popped open the wooden container she'd pulled from the closet. She rummaged past piles of pictures and postcards and pulled out an oval-shaped locket dangling from a long silver chain. She handed the locket to me.

"Berry Weatherly gave *this* to Mother, too," Cleo said. "He said it reminded him of better times. You can hear something rattling around in the locket if you shake it, but nobody's ever been able to get it open."

Cleo was right. I pried at the locket with my fingernails but it wouldn't budge.

"You can keep it if you want." Cleo shrugged. "I don't figure you can put much magic in a locket. It's safe."

The locket was kind of big and tacky but spindiddly, too. I looped it around my neck.

The lights flickered and dimmed, then flashed back to bright again.

"Cleo," Boone said thoughtfully, ". . . am I playing a cursed banjo?"

"Nah," Cleo said. "The banjo ain't cursed. It just doesn't make good music anymore."

"That's good to hear *now*." Boone pressed his palm against his forehead and wailed, "No wonder my career won't kick-start, Cleo! I'm playing a moody banjo!"

"Your ca-*reer*," Cleo huffed, "won't kick-start because you keep saying you're Boone Taylor instead of Boone Harness."

"Cleo," I interrupted, "you do know that Oliver Weatherly is . . ."

"Of course I know he's related." Cleo waved off my question. "But I don't want to talk to him about those brothers, and I don't want to talk to y'all about them anymore, either. That story is done; it was done a hundred years ago. We can't change the past. So I don't want to hear anything about it ever again."

"But, Cleo —"

"No. More. Questions!"

Lightning-colored words flashed against the wall:

FIERCE

DETERMINED

PURPOSED

I sat up tall and pushed my shoulders back. I traced my thumb back and forth across the smooth surface of Berry Weatherly's locket. "At least tell me what our curse says, exactly. I won't ask you any more about it after that."

"Not *our* curse," Cleo whispered. "*His* curse. When Stone Weatherly lost the duel, the old witch woman locked her hand around his wrist and said these words:

Foolish heart who fought and failed,
Where talent bloomed, your greed prevailed,
Cursed to toil, till labor-worn,
You'll spin up ashes, you'll harvest thorns.

Now pack your dreams, make haste, take flight,
You're cursed to wander through the night,
Till cords align, and all's made right.

Where sweet amends are made and spoken,
Shadows dance, the curse is broken.

"It means *we* . . ." Cleo's voice trailed off. She cleared her throat and said, "It means *he* was cursed to wander and never rest. Cursed to fail at everything he put his hand to. But that's only if you believe the stories, which I most certainly do *not*. And I don't want to talk about them again after this."

"Me, neither," Boone said. But he stared down at his banjo like it had betrayed him.

I traced my finger back and forth across the smooth face of the locket. I *did* want to talk about the curse. I had too many questions buzzing inside my brain now, such as, if the curse was real, had it traveled my family's history all the way to us? Did that mean us Pickles would always be wandering from town to town? That Boone would never catch a break? That Cleo would always have so much sad caught in her eyes?

And what about me and Frannie Jo? Would we fail at everything we tried?

What was the point of even trying to do the Duel if I was cursed to fail? What difference would it make for Mama to see me happy if she was cursed to keep on traveling?

I had too many questions fighting for the front seat on my tongue. Right at that moment, I didn't care about getting any answers. There was only one thing I wanted.

"I sure wish Mama was here." I gulped. Cleo kept the window shut that night because of the storm, so I couldn't smell the waffle cones baking. That smell always made me feel like Mama was safe, even if I couldn't see her. On my way home from the Gallery, the air hadn't smelled like anything at all. Instead, the wind felt too warm and too prickly. Electric, almost.

"I sure do, too," said Cleo. "I wish she'd stay here is what I wish."

As if we'd willed it to be, the front door burst open and Mama pushed her way inside. I squealed in relief just as the thunder *SMACKED*, so loud and clear you'd think somebody'd dropped the world and broke it in two.

"Tornado warning!" Mama said, locking the door behind her. As if that little bitty door lock could keep out a whole big tornado. "They let us leave work early. The radio says we need to get to a safe place."

We all looked at Cleo then. She was the only safe place any of us really knew.

"We probably ought to get in the bathroom," Cleo said, heaving as she got up off the floor.

Frannie Jo hopped up into Mama's arms. Then all three of us Pickles plus two Harnesses were picking up all our worldly possessions — which wasn't much — and running for the bathroom.

"Biscuit!" I ran for my dog's hiding place. But Boone was already kneeling down in front of the couch, pulling my dog up into his arms. I didn't know much about Boone Harness/Taylor, but I decided right then I loved him.

Mama and Cleo were already in the bathroom, hollering my name, but I ran to my backpack first. I wouldn't have been able to see anything if it weren't for all the purple lightning flashing outside. My heart was thumping *yes, yes, yes . . .* or maybe *RUN, RUN, RUN,* as I shoved aside all the crumpled homework papers and books. Finally, I found my blue book.

"We gotta go, Liss!" Boone hollered. He had a banjo on his back and a trembling dog tucked under his arm. And he was holding out his hand, waiting for me to grab on.

"One more thing!" I yelled. But the storm was yelling louder than me.

I ran to the corner of Cleo's apartment where we'd piled the grocery sacks full of clothes and junk that we'd brought from Kentucky. I dug through the bags until I found mama's paintbrushes, still tied together and wrapped in an old T-shirt. I held the brushes, and my blue book, tight against my heart, and I ran for Boone.

"Good girl," Boone said. His hand was strong around mine as he led me down the hall. I wasn't afraid of the storm at all right then, not with him leading the way. Not with my cursed family so close to me.

We all crammed into Cleo's dark bathroom and shut the door.

At first, none of us talked. We listened to the storm howling all around the apartment complex. I heard the rain whoosh up against the building. I was glad Florentine had her stupid burdens there with her on a night like this. At least they kept her safe from the wind and rain.

Mama sighed and stretched her arm around me to pull me close. She smelled like the sugar wind.

"What have y'all been talking about tonight?" she said. Her voice was tired.

I couldn't see Cleo's face in the dark, but somehow she told me, without words, to keep our conversation a secret.

So I leaned against Mama's shoulder and said, "Nothing."

And then lullaby music filled up the air around us. Boone strummed the sweetest tune on his banjo. The thunder outside was a rock song, electric and loud and strange. But the rain only whooshed and swooshed; the rain was a gentler song. Boone played like the rain.

Cleo didn't turn on the flashlight but if she had, I probably would have seen all kinds of dancing words. Words like *failure, fake, regret, curse.*

Cursed to wander through the night,
Till cords align, and all's made right.

Mama leaned over and kissed the top of my hair. I laced my fingers in with hers. I would keep her safe and steady in a world that kept rocking her soul.

Stay, I wanted to tell her. *Rest your heart here. Stay.*

But I knew I was no better at keeping her in this place than Cleo's door lock was at keeping out the storm.

✳ ◇ ✳ ✳ ◇ ✳ ✳ ◇ ✳

When the storm finally passed and we all shuffled back to our sleeping places, I flopped down on the inflatable mattress, thinking about all I'd heard, and all I'd seen.

"We're cursed," I whispered.

"We're Pickles," said Frannie Jo.

"Same thing," I said back.

I licked my chapped lips and reached over for the locket Cleo'd given me. "I wonder . . ." I held the locket up and let it swing back and forth. "I wonder if there's anything stronger than a curse," I whispered.

Frannie Jo didn't answer me. She was already breathing steady, sweet-dream breaths beside me.

Where sweet amends are made and spoken,
Shadows dance, the curse is broken.

I didn't speak the words out loud. I just moved my mouth around them, wondering what in the world they meant.

As I swung the locket back and forth, I heard something. A familiar something that sent shivers up my spine.

I sat up and lifted the locket up to my ear. Then I shook it.

I shook it again to make sure I wasn't imagining things.

Berry Weatherly's locket had the wind-chime wind caught inside it.

The next afternoon, Jonah told me to meet him at his mom's beauty salon. The shop is called

Jewell Pickett's Lube & Dye

because it happens to be the only salon offering beauty services and minor car repairs in the entire town of Midnight Gulch and possibly the whole world. Jonah said the shop came about because his mom, Jewell, had two great passions in life: tinkering with carburetors and coloring people's hair.

So Jewell signed up for beauty school on the same day she signed up for mechanic school. When she moved back to Midnight Gulch a few years ago, she decided to blend her two passions. Now every mechanic Jewell hires has to be well versed in rotaries and acrylic nails. And every stylist at the Lube & Dye knows how to change oil and cut a perfect mid-length bob.

I didn't need a perfect mid-length bob or an oil change, but I certainly had business to attend to at Jewell's Lube & Dye. Bad business. Awful business.

170

My business: I had to tell Jonah that the Duel couldn't happen. Somewhere way back in my twisty-turny family tree, I was related to a couple of dueling, feuding magicians who wrecked a whole town and cursed my family in the process. It didn't matter what spindiddly Beedle plan Jonah cooked up: Mama was cursed to wander. I was cursed to wander.

I dreaded the way Jonah's eyes would flicker from neon-happy green to mossy-sad all because of what I had to tell him. His know-how had never failed until me. I was broken up over it, too. I didn't want to leave the only place I'd ever felt at home. But there was no reason I should go through with the Duel, especially after Cleo's storm tale. I'd mess it up, no matter what. We would leave town, no matter what. I freewrote about my dilemma in the blue book:

Reasons the Duel Is Done

1. Because I still haven't written any poems worth dueling with.

2. Because there's an itty-bitty bit of Threadbare in me somewhere, which means I'm cursed to fail at everything I try.

3. Because I would much rather fail at something that doesn't happen in front of a roomful of people,

where I'll most likely refer to artists as fartists and various other stupidities.

Florentine was right. I did have magic in my veins. But it was the wrong kind of magic. My family magic was way worse than whatever she was packing along in her traveling bag. Worst of all, I didn't need to collect words or practice for the Duel anymore. So Jonah wouldn't have any reason to hang out with me.

As I shuffled my way toward the Lube & Dye, I imagined going through with the Duel, standing in front of the entire school, hoping the right words would work their way out. They wouldn't, though. And even though I was only at the Duel in my imagination, my hands trembled the same as if it were real. The skin above my lip got sweaty and the back of my head started to itch.

Itchy

Twitchy

Puke-ish

That's an awful way to be remembered. It was all for the best, really. As long as I didn't Duel, I wouldn't disappoint Jonah or embarrass myself.

"I'll tell him quick," I said to Biscuit, who trotted along beside me, wagging her tail. "It'll be like ripping off a Band-Aid."

Then I let out a sigh. I dragged my sneakers slower across the sidewalk. "You think he'll still be my friend? Even if I don't compete?"

I knew Biscuit wouldn't answer for real. But she stayed close beside me. Sometimes you don't need words to feel better; you just need the nearness of your dog. Or your best friend.

Biscuit and I stood outside the window of Jewell's Lube & Dye for a while, watching all the chatter and commotion happening inside. I could see Jonah sitting in the back of the room. He was polishing an elderly lady's nails.

Biscuit sat down and pressed her paw against my shoe.

"I know he'll be sad," I said. "But I have to tell him today. Wait here, okay?"

Biscuit lay down on the sidewalk, resting her fuzzy head on her paws.

The door jingled as I pulled it open. Jonah smiled at me from the corner of the room. As I made my way toward him, words fell down in such thick curtains I thought I might have to push them back just to get by. I'd never expected so many words in this place.

In Jewell's Lube & Dye, words were crashing into each other like bumper cars. And they were exploding up above me like fireworks. Some words looked extra lovely, though.

H o p e

Hope was lipstick red, reflecting back at me from the mirror over Jewell's station. On that same mirror, Jewell had taped a yellow ribbon and a picture of a handsome soldier: Jonah's dad. He looked brave and strong. Even in a picture, his eyes were full of love and sorrow. I wished he could climb out of the picture and see hope so close to him, right there beside him.

Hope didn't fade when I walked past Jewell's station. *Hope* doesn't fizzle or flicker or burn out. *Hope* isn't the same as other words. *Hope* holds steady.

I pulled the pen from the pocket of my jeans and wrote *hope* on the inside of my wrist. I'd put it in the blue book later. For now, I wanted it as close to me as I could have it.

Jewell Pickett was nodding her head *mmm-hmm, mmm-hmm* while she trimmed Elvis Phillips's hair. He tapped his foot to the music on the radio, antsy for his haircut to end so he could get back to dancing.

Most of the words above the rest of the clients were all people names:

Divinity Lawson
Burl Honeycutt
Cleopatra Harness
Holly Harness

My mama's name was fading, floating up slowly toward the speckled ceiling. I wondered which one of those clients had been thinking about her. I wonder if they'd said something kind or something sorrowful.

Jonah waved me over to the corner table where he was sitting. Working beside Jonah was a rotund man with a shiny bald head. He wore sparkly diamond earrings and had muscles in his arms the size of cantaloupes. The man had tattoos from his wrist to his shoulder, bright pictures of dragons and angels with wings of fire.

"This is Big Bruce." Jonah nodded toward his coworker. "He used to do detail work out in the shop, but he missed the personal interaction with the clients."

"Gets lonesome dealing with motors all day long," growled Big Bruce. He was gently holding Ponder Waller's hand, painting little yellow flowers onto her nails.

"We sure get lonesome without you in here." Ponder batted her eyelashes.

"Huh," Big Bruce huffed. But his ear studs seemed to sparkle extra brightly at her compliment.

Jonah picked up a bobby pin and used the tip to add tiny blue polka dots to the freshly painted nails of the old lady in front of him.

"Pull up a chair, Felicity," Jonah said. "I wanted you to meet my dear friend Rosie Walker. Miss Walker, this is my best friend, Felicity Pickle."

Rosie Walker's milky-blue eyes met mine. She smiled and said, "You doing okay, child?"

I said, "Yes, ma'am." Even though that was a lie. I wasn't okay at all. I was plumb *awful* because of what I had to tell Jonah. I didn't want to tell him in front of Rosie Walker, though. I figured I could at least wait until he was finished doing nails to break his heart.

"Sit here beside me, Felicity," said Rosie. Her voice was a pretty old-rasp, like the rush of pages in an old, dusty book. "I do love your name. *Felicity*. It sounds so lovely to say, doesn't it? Like a secret."

"I like your name, too," I said. And I also liked her dress: because it was as bright red as a summer tomato. Rosie's skin was pale, brittle-looking as a piece of crinkled paper. Her white hair was fuzzed out and fluffed high up on her head. She had a red flower pinned tightly in her nest of white hair. I liked that, too. And when she crossed one leg over the other, I saw her cowboy boots. They were scuffed-up brown and embroidered with red roses. I crazy-liked those cowboy boots.

Jonah must have noticed me checking out Rosie's fancy boots, because he said, "Rosie Walker is a famous country music singer."

"I *was* a singer," Rosie corrected. "I lived in Nashville for a time. I wasn't Rosie Walker out there, though — I was Ramblin' Rose. I sang songs I wrote myself. And people came from a hundred miles away just to hear my voice."

"My uncle is a musician," I said. "His name is Boone Harness and he played in Nashville. He had a stage name, too — Boone Taylor. Do you know him?"

"Been years since I've been to Nashville, honey," said Rosie Walker. Even though she smiled at me, I could hear the sadness crackling in her voice. I saw words shimmering against the fabric of her dress, inching up her sleeves as slowly as silkworms:

Saturday song

Lonesome sky
Rebel
Scandal
Summer rain

Jonah smiled proudly and said, "Miss Walker played at the Grand Ole Opry. She sang on stage with Minnie Pearl."

"I'm a blessed woman. I saw every one of my dreams come true," Rosie Walker stated. "I'm proof that it's never too late to take hold of a dream. I thought I was too old to set out for Nashville and be a singer. I thought nobody'd listen to me since I wasn't no young, flouncy little spring chicken. And I always thought my songs were just for me, to keep me busy, to keep my mind moving. But God bless the Beedle."

Rosie didn't look at Jonah. I glanced his way, but he stayed focused on his polka-dot project. She didn't know the Beedle was sitting right across from her.

"What'd the Beedle do for you?" I asked.

"Twenty years ago, the Beedle left me a guitar and a hundred-dollar bill on the front porch of my house," said Rosie. "There was a red ribbon tied around the guitar. And slid in underneath the ribbon was a note with very specific instructions. That's a special guitar the Beedle left me, you see."

Rosie leaned over and whispered to me, "The Beedle said my guitar originally belonged to one of the Brothers Threadbare."

Of course, I'd figured that out already. But the shine in Rosie's eyes was so pretty when she told me, that I pretended to be surprised all over again.

"The note told me that every time I played that guitar, I had to lead off with the same song. I could play anything I wanted after that, but I had to start with the same tune. It's an old mountain song, the very same one the Brothers Threadbare started their shows with. I knew the tune, of course. Everybody in the mountains knows that tune."

A sad smile stretched across her face. "Not a single note of music would come outta that guitar unless I started my set with that song. If I sang 'Fair and Tender Ladies' first, then everything else I played sounded lovely. Otherworldly, even. That's magic if I ever heard it."

Rosie inspected her polka-dot nails and thanked Jonah for his hard work. "I was fifty-seven years old when I set out for Nashville. I embroidered red roses on my favorite pair of cowboy boots. I put new strings on that magical guitar. And I lit out. I played on the sidewalks of Nashville for a time; that's the only place I could play. I played for pennies and day-old coffee. I played through the storms and through the rain. Some people didn't listen at all. Some people listened and told me I was no good. But I've always had a heap of determination caught up in me. So I kept on playing. And I played my way all the way to the stage at the Ryman."

"What's a Ryman?" I whispered.

Because the way she'd said the word made it sound like some dreamy, fog-covered castle.

"The Ryman is a place where people go to play music and to hear music. Before it was a music hall, it used to be a church. The pews are all still there. That building's got stained-glass windows and beer-stained floors. There are thousands of prayers and songs caught in the bones of the walls. You can feel them — the prayers, the music — all around you whenever you sit down in that place."

"Then why'd you stop going there?"

"Yeah, Rosie," Big Bruce sniffed. His eyes were sparkling with tears. "Why'd you stop playing?"

"I know when it's time to bow out," Rosie said sadly. "But I'll tell y'all this: The Ryman is sacred. And the Ryman is wild. And when you find a place like that in this world, a place that is wild and sacred, you should treasure it."

"I wonder if Uncle Boone has played at the Ryman?" I asked.

Rosie nodded. "I'm sure he wants to. Anybody who sings a note or strums a string wants to play there."

"Felicity is a storyteller, Miss Rosie," Jonah said. "She sees words hovering in the air and shining over people's heads and stuff. She collects the ones she loves the most. That's how she's going to win the Duel."

My heart flopped down into my stomach again.

"Is that right, Felicity?" Rosie asked.

"I collect words," I said. "But I'm not much at making them into anything."

"Word collecting is a special gift," said Rosie.

"And a curse," I barely sighed.

Rosie chuckled. "Jonah, I like Felicity. She seems unique."

"Felicity is enchanting," Jonah said. And he said this as though the word had been on the tip of his tongue, ready to break loose and be said for weeks.

Enchanting

The word perched on Jonah's shoulder like a tiny silver songbird.

I leaned over and wrote *enchanting* on my shoe in big bubble letters. I never wanted to forget my songbird word. I never wanted to forget it was mine.

Plumb pretty

Poet

Enchanting

Those were all words Jonah'd given to me because he believed they were true. He believed I *was* those things. And I was minutes away from telling him that he'd believed for nothing.

Rosie turned toward Jonah. "I'm not wearing my glasses. Is Felicity as cute as she sounds?"

"Felicity has gray eyes," Jonah said. "They almost look silver sometimes, the same color the river turns when a big rain comes through and it's about to overflow. She has sad eyes, but she's not a sad girl, not always."

Jonah finally looked up at me. "Maybe a little bit today, though." His forehead wrinkled when he concentrated on my face. "Why are you sad today, Felicity?"

"Jonah." I had to do it now. It was pure torture to put it off any longer. "I came to tell you —"

But I didn't get to tell him a thing because suddenly the doorbell clanged and Oliver Weatherly shouted "Hey-yo!" from the doorway. He wore overalls, a white T-shirt, and a big smile. He held a large red cooler in his hands. Oliver hoisted the cooler above his head like it was full of treasures and said, "Free ice cream for everybody!"

"Woo!" Ponder Waller raised her hands in the air.

"Your nails are still wet!" Big Bruce hollered at her.

But she didn't hear him because the folks getting their hair done and the people out in the shop all started hollering out their favorite flavors:

"Virgil's Get-Outta-My-Face Fudge Ripple!"

"Bobby's Buttered Avocado!"

"Suzie's White Chocolate Cherry Walnut!"

"Aunt Ruth's Pumpkin Sampler!"

"I could sure use a Blackberry Sunrise," said Rosie Walker, so softly I didn't know if anybody besides me had heard. "I'm in a remembering way."

"I'll get it for you!" Jonah said. He wheeled away and I stood to follow him, but Rosie Walker caught my wrist with her bony hand.

"Felicity darlin'," she drawled, "you know what helped me figure out how to put my words together? *Music*. Music gets my words where they need to go. So you keep catching them words, you hear? Pluck them out of the wind. String them together like the finest set of pearls. Line them up on paper. And if it hurts too much to say them, then you sing them, or whisper them, or write them into a story. But don't waste them. Your words matter more than you know. You hear?"

I nodded sadly. "I'll try."

"That's all you have to do." Rosie patted my arm. "The rest takes care of itself."

Jewell Pickett walked to the front of the shop and stared down into the wondrous abyss of Oliver's cooler. "What's the occasion, Weatherly? And what are you doing here so early? Your appointment ain't till four!"

I liked Jewell Pickett's voice because it sounded like it had a laugh caught up inside it. I could tell that some of Jonah's weirdly-wonderful had come straight from his mother. She smiled the same way Jonah smiled. And her hair was blond and prickly, like his.

"No occasion!" Oliver said. "I figured I'd scoot in early. Share some ice cream and shoot the breeze."

"All he's good for is shooting the breeze," said an old man in a plaid shirt and dirt-stained blue jeans. He tried to sound tough, but a kind smile stretched across his face. "I never met a man that told more tall tales in all my life."

"There's more truth in my tall tales than your weather reports, Virgil," Oliver said as he tossed the old man a carton of ice cream. They both laughed. If there's one thing I dearly love, it's a chorus of that kind of laughing. Happy laughing. It's as fine as any symphony.

Survivor
Safe harbor
Sweetheart

Anchor

Those were Virgil's words. They clung to his arms. And I could tell — by his strong shoulders and bold words, and by the twinkle in his eye — that he was a man who'd been dearly loved.

Virgil scratched the scruff on his jaw. "You might as well settle in, Weatherly. Spin a few of those tales, since you're here."

Oliver plopped down underneath one of the hair dryers and propped his boots up on the footrest. "Any requests?"

"Tell us about sweet Eldee Mae!" said Big Bruce.

"Tell us about the Duel!" hollered Harriet Bond, Jewell's lead mechanic, through the window connecting the salon to the body shop. She waved to Oliver from underneath the hood of an old Ford truck. "That Duel Miss Lawson's cooking up's got everybody talking about the Brothers Threadbare again."

The last thing I wanted to hear more about was the Duel.

There was another story I wanted to know about.

"Tell us about the witch of Midnight Gulch," I said.

Even though I said it quick and quiet, you'd think I'd shouted. The room fell silent. Folks cranked around in their seats to stare at me.

Elvis Phillips tapped an anxious rhythm against the swivel chair. "What witch?" he asked. "I've never heard anything about any witch . . ."

"Everybody hush." Jewell raised her voice over the chorus of mumbles and grumbles. "Let Oliver tell the story."

The dark clouds that had been slinking in and out of the mountains ever since I got to town rumbled low across the sky, like a warning.

Oliver laced his fingers together over the paunch of his belly. He sighed, as if he'd been expecting me to ask that very thing. He leaned back in his seat and began, "All right, then."

And I leaned in close and prepared my heart for a storm of a story.

Biscuit was thrilled when Jewell told me I could let her inside the Lube & Dye. She zoomed in and shook the raindrops out of her fur and then she walked around, getting to know people. Every hairstylist and mechanic and client in the whole shop reached out to pet her, which Biscuit didn't mind a bit. When it comes to affection, she knows how to dish it out.

I helped Rosie Walker to a seat closer to the front of the shop, where she could hear Oliver's story. Rosie had just sat down when Biscuit pounced up in her lap. At first Rosie let out a surprised "*OOOOF!*"

But then Biscuit turned toward Rosie and nuzzled her cheek.

Rosie smiled. "Well, hello there, darlin'!"

Once I'd seen that the two of them were settled, I pulled a seat for myself beside Jonah and told him, "Don't forget . . . I need to talk to you about something later. It's an important something."

Jonah's smile pinched into a frown. "Important how?"

"I'll tell you later," I said. Because I had more important things to focus on. Things like who the hayseed the witch woman was and how the heck I was going to undo her stupid curse.

The room got quiet as we all settled in for Oliver's tale. The only sound I could hear was the *snip-snip-snip* of Jewell's scissors.

Oliver tapped the dimple on his chin, collecting his thoughts. He started his story with the part I knew but never got sick of hearing:

"Many years ago, Midnight Gulch was a secret place. The mountain hid the town high-up-away from the rest of the world. And the river surrounded the mountain and kept it safe. And the forest stood up tall around the river, and caught all of the town's secrets and songs in its branches. The town *had* to stay secret, you see, because the people who lived there had magic in their veins.

"Some families had more powerful magic than others, of course. Some families, like the Tripletts, had flashy magic. They say Owen Triplett could catch starlight in glass jars. He got in trouble for selling his starlight jars to tourists, though. People'd no more than pay for their jars when the starlight would bust loose and head back for the skies. Starlight doesn't take good to domestication."

"Note to self," Jonah whispered to me. "Stars don't make good pets."

"Duly noted," I agreed.

Oliver continued, "Some families had a purpose to their magic, though. The Terrys could conjure up the rain. The Smiths could bake secrets into their pies."

"Tell about the Hancocks!" Charlie Sue yelled.

Oliver rolled his eyes. "The Hancocks could turn themselves invisible." He closed his eyes and sighed contentedly. "I wouldn't mind if they started doing that again, honestly."

"Me, neither," Charlie Sue chimed in. "I'd follow you around all day and bug the daylights out of you."

"You already do that every day," Oliver laughed. He cleared his throat and continued, "And when the Weatherly boys played music, the whole world danced and sang.

"But there was another powerful family back then — the Thistle family. Nobody talks about them much, but they had the strangest and most exciting magic of all.

"In fact, back then, the most notorious woman in all of Midnight Gulch was a young lady named Isabella Thistle."

Thunder rumbled low and long over the rooftop. I didn't know if it was the thunder or the name Isabella Thistle that sent the shiver down my spine. And it wasn't just me: Everybody in the beauty shop shivered or rubbed their arms.

"Now, the men in the Thistle family weren't much tootin'," Oliver said. "The most magical thing those men ever did was drink their weight in moonshine. But the Thistle women were powerful creatures. And Isabella was the most powerful of them all."

Even though my heart was already drumming *yes*, I asked Oliver, "So Isabella was the witch woman?"

"Eh." Oliver shrugged his shoulder. "She was no more of a witch than any other woman in the Gulch. Lots of women had magic in their veins. The problem was that most women despised Isabella Thistle. They were jealous of her because the Weatherly boys liked her so much. They hated her because she spoke her mind even if it made folks angry. They hated her kind of beautiful. I always heard tell that, if you passed Isabella Thistle on the street, you'd think she looked very ordinary. But she had a way about her: an easy laugh and a strong will. She didn't care what people thought of her. She was bossy, opinionated, and feisty. Isabella wore her hair in a long, black braid. She kept a yellow flower behind her ear. To be in her presence, they said, was enchanting. And that's why some people called her a witch. They said she wasn't pretty enough to get the Weatherly boys' attention. They said she must have put a spell on them somehow."

"But you don't think she did?" Jonah asked around a mouthful of ice cream.

"Jonah," Oliver sighed. "I'm about to give you some advice about women, man to man."

"Here we go." Jewell shook her head.

Jonah settled his carton of Aunt Ruth's Pumpkin Sampler in his lap. "I'm listening."

"Here's what you need to remember," said Oliver. "Women who make you laugh, and who make you think, and who also happen to wear yellow flowers in their hair are always dangerous. And if they happen to have magic in their veins, then heaven help us all. You either give up and fall in love or get out of town. Isabella wasn't a witch no more than I'm a trapeze swinger. And she didn't cast any love spell on the Brothers Threadbare, either. They both fell in love with her. She fell in love with both of them."

"Both?" I blew my too-long bangs away from my eyes. "How's it possible to fall in love with two people?"

"Stone Weatherly courted Isabella first." Oliver popped open a carton of Blackberry Sunrise. He was quiet for a time as he considered the memories melting in his mouth. "Nobody knows what went wrong, but Stone and Isabella broke up. Not long after, Berry started courting her. I don't know if Stone still took a shine to Isabella or if he hated the thought of his brother courting her, but that's how the jealousy first got stirred up between them. The Weatherlys weren't jealous of each other's fame, the way most people think. They were both plumb crazy over a girl.

"Isabella wouldn't have it. She ended up turning both of the boys down on account of their stupid antics. And that turned both of them bitter and angry and sad. Eventually, the brothers had enough of each other and they came up with the Duel. And because they didn't know anybody who could twist magic like Isabella Thistle, they asked her to come up with a curse. And she was so mad at both of them, she agreed. It was a strange magic those Thistle women had. *Sad* magic."

"And it worked?" I asked. My voice came out like a bullfrog croak. Of course, I already knew the curse had worked. I'd traveled enough dark nights in the Pickled Jalapeño to know it was still working just fine.

"*They* believed it worked," Oliver said to me. He set his eyes directly on mine, the way you do when you want somebody to hear more besides the words you're saying out loud. "*They* believed it," he repeated. "I doubt there was any real magic to that curse. But Stone Weatherly believed he was a cursed man, and that's all that mattered."

Rosie Walker cleared her throat. She was still holding Biscuit, scratching behind my dog's ears. Biscuit panted happily, her mouth wide open with a very satisfied smile.

"Sorry to interrupt," Rosie said. "But this witch woman — you said her family had a peculiar kind of magic. What was it, exactly?"

"Legend says that the Thistle women were shadow catchers. Way back, during the War Between the States, soldiers would pay the Thistles to catch shadows and turn 'em loose over paths and trails to scare off the other side. People say Isabella used to hide bird shadows inside the hymnals at the church. When the choir stood up to sing, a hundred shadows came fluttering up off the pages, and people started shouting and hollering and carrying on. She had the gift. Seems a sad way to live, though. Collecting shadows. If ever there's a waste of magic, I reckon it's that."

"I'm sure it didn't start out as a waste," Rosie Walker drawled. "Maybe the Thistle women collected sunsets, once

190

upon a time. Maybe they trapped stars in Mason jars or maybe . . . *maybe*" — her hands fluttered excitedly — "maybe they collected memories. I've heard tell of that, about mountain people who could keep memories and songs, hush them up for decades inside boxes and bottles."

Oliver tapped his finger against his lips, choosing his words extra carefully. "A feller once told me that Isabella Thistle took something that belonged to the Brothers Threadbare. Right after she set the curse on them, she stole something that belonged to them, and then she lit out of town. Of course, most people think she took money. But I don't think that was it . . ." Oliver shrugged his shoulders. "Don't matter much what she took or what those brothers did. We can't undo what's been done."

Elvis ran his fingers through his hair and said, "Reckon there's no magic left in Midnight Gulch."

And most of the folks in the shop all shook their heads and mumbled their *reckon not*s and *you got that right*s.

I knew better, though.

Words as beautiful as magic spells — hidden to most people, but shimmer-shining at me — threaded all across the ceiling of Jewell Pickett's Lube & Dye:

Winsome

Wonder

B e l i e v e

I didn't have to reckon anything about what magic might be left in Midnight Gulch. I knew it was still there.

"Sure wish they'd have made amends," Oliver said sadly.

"Tell you what I wish." Jewell swept around her station. "I wish somebody'd redo that trashy looking Gallery out there. Why don't you get to fixing that, Oliver?"

"Aw, shoot," said Oliver. "Nobody in this town could paint that thing right. I suppose I could have somebody plow it down, but that makes me too sad to think on. Too much history in that wall. I'd like to see it painted up again, but nobody here can do it."

At exactly that moment, I saw one of my favorite words shimmering against the big window of Jewell's shop:

Holly

"Mama!" I hollered. Everybody in the shop stared at me. "My mama could paint the Gallery, easy. She'll paint something wonderful and winsome all over that wall. She's an exceptional artist."

"She really is," Jonah quickly agreed. "She has a portfolio and everything. Holly's painted murals all over the southeastern United States."

"Why hasn't anybody thought of that until now?" Ponder Waller asked. "I've always said Holly Harness was the most talented girl ever to come out of Midnight Gulch. You think she'd be willing to paint the Gallery, Felicity?"

"She might," I said, as the most wonderful feelings came swirling up inside my belly: hope and pride and happiness. They snuffed out all the sad I'd felt over the Duel and over leaving Midnight Gulch. Holly Harness might paint again. This was the best kind of happy I'd felt in ages.

Also, the Gallery was gargantuan.

We'd have to stay in town at least until it was done.

Oliver thought that was a fine idea. I locked eyes with Jonah and saw a halo of words spinning around his spiky blond hair:

Clever

Stalwart

Brilliant

Splendiferous

"Spindiddly plan, Felicity Pickle." Jonah grinned.

That night, while everybody else was sound asleep, I sat on the floor of my makeshift bedroom, spilling my heart out to my dog. "If Mama starts painting again, that doesn't mean the curse is broken. But it means there's hope. Right?"

Biscuit pressed her paw against my hand.

"The thing is, Isabella Thistle wasn't some mean old witch out for revenge. She said the Threadbares were cursed *until* cords aligned. I don't know what the hayseed *cords aligning* means . . . " My voice trailed off as I fumbled with the locket around my neck. "But I'll bet the Threadbares figured it out. Maybe that's why they tried to find each other."

Biscuit cocked her head sadly.

"You're right," I groaned. "We're doomed." I flopped back on the floor. Biscuit snuggled against my arm and fell asleep.

I should drop out of the Duel. I should pack my bags and give in to my rambling fate. I knew the facts: Pickles are cursed with wandering hearts. We're cursed to fail at everything we try.

But I also knew this fact: Once upon a time, Midnight Gulch was a magical place. And the Brothers Threadbare were two of the most magical people who ever lived here.

I shared Stone Weatherly's gypsy fate. Did I share his magic, too?

"There's still magic here," I dared to whisper, even though nobody was awake now except me and the midnight moon.

I'll bet the midnight moon had a good laugh over that. Because the kind of magic that found me the next morning is definitely not what I was expecting.

"Let me in, quick!" I banged my fist against the door of Oliver Weatherly's mansion. I could feel the rain beading on my face and dripping off the tips of my bangs. "Hey-yo!" I hollered again.

Charlie Sue Hancock swung the door open and pulled me inside. "Felicity!" She helped me out of my jacket, which was so wet that it popped and snapped like rubber bands against my arms. "What are you doing out in this mess?"

"I have to see Oliver now," I sniffed. My nose sucked in a mix of rain and snot. "Is he home?"

"He sure is." Charlie Sue wrapped a blanket around my shoulders. She led me up a swirly, spiraled staircase to the second story of Oliver's mansion.

"Hey-yo, Miss Felicity!" Oliver's voice seemed as surprised as Charlie Sue's when she first saw me. "I wasn't expecting you today. Is Jonah with you?"

"Just me," I said. "I've got a big problem that only you can help me with. I woke up this morning and found this . . ."

I pushed back my sleeve and flipped my hand so Oliver could see the inside of my wrist and what appeared to be the freshly drawn image of a dove. The very same dove that had been on Oliver's arm only a few days ago.

"It won't come off," I hollered. "And I have no idea how it got there!"

Frannie Jo had noticed it before I did. We were eating a healthy breakfast of Cheetos and Pop-Tarts when Frannie pointed to my arm and said, "Don't let Mama see that. She gets mad whenever I draw on myself."

I nearly spewed milk all over Cleo's table when I realized what she was talking about: Oliver Weatherly's tattoo. On *my* arm. I ran down the hall, hurdled over Boone — who was still snoring in the hallway — slammed shut the door of Cleo's bathroom, and tried to scrub the bird away. The skin of my wrist turned blotchy red, but the bird stayed put.

"I can't get it off!" I hollered at Oliver.

But Oliver didn't look perplexed, despite my yelling. Charlie Sue patted my shoulder. "Why don't I make the two of you some hot cocoa?" she said. And she shuffled back down the hallway.

"Fine idea," Oliver said. And then he nodded to me and smiled. "You don't need to worry about getting it off. The bird comes and goes as it pleases."

"This isn't a bird," I said. "It's a . . . *tattoo*."

And I gulped as I remembered what Mama had said when I saw the tattoo on her shoulder. The word *peace*, in such tiny letters they looked like a sparrow's footprints. My mama was the only person whose words I had never been able to see. I told her how much I liked it and she said she liked it, too. And I told her I wanted *peace* on my shoulder, too, and she said if I ever got *anything* tattooed on me before I was at least forty years old, she'd ground me for life.

"It's not exactly a tattoo," Oliver said, leading me to the big stuffed chair across from his desk. He settled across from me. "The bird first showed up on my arm the same morning I saw the hot air balloon. You remember that story, right?"

"Yes, sir," I said. "Hope came down."

"Exactly!" Oliver's eyes sparkled. "Hope came down. But the bird came first. Most of the time it stays put, right here on my arm. But sometimes the bird ends up on somebody else for a while. Seems like it knows when people need it most, when they're most fearful, most uncertain, most unsure. When the bird shows up, that means hope's coming down."

"The bird tattoo is a snicker of magic?" I asked.

"Exactly!" Oliver clapped.

Charlie Sue came back into the room and handed me a steamy mug of cocoa and smiled. "Better than my family's snicker of magic."

"Your people used to go invisible, right?" I asked, remembering Oliver's story from the Lube & Dye.

"Used to." Charlie Sue propped her hand on her hip. "But now we just go blurry in pictures."

Oliver chuckled.

I looked down at the inky dove on my wrist. "I could use a little hope," I admitted.

Oliver nodded. "You mean for the Duel, I reckon. When Jonah told me about that, I had a feeling the bird might show up on you. It'll sure stay with you through the Duel. That bird means good is coming your way." Oliver grinned. "You got nothing to worry about now!"

"I guess that's okay, then." I finally touched my finger to the bird's wings. It didn't feel feathery or magical; it just felt like my skin.

"That bird doesn't attach itself to people for nothing," Oliver said. "You must have something good worth saying if the bird showed up on you. Wear it well, you hear?"

I breathed easier then, first because the tattoo would be gone in a few days and that meant I wouldn't be grounded for life. But I also couldn't help but wonder if that meant everything would be okay, maybe better than okay.

Yes, my heart agreed.

      Yes,

            Yes,

                  Yes!

✳ ◇ ✳ ✳ ◇ ✳ ✳ ◇ ✳

The rain let up long enough for me to run to Jonah's house on Chicken Bristle Lane.

As soon as he opened the door, I held out my wrist. "Look," I said, "I got a tattoo."

"Spindiddly wicked!" Jonah grinned. "You got Oliver's bird!"

I told Jonah all about my crazy morning as I followed him into the kitchen. "Oliver says it's a little snicker of magic, my good luck charm for the Duel. Kind of like a lucky rabbit's foot but way less disgusting —"

I stopped so abruptly that my sneakers squeaked against the black-and-white kitchen tiles. Toast Terry sat at Jonah's kitchen table, with a carton of Dr. Zook's in front of him. Two thick books were fanned open on the table. Since no words were spinning up out of them, I figured they were math books. Numbers tell all sorts of stories to some people, but they've never done so much as whisper at me.

Toast nodded in my direction. "How goes it, Pickle?"

"Okay." I smiled.

Jonah wheeled around me toward the refrigerator. "Toast is helping me with math stuff."

"*You* need tutoring?" I flopped down in the empty chair. I didn't mean to sound so surprised, but Jonah didn't look offended. He just laughed.

"Decimals are my kryptonite. We were talking about the Duel when you walked in. Tell her your talent, T."

"I can make grilled cheese with a clothes iron." Toast grinned proudly. "That's how I got my nickname,

Toast. Someday I'm going to be a chef and make gourmet grilled cheeses. The space llama will be my trademark."

"That's a spindiddly life goal," I said.

Toast raised an eyebrow. "Spin-whatty?"

"*Spindiddly* is Felicity's word for 'awesome,'" Jonah clarified, coming to join us. "Toast has a good luck charm, too."

"Yeah, I do!" Toast beamed. He leaned in and pointed to a lone whisker squiggling out of his chin. "I named it Goliath."

"You named your facial hair?" I asked.

"Course he did." Jonah beamed, reaching across the table to give Toast a fist bump. "That's a monumental achievement."

Toast laughed as he stood up and stretched his long arms. "I need to use the facilities. Be right back."

Once I knew Toast was out of earshot, I said to Jonah, "I've never seen him so laid back. I've barely ever heard him talk. Honestly, I didn't think he liked me very much."

"He's just shy," Jonah said. "The two of you have a lot in common, actually. Toast is self-conscious about his voice and you're afraid to use yours."

"So you got a know-how over Toast? He's a Beedle project?"

"No," Jonah said quickly. "He's not a Beedle project. He's a friend. You're a friend, too. If I get a know-how over my friends, that's just a bonus."

I flicked at the lid of my Dr. Zook's carton. "Does he know you're . . . pumpernickel?"

Jonah shook his head. "Nope."

I couldn't help but smile as I looked down at the bird on my wrist again, traced my finger along the tips of its inky-black wings.

"He'll do great in the Duel," Jonah said. "That grilled cheese thing is pretty darn spindiddly, right?"

"Better than reading poems," I sighed, tracing the pointy tip of the bird's beak.

"You *are* still competing in the Duel? Right?" Jonah's eyes looked all swampy green and sad. "Because I thought after you figured out the Threadbare connection, you might not . . ."

"You knew my family was cursed? And you didn't tell me?"

"I must have figured it out at the same time you did. Mama told me your family was kin to the Weatherlys." Jonah shook his head. "But you heard Oliver. Nobody knows if that curse was even real."

"After all I've told you about Mama's rambling habits, you don't think the curse still exists?" I swallowed. "*Not even a little bit?*"

"Maybe you only have a snicker of it," he conceded.

"A snicker's enough to do plenty of damage."

Jonah moved his hands closer to me and I thought he might touch the bird on my wrist, but he didn't. "You know, if you don't want to do the Duel, I won't be mad. It's not like we'd stop hanging out or anything."

I raised my eyebrows. "Seriously?"

Jonah nodded. "I only want you to do the Duel because —"

"Something good will happen there," I sighed. "I'll do the Duel. I already told Mama and Cleo I would. I don't want to disappoint them by backing out. Plus . . . I have a plan B."

Jonah raised an eyebrow. "Plan B?"

"I thought maybe I . . . maybe *we* . . . could figure out Isabella's riddle. Then we'd break the curse."

"You're not a Threadbare, Felicity. Even if you're related to them, so what? You're related to lots of other people. You're part Pickle, part Harness, part . . . who knows what else. They're a part of who you are but you are the only *Felicity*. I think Oliver's right; the curse only matters if you let it."

"But all the same," I said, trying not to sound like I was begging, "there's a chance we could break it. The last Duel was when everything went wrong. What if this is the Duel where we make everything right? I'm part Threadbare. What if I'm here for a reason? What if I could do it?"

Maybe Jonah didn't believe in a curse, but I could tell he was interested. Just as he started to answer, we heard Toast bellow from somewhere in the house:

"Pickett! Okay if I play your piano?"

202

"Sure," Jonah yelled back. His yell must have woke up the storm, because suddenly the clouds split apart and the rain fell, hard and heavy against the roof.

Deluge

Waterwall

Silver, stormy, star curtain

I wrote down the words dripping down the windows of Jonah's kitchen.

"Let's focus on you doing the Duel," Jonah said. "But maybe we could look at the riddle, too, if that makes you feel better."

"Yes! I made you a copy." I ripped the page I'd written for Jonah out of my book. He just sighed and shook his head. "Have you written any poems yet?"

"Not yet," I admitted. "But Florentine says she'll help me."

As Jonah popped open the container of Dr. Zook's Mean Gene's Mocha Coconut, the sound of soft piano music drifted through the house. As I listened, I wondered if there was any story in the world better than music, a wordless and weightless lullaby wind, prone to fly right off pages and strings. No wonder people in Midnight Gulch could put their problems aside back when the Brothers Threadbare were around. No wonder it was the happiest town in the world.

Truly, when Toast said he wanted to play the piano, I thought he'd pound out something like "Jingle Bells." I didn't know he was a bona fide baby Mozart. "He can play the daylights out of that piano, can't he?"

"He can play anything. It's like he makes an instrument say everything he's afraid to say for real." Then Jonah grinned at me in his secret-keeping way. "I call this tune 'The Storm Song.' Watch the windows, Flea. You're gonna love this. . . ."

As the thunder growled louder, Toast pounded the piano keys harder, and the song changed from something lonesome and haunted to a peppy tune that belonged on a Broadway stage. The song sounded bright, and happy. It reminded me of sunlight and wildflowers, leaps and kicks.

Suddenly, the thunder stopped rumbling.

The rain squiggling down the windows paused midway.

The shy September sun peeped its bald head through the clouds and shone through the kitchen windows.

My heart kicked in rhythm with the plucky piano music:

Yes and

Yes and

Yes, yes, yes!

By the time the music died down, the storm was over.

"Guess I better head out." Toast trudged back into the kitchen and shoved his books into his backpack. "Later, Pickle. Later, Pickett." He saluted us both from the doorway.

I said good-bye but I don't think Toast heard me over the kitchen door banging shut.

"Jonah. Did he just make the storm stop?"

Jonah grinned. "Have I told you about the Terry family magic?"

Jonah pushed a carton of Blackberry Sunrise across the table. I pushed it far away from me and reached for the Mocha Coconut instead. Jonah didn't miss the movement of my hand. He scrunched his eyebrows, but didn't ask any questions.

"Nope," I said. "But I heard Oliver say something about them yesterday."

"They were storm catchers," Jonah said. "Whenever the drought came and the corn bowed down and the leaves dried up, farmers called on Maude Terry. She'd go stand in the field and sing and the clouds would come rolling in, peaceful easy. The rain lasted for days if Maude Terry called it up. The only problem is that, after she sang up the rain, Maude Terry would lose her voice for a long time. And people called on her so often that she never had a chance to say much. So whenever she was out in the fields, she sang as loud as she could. She sang clear and strong and she tried to make the song even more beautiful than it was the time before."

"Couldn't her family help out?" I asked. "You said it was Terry magic. Why'd Maude always have to lose her voice over it?"

"The rest of the Terrys only had a snicker of Maude's gift," Jonah said. "Her girls could call up an hour or two of rain, but they moved out of town as soon as they could. And poor old Jester Terry" — Jonah shook his head — "he just sang up swarms of bees. And Maude's older sister, Hester Terry, sang so screechy-loud that every dog in Midnight Gulch started hollering."

That made me laugh.

"Nobody had the knack like Maude did," Jonah said. He inclined his head toward the door. "But I think Toast has a snicker. Maude was his grandmother. Good magic runs in families, too."

"How do you know so much about so many people?"

"My dad told me her story. After he told me, he always asked me what I'd say if I knew I'd lose my voice — for a year, for a day, for forever."

Now it was Jonah pushing the Blackberry Sunrise away. "My dad said he heard Maude sing once, back when he was a boy. He said she walked out in the middle of the field and lifted up her arms toward the silver skies. He said the cold wind came first, and rippled against her dress and blew her gray hair away from her face. She sang until the rain fell on her face. She sang until her voice ran out. That was my dad's favorite story to tell. He says that's why the weather's so crazy in Midnight Gulch now, because Maude's not here to sing to the sky."

"Tell me more about your dad?" I asked.

I didn't look at Jonah. I looked at my blue book instead. When he didn't answer my question right off, I was afraid I'd hurt his feelings or drudged up bad memories.

"You're stalling, Flea." Jonah's lip quirked in a half smile. "You need to get some poems down or we won't have time to practice before the Duel."

"Practice won't help," I assured him.

"Oliver's bird won't write a poem for you," Jonah said. "It just gives you courage."

"I wasn't talking about the bird." I pushed my bangs down over my eyes. "It won't matter because I'll still find a way to mess things up."

"You don't mess up when you talk to me."

"Talking to you is different than talking to a big room full of people."

Jonah picked up the ice-cream container and squinted his eyes toward the trash can. He arched his arm and tossed the carton toward it. *THUNK*. Perfect shot. Of course it was. Jonah never missed. "Why's it different?"

"Because I know my words are safe with you," I said. And my face got hot and tingly. I wiped the side of my face like I could wipe the tingly feeling away. Then I stared down at the blue book.

I heard the whir of Jonah's wheelchair backing away from the table. He reached for a tall jar on the counter, then settled it gently on the table, right in front of me. I saw little curls of paper tangled up inside.

"My dad's name is Arly Pickett," Jonah said. His eyes looked extra-neon green right then. I had a feeling he was about to give me something way more important than a hope tattoo or a carton of ice cream. "He gave me this jar before he got deployed. He filled it up with 365 strips of paper. He told me to pull one piece of paper every single day — but only one. And he said when I got to the last slip of paper . . . that's when I would know he was about to come home."

"He's coming home soon, then." There were only a few curls of paper left in Jonah's jar.

"I hope so," Jonah whispered.

"What did he write on the papers?" I could only see scribbles on the paper scraps, but full-blown words were floating around in Jonah's jar:

Hockey puck
Guitar pick
Fishing lure
River run

"He wrote down the things we'll do together when he gets home again."

"How do you play *hockey*?" I asked.

"I play my own way," Jonah said. "I can't stand up to hit the puck, obviously, but I can —"

"I didn't mean that," I said. "I mean that it's too hot here. There's no lake frozen enough to skate on."

"Street hockey." Jonah smiled. And then he countered, "More like garage hockey, actually."

"Chicken Bristle hockey?" I grinned.

"Exactly!"

"Tell me something else about him," I said softly.

"He met my mom when they were both in mechanic school. They drove off to their honeymoon in a car they fixed up together." Jonah reached deep into his pocket. He dropped a small, thin piece of red metal onto the table. "Before Dad got deployed, he gave my mom half of a red heart that he'd made out of a piece of sheet metal. He gave me the other half and told us both that, no matter where he was, no matter how much of the world was sitting between us, his heart was right here."

Jonah picked up the metal scrap and twirled it between his fingers. "I keep my half in my pocket during the day. At night, I keep it beside my alarm clock. But whenever I wake up in the morning, I'm always holding it tight in my fist. Always. I wish I'd given him something, too, to help him remember me when he's over there."

"He doesn't need any help remembering you," I said. "Forgetting people you love is impossible. It'd be like forgetting how to breathe."

"I still wish it, though," Jonah said. "I knew I wouldn't be seeing him for a year and I still didn't give him anything to keep."

"He keeps all this." I tapped my fingernail against the jar. "You know how Oliver keeps all those pictures on his bookshelves? I'll bet your dad keeps all those memories propped up on the walls of his heart. When he gets lonely, he takes one down and thinks about you and remembers."

Jonah flicked at the tip of the red metal heart. "When he left, and when I talk to him on the phone, I tell him that I love him. That's all."

"That's everything," I said.

Jonah's smile faded as he twirled the jagged metal heart between his fingers. He flicked the heart against the table, spun it like a top. "I need to be honest with you about something. I'm not as good as you think I am. Sometimes the best thing about doing Beedle stuff is that it keeps my mind occupied, so I don't think about what might happen to . . ."

Dad.

Jonah didn't say the word. Instead, he flicked the heart so hard it nearly spun off the table. I caught it in my hands and pressed it flat in front of him. I knew the weight of that word. I knew how hard it was to say.

"I still think you're good. You might as well save your breath from convincing me otherwise."

Jonah leaned over and tapped the bird on my wrist. "Hope's a good thing to hold on to, isn't it? I hope he comes home soon. And I hope we make a million more memories together."

"I hope for that, too," I told him.

Jonah glanced up and smiled at me. I smiled back at him.

And no more words passed between us. That day Jonah became more than just a friend who kept my words safe. I realized he was the kind of friend who didn't mind the silent places. The quiet fell between us like a comfortable old quilt and we both settled into it. Jonah scanned the paper for do-goods. I listened to a bird chirping outside, taking its rare opportunity to sing up at the sunlight. No wonder the storms are so loud and mean in Midnight Gulch, I thought. I'll bet the sky missed Maude Terry's sweet lullabies.

"I ain't dancing!" Cleo hollered. "If I start stomping and jumping, everybody in this building will think there's an earthquake."

"Have it your way, then!" Boone shot up off Cleo's couch and tightened the banjo pegs. His left hand curled around the banjo's neck. Next he stretched out his right hand. Boone's banjo picks weren't flat like guitar picks. Instead, they were pointy and silver and curved like little crowns over the tips of his fingers.

"Holly?" Boone asked. "I know you wanna dance. We got lots to celebrate!"

"What I *know* is that I haven't danced in years or painted in so long that I'll probably make a mess of that Gallery. . . ."

"No more talk like that!" Cleo gave Mama such a hard push, she nearly fell out of her chair. "Cut loose, Holly!"

Boone started picking the banjo so fast I thought sparks might flick off the strings. First, Boone shook his hips back and forth. And then he started shuffling around the floor in his mismatched socks. Biscuit was sniffing out the cowboy boots Boone had kicked off by the couch. This night was definitely a celebration; Boone didn't kick off his boots for anything.

"Get up, Holly!" Boone hollered.

Mama shook her head *no* but her foot was already tap-ping *yes, yes, yes.* I guess some people love music so much it gets caught up inside them.

Suddenly, Mama shot up out of the chair and twirled around so fast that her hair came loose from its elastic. "You gotta dance, too, Frannie!"

Cleo started clapping a loud rhythm to Boone's music and so did I. Frannie squealed as Mama spun her around.

"You, too, Felicity." Mama pulled me up out of my seat. I tried to dance the same as Mama; I let the music tell my feet what to do. I closed my eyes and shuffled back and forth. Then I kicked and I jumped and I spun around so fast that the locket flung up and whopped me in the forehead.

"I love this more than Friday!" Frannie Jo yelled. "I love this more than fireflies! I love this more than cake icing!"

I spun around once more and plopped down in the floor, spindiddly dizzy with happiness.

Until I noticed the brochures sticking out of Mama's purse.

Seattle. Silver city skylines and squiggly roads on a map. I wondered if the miles would feel even longer now that they'd be separating me from so many people I loved. I thought about Jonah and his dad, how they still talked to each other weekly on the phone, thank goodness. But Jonah missed the physical presence of his dad, too.

I pushed back my sleeve and traced my ink bird. *Hope's coming down for all of us*, I reminded myself. Hope was coming down for me at the Duel . . . once I figured out how to break the curse.

But I had a sudden and fantastical idea for sending hope out to someone else. Someone who needed it even more than me.

Once all the Pickles and Harnesses were snoozing, I snuck down the hall, around Uncle Boone's sleeping bag, over to the window of Aunt Cleo's apartment and pushed it open.

SQUEEEEEEEAK.

I cringed at the sound and waited for Cleo to run out of her room, flinging her broom, looking for an intruder. That's what happened the other night when Boone got up to get a drink of water. Apparently, Cleo forgot he was here and ran in the kitchen and whacked him so hard with the broom that she nearly knocked him into next week.

Nobody got up this time, though. I waited until I heard Boone snoring again. Then I took one of the table chairs and pushed it up close to the window.

Something cold clutched around my ankle and I nearly screamed. Luckily, I glanced down in time to realize it was Frannie Jo and not some mean old shadow. Isabella Thistle's magic didn't sound very creepy in the daylight, but it was sure bothering me tonight.

"Go back to bed," I whispered to Frannie.

"What are you doing?" She climbed up on the chair beside me. "You can't fly!"

"Why would I try to fly?" I whisper-yelled. "Do you think I'm an idiot?"

Frannie Jo didn't answer.

I sighed. "Stay here if you want but stay quiet. I got work to do."

"You'll get in trouble for drawing on yourself."

"You'll get in trouble for being out of bed." I pushed my sleeve up to my elbow and looked at my hope tattoo.

You could win the duel with that, said the selfish half of my brain.

But you don't need more hope, said the do-good half. *You've got enough inside you and all around you. You've got it in your friends. You've got it in your family. You've had it all along.*

I touched the fine tip of the pen to my wrist, right along the upturned feathers of the dove. The ink was so cold I felt every letter as I wrote the words on my skin. Sweet as cotton candy:

Love you

And then I threaded the rest of the letters underneath it:

That's all

That's everything

Next I pressed my lips against my wrist. "I know you're not a carrier pigeon," I whispered. "And I don't know if you fly long distances. . . ."

"*Why* are you talking to it?" Frannie asked.

"Shhh," I told her, returning my full attention to the bird. "I don't know exactly what you do, but I'd be

214

grateful if you'd deliver that message to Arly Pickett . . . for Jonah."

"*Jooonah*," Frannie Jo said. She made kissy noises with her mouth.

"Hush," I said.

"You hu —" Frannie gasped. "Felicity . . . your ink bird . . . it's fluttering."

Sure enough, the bird on my wrist shook out its feathers until it was puffed up proud and strong. Then it stretched its wings open wide and flew off my wrist, taking my words along with it. I saw one last flicker of Oliver's bird before it sailed out the window and blended into the night.

"The bird was my only good luck charm." I gulped. The Duel was coming. Mama was leaving. And I just sent all my courage out the window. "Guess I'm on my own now."

Frannie Jo slipped her hand inside mine. "You're not on your own. You still got me."

"Tell me the truth, Florentine. Don't hold back. I can handle constructive criticism." I wrung my hands together, round and around, while she scanned my first poem. Showing Florentine my words made me so nervous that I couldn't shut up talking. Florentine read silently. I figured she was trying to think of a nice way to tell me the poems stunk. I sighed. "They're horrible, aren't they? I can write a new batch. I still have a few days."

"They ain't horrible." Florentine turned the page, her dark eyes scanning my next set of lines. "These words are marvelous."

I felt light-headed. ". . . Really?"

Florentine nodded. "These are fine words you got here. And Jonah says you got Oliver's dove to keep you calm and steady on stage. I'd say you're about to have a fine dueling day." She winked at me and handed the blue book back.

I didn't tell Florentine about hope flying the coop. The thought of the bird tattoo flying across the ocean and

216

landing on the wrist of Arly Pickett made me happy. I wanted him to have hope. I wanted him to come home to his family. But I missed having a snicker of magic on my wrist. I blinked up into the face of the September sun, wondering where the tattoo was right at that moment.

Florentine propped her hand over her eyes to shield the light and glanced up at Mama, who stood beside us with her hands on her hips, staring at the Gallery.

"You been staring at that wall for twenty minutes," Florentine said to her. "You think it's gonna paint itself?"

"I need to figure out how to get the graffiti off first," Mama said. She stepped closer and gently traced her fingers across the letters somebody'd painted on the bricks. I watched each word ripple beneath her touch. "I need a blank canvas when I start."

"Not this time you don't," Florentine chuckled. "Whoever painted those words? They were mad. They painted 'em in deep. Heartbreak always makes the words stick extra deep."

Mama looked down at Florentine. "How do I get them off, then? They'll probably bleed through the paint."

"Probably." Florentine nodded. "But you do what you know how to do: You paint something new."

"Been too long since I've done this," Mama sighed as she eased down on the sidewalk. She hunched her scrawny shoulders and buried her face in her hands. "I don't even know where to start. That's what happens when we're in a place too long. My creativity's just . . . gone. I feel stuck."

"That's not why you're stuck," I said quickly. "You just haven't painted in a long time. Start in the center, like you tell me," I said.

We've done a bunch of traveling in the Pickled Jalapeño. And on warm summer nights, after sunset, before the dark drops its curtain, I like to stare out the window and wonder. I've seen mountains and wildflowers and wild animals and storms. I've seen the ocean; I've felt it lick up around my ankles like it's something frisky and playful. And I've seen it crash against the rocks, dangerous, a silver-tongued monster. I've seen sweet things like Frannie sleeping and Biscuit snuggling close to me and Cleo slipping extra cash into the pocket of Mama's work uniform. My eyes are tiny, but they've taken in a world full of wonderful.

So I can't even imagine how it must feel to see all that wonderful and then be able to touch a paintbrush to a piece of paper, or pavement, or brick, or brittle rock and leave that image right there, exactly the same way your eyes took it in. Mama doesn't just paint mountains or moonlight or people's faces; she paints memories. She paints the joy you feel when you see something wonderful for the very first time.

But Mama wouldn't even look at the Gallery.

I clutched the locket so tight in my fist, I wondered if it'd crumble. Enough magic to take her sad away, that's what I wanted. I didn't have that.

But I did have my words.

"Miss Florentine," I said, "I'd like to tell you a few things about my mama, Holly Harness Pickle. Do you mind?"

"Sure don't," Florentine drawled.

Mama didn't look at us, but I could see her cheek dimple in an almost-grin.

"Okay, then," I began. "The first thing I painted with Mama was rocks, river rocks we saved from the Cumberland River. We all took home a rock and we painted one thing we loved on it. I painted the dog, and Frannie painted a piece of cheese."

"That's fancy." Florentine nodded.

"It truly is," I agreed. "And then when we lived in Birmingham, Mama painted red roses on paper plates and she taped the plates to my wall. She told me I could fill my garden with any flower I wanted. If I could dream it, I could paint it. That's what she told me. But quite honestly, I can dream up some pretty weird stuff. And it never looked so good when I painted it. When Mama did? It looked even better than it did in my dreams. By the time we moved from that place, the entire wall of my and Frannie Jo's room was covered with paper flowers."

Mama wasn't looking at the wall anymore. Her body was still turned toward the Gallery. But she'd turned her face toward me, listening.

"Once, Mama painted a map on the roof of the Jalapeño. We called it the Kingdom of Spiderberg. Every night we told a story about a new place and then Mama would paint a new castle on the map. I was the Queen of Spiderberg."

"Rightly so." Florentine nodded.

"I told Mama maybe we should paint stars up in

Spiderberg, too." I gulped. "But instead of grabbing her paintbrushes, she pulled me and Frannie outside and we stared up at the stars and spun around underneath them until we got spindiddly dizzy. She said stars don't mind being painted. And they don't mind sonnets or songs or poems, neither. But they'd rather just give you light enough to dance by. That's what she told me."

"Okay," Mama breathed. She wasn't talking to me or Florentine. "Okay," she said again, like she was answering some deep-down question she was afraid to ask out loud.

Her hands trembled as she picked up the can of white paint and poured it into her paint tray. She pushed the big paint roller down into the paint until it soaked up all the color.

SWISH. The roller swiped up and down, over the brick, over the words, over every picture that had been painted there before.

My heart felt heavy in a good way again, holding me still in that memory.

"Mmm-hmmm." Florentine grinned at me. "I just heard you speak hundreds of words, Felicity Pickle. Every last one of them came out of your mouth fine. Mighty fine, in fact."

"My words are different when I talk about people I" — I gulped — "love."

"Exactly," Florentine said softly.

The wind-chime wind tunneled down Main Street. Florentine groaned and pulled her traveling bag close to her side. I stood up and clamped my hand tight around the locket.

The wind didn't rattle Mama, though. She kept swiping the paint roller back and forth across the brick. I watched new words appear, then fizzle, with every stroke:

Sandstorm

Avalanche

Fly

Away

Home to visit

Home to stay

You don't have to leave to find a new beginning, Mama. You can begin again exactly where you are. That's what I wanted to say to her, but me telling her wouldn't matter. Mama had to see that we were home for herself. Painting the Gallery might help a little bit.

But breaking the Weatherly curse would set Mama free forever. I could feel it.

* ◇ ✳ ✳ ◇ ✳ ✳ ◇ ✳

After Mama'd been working for a few hours, I jogged across the street to see how the Gallery looked from far off. As I spun around to take a seat on the red bench, I heard Florentine hollering my name from back at the wall.

"Don't sit there!" she yelled.

I froze, half squatted, ready to plop myself down. "Why?"

Florentine slung her traveling bag around her shoulder and crossed the street. " 'Cause that bench belongs to Abigail Honeycutt."

I glanced back at the empty bench. "You think she'll mind if I sit on it?"

"Probably not," Florentine said. "But she'll sure mind if you sit on *her*. She's invisible. Maybe ask first and make sure she's not there."

Mama had already told me that Florentine was probably crazy, but crazy in a sweet way, not crazy-mean. I knew then that Mama's words were most certainly true. All the same I said, "Uh . . . Miss Honeycutt?"

When nobody answered, Florentine said, "You're fine, then. She ain't here."

"Who is she?" I whispered, sitting down easily onto the bench.

"That's a better story for Oliver to tell. He tells it right."

Florentine pulled her bag tight against her side. "I only know bits and pieces about people who used to live in this town. I don't know the full story."

* ◇ ✳ * ◇ ✳ * ◇ *

"Thanks for all those kind things you said back there," Mama said as we walked back to Cleo's. She leaned down and kissed the top of my head.

I flung my arm around her waist and said, "You're welcome. I can't wait to tell Jonah what Florentine said about my poem."

"I've been meaning to ask you something about Jonah," Mama said, turning us down Main Street.

Just when she was about to ask, we passed Dr. Zook's Dreamery Creamery. The door swung open, and Uncle Boone walked out carrying two ice-cream cones. "Perfect timing!" he said. He gave one cone to Mama and one to me. Boone's banjo was strapped to his back, like always. He slung it around in front of him and winked. "I figured I'd play y'all home. How does that sound?"

I wished every day could end that way, with banjo music, sweet ice cream, and street shadows painted long by the setting sun. The world was so beautiful I nearly forgot about my troubles.

"About Jonah Pickett." Mama glanced down at me. "Do you have a crush on him?"

"Not a crush." I shook my head. "More like an inflate. He makes me feel the opposite of crushed. He makes my heart feel like a balloon, like it's going to blow up and fly right out of my chest."

Boone sighed. "I might have to use that in a song, Felicity Pickle."

"Jonah's a sweet boy," Mama said. "But you know you don't have to participate in the Duel to impress him, right? You can back out if it scares you."

"Why would it scare you?" Boone asked. "You didn't get worked up over that stupid curse did you?"

Mama stopped walking. Her hand clamped down tight on my shoulder. "Why would she know about that?" She narrowed her eyes at my uncle.

Boone shrugged. "You know how people talk. It doesn't matter anyway. It's a story, Liss. It's got nothing to do with you."

"Boone . . ." Mama warned. Then she looked down at me. "You are *not* cursed, Felicity."

I nodded, even though I didn't believe her. Even though I was pretty sure Boone didn't, either. The curse had everything to do with me, which is exactly why I had to figure out how to break it.

"You don't have to do the Duel." Mama tightened her arm around my shoulders. "If you change your mind . . . if you get nervous . . ."

"I am nervous," I admitted. "But I'm not going to run away."

"Atta girl!" Uncle Boone cheered. Mama only sighed.

Boone strummed a sweet tune as we walked through downtown, toward Cleo's apartment. The first evening star showed up in the sky and winked at me. The wind rolled through the streets. The trees shook their branches and beat their tambourine-leaves in a strangely perfect rhythm. Almost like the trees were clapping along to Boone's music.

Jonah and I sat side by side on the bench seat of a Dr. Zook's delivery truck. Oliver was behind the wheel, driving a little bit too fast down a dusty country back road.

"Slow down a little bit!" Uncle Boone yelled from the back. "Or this piano's gonna smash me flat."

When I woke up that morning, I had no idea part of my day would include a full-blown Beedle mission, but soon enough, Jonah was calling about a know-how, a delivery truck, a piano, and making Boone a Beedle associate. Because we needed somebody who could do the heavy lifting. One perk of having a do-gooder best friend is every day's got an adventure tucked away in it.

"We're delivering a piano to Toast Terry," Jonah said to me at school. His eyes were sparkly bright, the way they always get when he's plotting good deeds.

"A piano?" I squealed.

"Shhhhh!" Jonah chided. "It's not like a baby grand, just a little upright. It'll fit in the back of the Dr. Zook's truck. But Oliver threw out his back at square dance lessons with Charlie Sue. Do you think Boone will help?"

So I asked Boone if he'd do me a favor and he said, "Anything!" And so off we went. Big Bruce helped Jonah into the front of the delivery truck, then loaded the wheelchair into the back with the piano. Boone stayed in the back, too, so he could keep the piano from scooting around whenever Oliver took turns too fast. The ice-cream delivery trucks didn't need freezers, thanks to Oliver's marvelous invention. But I was still a little bit worried about Boone getting piano-smashed. Big Bruce was back there with him, mumbling something about how he might as well just unload the piano by himself since Boone was about the size of a skinny pencil.

According to Jonah, Big Bruce was part of a small, secret group of Beedle associates. Jonah said he never had an accomplice before me. But he and Oliver knew every so often, in emergencies, they'd need help with logistics, deliveries, and heavy lifting. Up until now, Big Bruce and Jewell Pickett were all the help they'd ever needed. But with Oliver's back out, and Jewell working overtime to keep her mind busy, we needed Boone, too. I figured Boone would be thrilled about joining me on Team Beedle. I guess he was, a little bit. But he didn't much care for the heavy-lifting part.

Jonah flicked open a small door on the dashboard, which probably had a glove compartment at one time. Now it was refitted to carry small pints of ice cream. He pulled the lid off a pint that smelled like pancake batter.

"Ah!" Oliver grinned, recognizing the smell. "That's a new flavor called Sarah's Sunday Breakfast. What's the verdict?"

"Pretty good," Jonah said. But he only took a couple more bites before he passed the pint to me and reached for the Blackberry Sunrise.

Jonah cleared his throat and tried to refocus on the folded newspaper in his lap. But I could tell he was too excited about our mission to focus. "Toast is gonna love this," he sighed. "He saved up for a piano last year, but his dad was let go from the water plant. Toast gave his savings to his parents. He never told me that. His mom told my mom that he'd done it. He deserves something spindiddly as this."

"Are we just gonna drop a piano in his front yard?" I asked.

"Front porch," Jonah clarified. "I figure they can wheel it inside from there."

As Oliver drove, Jonah read tidbits of news from seven different counties. He'd circled stories and pictures and classifieds, anything that gave them a clue to what somebody might need.

"The Freely family down in Sweetwater needs an air conditioner," said Jonah. "We can take care of that, easy."

"There's an obituary in there for Delora Riggins," Oliver sighed. "I know her husband, Clifford. I'll drop by Ponder's and get a pie for him. Maybe run over there and give him some company."

And on and on they went. You'd think after reading about so many needs, they'd start feeling tired, but they never did. They only got more excited about figuring out ways to help.

"Is something troubling you, Felicity?" Oliver asked. "You're awfully quiet."

"There is one thing I'm troubled over," I said. "Florentine had me believing I was about to sit down on an invisible person. She said you could tell the story better than her."

"Ah! Abigail Honeycutt." Oliver nodded. "She ain't invisible."

"That's what I figured," I sighed.

"She *was* invisible," Oliver said. "She's long gone by now. You remember Charlie Sue telling you that her family used to be able to turn invisible? Same with Abigail Honeycutt. The difference is that Charlie Sue's people knew how to pull out of it. Abigail didn't."

"How the hayseed does somebody go invisible?"

"It's easier than you think," Oliver said.

"Are we almost there?" Boone yelled from the back.

"Not even close," Oliver hollered. Then he got back to his story.

"That bench Florentine told you not to sit on? That's where Abigail Honeycutt sat, right up till the day she faded away."

"She died?" I asked softly. I felt Jonah's shoulders stiffen. He'd been extra-especially quiet during the past few days. He said it had to do with only having a few pieces of paper left in the jar. He said he knew he should be excited about his dad coming home. But he couldn't help but worry, too.

"She died eventually," Oliver said. "Everybody does, of course. But nobody knows when she passed because she faded first."

I blew my too-long bangs out of my eyes and said, "You better start explaining."

Oliver said, "Abigail Honeycutt was married to the only man in town wealthier than the Weatherlys. His name was Lionel and he was the kindest, most gentle soul you'd ever meet. Lionel and Abigail had a son, Burl. And shortly after Burl was born, they built Dr. Zook's Famous Ice Cream Factory. The name came from a bedtime story Abigail made up for Burl. Dr. Zook was a superhero in disguise. A frazzled chemist by day. A crime stopper by night. That sort of thing. The Honeycutts set up the ice-cream factory, then put the parlor on Main Street. They brought thousands of jobs into Midnight Gulch. I saw an old newspaper clipping about it, and the reporter said that's the happiest people had been since the Threadbares were here."

Oliver slammed on the breaks, just in time for a fat white cow to meander across the road. He honked the horn, which made a sound like *waaaah-uuuuuu-guh*. Boone screamed an unsavory word as he tried to brace the piano.

"Most of their success had to do with hard work," said Oliver as he stomped back down on the gas. "But folks know some of it had to do with Abigail's magic. She was kin to the Smiths — so she knew all sorts of wild recipes —

229

cookies that gave people laughing fits, and punch that turned shy people feisty. Her most famous recipe had to do with memory; she baked homemade biscuits with black-berries and sugar stirred into the dough. Her blackberry biscuits helped people remember things; sometimes the memory was good and sometimes it was bad. But it needed to be remembered."

"Like the Blackberry Sunrise," I said, staring down at that infernal carton in Jonah's hands. The carton I refused to touch.

"Exactly," said Oliver. "That's where the idea for the ice cream came from."

Oliver continued, "The Honeycutts were older than most folks are when they had their baby, so they doted extra special on little Burl. He was a real creative soul, helped them name all the ice-cream flavors. Every year on Burl's birthday, his parents took him on a trail walk down by Snapdragon Pond. They'd sit on the banks beside the tall reeds and watch the sun creep higher and higher above these sleepy old mountains. One day, the sun turned the sky lavender and gray and then silver metallic. The morning glories fanned open their petals. The wind blew ripples across the water. And Burl told his parents he'd never been happier. He said he wished every day could be a black-berry sunrise. And so, as a gift, Abigail mixed that memory into the ice-cream recipe. Every time Burl tasted it, he remembered that morning. Blackberry Sunrise was his favorite flavor."

"Mine, too," Jonah said, and he held the carton of ice cream up like he was about to make a toast. "Then what happened?"

"Just a sec," Oliver said as the delivery truck slowed to a creeping crawl. He drove along a tangle of old barbed wire fence until he came upon a gravel road that led to a sweet little house in the middle of a sunflower field.

Jonah nodded. "Charlie Sue was right. Nobody's home yet."

"Perfect," Oliver said, and he threw the truck into reverse and backed into the driveway. "Y'all can leave it on the porch!" Oliver hollered to Boone and Bruce. "And don't forget to stick that red ribbon on it."

I heard Boone huff and puff while he tried to get a good grip on the piano. Somehow, they managed to haul it out of the truck. Boone puffed out his cheeks, and his face turned stop-sign red as he helped Bruce carry it up on the porch.

"I'm gonna owe him big-time," I sighed.

Jonah elbowed Oliver's arm. "What happened to Burl?"

"Burl grew up," said Oliver. "Burl's dad wanted him to take over the ice-cream factory, but that's not what Burl wanted. Burl loved the stage; he wanted to go to New York City first, see if he could make it as an actor. But his father didn't even want him to try. They had horrible fights, the two of them."

Oliver took off his glasses. Before he wiped the lenses clean, I saw a cluster of tiny words forming, and fading, against the glass:

Hear and remember
Hear and hold close

"So one day," Oliver continued, "Burl climbed the bus headed north and he never came back. He didn't tell his parents where he was going or how long he'd be gone. He only left a note for his mother. It read:

" *'I love you. I'll never forget my Blackberry Sunrise. Love, Burl'* "

"And then . . ." I waited. "When did he come back?"

Oliver shook his head. "Never. Nobody saw Burl Honeycutt again after that."

"That's awful," I said.

"It was indeed," Oliver agreed. "Abigail sat on that red bench every day at noon for ten years. The bus stops there by the bench. So Abigail would go and wait to see if her son got off the bus. When she finally realized he wouldn't be doing that, she took all of her memories — all the good ones — and all the bad ones — and she steeped them in a teapot. Then she walked down to Snapdragon Pond and poured every last drop in the river.

I heard the heavy thud of Boone's cowboy boots climbing up into the back of the delivery truck. "Done!" he hollered, raising his arm in victory.

Big Bruce rolled his eyes.

Jonah pointed to the ice-cream box. "Toss them some ice cream, Flea."

I picked two pints, Rosie's Strawberry Rhubarb and Bridgett's Hawaiian Pineapple, and tossed them into the backseat.

"Hallelujah," Boone sighed.

"Uh-oh." Jonah pointed toward the far-off edge of the dirt road. "Car's coming! Haul out, Oliver!"

Oliver stomped down so hard on the gas that my body slammed against the seat. I heard a loud *FWOMP* in the back of the truck, followed by another unsavory word, which no doubt came from Boone. He and Cleo are alike in lots of ways.

"You think they saw us?" Jonah asked.

Oliver smiled proudly and shook his head. "We barely made it."

"Finish telling about Abigail," I said.

Oliver nodded. "As time dragged on, the strangest thing began happening to Abigail Honeycutt. First her color started to pale a little. The bright orange dress she liked to wear faded to peach. Her black hair faded to brown. Her pale skin got even whiter. Then she started looking like she stepped out of a black-and-white photograph. And then she started to look transparent. Lionel gave her a red umbrella to carry so people could see her. So they wouldn't run through her. But soon she'd faded completely, and the red umbrella was all anyone could see. One day the wind came and lifted that umbrella and spun it up into the stars."

"She got rid of her memories because they hurt too much," I said.

"They sure do hurt," Oliver said. "They hurt like the dickens."

Oliver patted his shirt, right over his heart. "They'll help heal you, too, though, if you'll let them."

✳ ◇ ✳ ✳ ◇ ✳ ✳ ◇ ✳

"Are you still trying to figure out Isabella's riddle?" Jonah asked me. I stood on Oliver's porch, kicking my shoe back and forth.

"Definitely." I nodded. "But even if I figure it out, I'll compete in the Duel." I told Jonah what all Florentine said about my poems. He nodded along, but didn't have much to say. Big, fat raindrops plunked down from the sky. I pulled my hood over my head and smiled. "You're being awfully quiet."

Jonah tugged on his hair, pulling his words together slowly. "I'm trying to figure out how to tell you something. . . ."

I raised my eyebrows. "That doesn't sound good."

Jonah laughed nervously. "The thing is . . . I want you to know . . ." He took a steadying breath and looked up at me. "Even if I didn't get a know-how over you, I still would have found an excuse to talk to you. When you stood up in front of Miss Lawson's class and said 'My name is Flea . . . ,' I wanted to be your friend. I'll be your friend no matter what. I feel kinda guilty for pushing you so hard to do the Duel. I mean, I've been trying to talk you into doing something you are morbidly afraid of. You know what I'm afraid of?"

"Nothing."

"Wrong," Jonah sighed. "I'm afraid of clowns. And if somebody tried to get me to shake a clown's hand, or wave to a clown, or even touch a clown with the tip of a vaulting pole . . . I wouldn't do it. I'd tell that do-gooder to buzz off."

"I don't want you to buzz off," I said. "And clowns are severely creepy. They have painted smiles."

"I don't like painted smiles," Jonah said.

"Amen." I nodded.

"Hallelujah!" Jonah grinned. "If I start pushing you too hard, just tell me to back off. Okay?"

"I'm plumb flattered you'd want to help me," I admitted. "I've never had a friend like you."

I looked out toward the end of Oliver's driveway. Past the gate was downtown Midnight Gulch and past the Gulch were the gray mountains that hemmed us in and kept us safe. How strange, I thought, when you can see what's way out ahead of you but not what's right up close. "We're leaving soon, if the Duel doesn't work." I swallowed. "I wouldn't be surprised if we're gone by next week."

"The Duel's going to work," Jonah said. He pulled his backpack around and fished a carton of Blackberry Sunrise out of it.

"Geez," I said. "I've never met anybody who eats more ice cream than you."

"I consider that a compliment." Jonah held the carton out for me. He'd tied a red ribbon to the top. "But this one's not for me. It's for you. I got a know-how over you. . . ."

"Again?!"

"All I know is that if you eat this ice cream, you will do great in the Duel. This is from the Beedle," Jonah said, "when you're ready for it."

The carton of Blackberry Sunrise was so icy cold that it stung my fingers. I knew Jonah meant well, but I had absolutely no desire to eat that stuff. Ever. I swerved around to fling the pint deep into the abyss of my backpack. Before I did, I noticed something unusual on the carton. Two somethings.

"Did you write this?" I squinted my eyes.

"Write what?"

SWEET

AMENDS

Those two words were golden, glittering. They'd become familiar to me already, but I'd only seen them scrawled in my blue book. I'd read Isabella Thistle's curse a zillion times wondering what the hayseed *sweet amends* meant. And now, here it was, out in the wild.

Maybe biting into that ice cream would help me break Isabella's curse, but I didn't care. I couldn't eat it. I'd find another way. I shoved the ice cream deep into my backpack and cleared my throat. "I'm going to miss you and your crazy know-hows."

"You're not gone yet. The Gallery's not even done."

236

I was as good as gone, but I didn't want to think about good-bye. Not right then. So I smiled and gently punched Jonah's arm. "You're splendiferous, Jonah Pickett."

I walked down the ramp, toward Oliver's spiraled gate. I was nearly to the balloon-shaped hedge when I heard Jonah say, "You're spindiddly, Felicity Pickle."

Mama marked out the scene she wanted on the Gallery wall: the blue sky, the silver river, some of the buildings on Main Street, the fields, and the forest. I hoped as soon as Mama started painting, she'd remember how much she used to like it. I thought it all looked spindiddly.

But the more beautiful the Gallery became, the more frustrated Mama looked.

She'd just painted a cluster of river rocks when she stepped back, crossed her arms, and squinted her eyes. "It's all wrong."

"It's all going to come together," I assured her. "Take all the time you need!" And then more quietly, just so she'd hear me, I said, "Maybe it would be better if you didn't have so many people watching you work. . . ."

Since the Gallery painting was the most newsworthy thing to happen in Midnight Gulch in years, I wasn't surprised to see townspeople wandering by all day long. Elvis Phillips serenaded us for a time. Day Grissom brought us sandwiches from Ponder's Pie Shop. He brought one for

Cleo, too, but I told him she was busy back at the apartment. Day frowned and gave the sandwich to Biscuit instead.

"That's not it," Mama sighed. "And anyhow, it's everybody's Gallery. I like them being part of it. It's me that's the problem; my work's not good anymore."

When I'd suggested Mama could paint the Gallery, I thought it'd be great for her. But I could see now I was wrong. Mama was so frustrated by her own lack of inspiration that she was eager to quit, and therefore even more eager to bolt. I could see it in her eyes.

I watched folks come and go from Abigail Honeycutt's bench. Jonah parked beside me, scanning the paper for dogoods. Boone sat on my other side, strumming his banjo.

"Wonder where Florentine is?" I asked Jonah.

"Probably trying to find a place to put her burdens down," Jonah said. "That's where I hope she is."

"Me, too," I said as I flicked the locket around my neck. I pulled my legs up pretzel-style on the bench, then slid my blue book out of my backpack. I needed to concentrate on Isabella Thistle's curse.

Foolish heart who fought and failed,
Where talent bloomed, your greed prevailed,
Cursed to toil, till labor-worn,
You'll spin up ashes, you'll harvest thorns.

Now pack your dreams, make haste, take flight,
You're cursed to wander through the night,

Till cords align, and all's made right.
Where sweet amends are made and spoken,
Shadows dance, the curse is broken.

"What's that noise?" Boone stopped playing. "Y'all hear it? That creepy-tingly sound?"

"The wind-chime wind!" I slammed the blue book shut. "You hear it, too?"

"Hear what?" Jonah asked.

"Of course I hear it." Boone shivered. "It's . . . weird."

"Plumb weird," I agreed. "I think it's a snicker of magic."

"Why don't I hear it?" Jonah asked.

Because you're not cursed is what I wanted to say. But I just shrugged my shoulders.

Boone played his banjo louder and faster to try to drown out the wind-chime sound. I saw Elvis Phillips start tapping his foot to the music. I thought he might pick up his microphone and start singing again, but instead he said:

"Hey, Boone! You know any songs by the King?"

"I know a few." Boone smiled. "I've never tried to pluck them on a banjo."

Elvis nodded so sadly that it got to Boone. So Boone said there was a first time for everything and he shrugged and gave it a whirl. Elvis Phillips sang along till he was red faced.

"I got a request, too!" said Day Grissom, who was busy refilling Mama's paint trays. "Could you play 'Foggy Mountain Breakdown'?"

"Sure." Boone flashed his eyebrows at me while he tuned. He whispered, "Cleo and Day used to play bluegrass together, back when they were young and in love. She ever tell you that?"

Jonah put down the paper. "*Day* and Cleo?"

"No way!" I whispered.

"Way." Boone nodded and spun back around. "Foggy Mountain Breakdown" wasn't the sort of song he could play standing still. The music spun him around a few more times before he was done.

"Now I have a request," drawled somebody behind us.

All three of us looked back in time to see Rosie Walker shuffling toward the bench, her cowboy boots scrape-scraping across the sidewalk. As soon as Rosie sat down, Biscuit crawled out from under the bench and jumped up in Rosie's lap. Biscuit gave Rosie a big sloppy kiss on the cheek.

Rosie chuckled. "I do love this darlin' dog."

Boone looked shell-shocked. His face went pale. Puke-ish pale. The kind of pale I get when somebody mentions the Duel. "Ramblin' Rose?" he whispered.

"Once upon a time I was," Rosie said with a nod. "And you must be Boone Taylor? I've heard good things about you."

"I'm Boone Harness, actually." Boone held his banjo steady, right over his heart. He looked down at the strings, like they might tell him the words he needed to say. "I'm such a big fan of yours. You've really heard of me?"

"Yes, sir." Rosie nodded. "Now you better play me a tune so I can tell if I heard right. My favorite song is an old mountain tune, 'Fair and Tender Ladies.' You know it?"

"Yes, ma'am," Boone said. He took a deep breath and tightened the banjo pegs, looking for the right note to start on.

Boone played the song so gently, strumming across the strings as softly as the summer wind rolls over the river. It seemed like that banjo was made for that song. Then he sang out the words. Boone didn't get red faced when he sang, like Elvis Phillips did. Instead, he closed his eyes and let the lyrics roll out peaceful and easy. I was spellbound. If Boone's music painted pictures, that song was a sunset.

The painting party all took a break to hear Boone sing. I saw a tear sparkle down my mama's face, even from all the way across the street. Day Grissom took his hat off his head and held it over his heart.

Something was happening in my heart, too. At first, I thought I was getting sentimental on account of Boone's sweet music. But then the little circle of warmth I felt heated into an almost-burn, and then the almost-burn scorched its way into an almost-sorta-deep-fry. And then I realized the heat wasn't coming from inside my heart but right over the top of it.

Stone Weatherly's locket was burning red-hot against my skin.

I gasped as I yanked the locket off my neck and flung it onto the sidewalk. Boone was playing so loud, and people were so lost in his music, that nobody noticed what I'd done. Nobody except Jonah.

"Flea?" Jonah raised his eyebrows. "What's your —"

But he never finished his sentence. As Jonah gasped softly, I knew he was looking at exactly the same thing as me: The air around the necklace rippled in time to Boone's music. And as Boone strummed his last note, the air around the locket shimmered one final time. And then . . . stillness.

Nobody except Jonah and me noticed it. Everybody else clapped and whistled and hollered out more songs for Boone to play.

But I kept my eyes on the locket. I wondered if it might burn a hole in the sidewalk.

Jonah punched my arm. "Pick it back up."

I punched his arm harder. "You pick it back up."

Jonah rolled his eyes and reached down to grab it, but I didn't want Jonah to think I was too girly. So I snatched it up first. The locket felt the same as always: big, tacky, shiny, and cold against the palm of my hand.

And sealed tightly shut.

"Well, Flea." Jonah reached for the locket and let it fall long, swinging it back and forth in front of his face like he was trying to hypnotize himself. "There's something weird about this locket."

I rolled my eyes. "You think?"

Jonah chuckled as he passed the necklace back to me.

"There's something weird about that old song, too," I said, rolling the pendant over in my hand. Boone had already launched into another tune, but nothing strange was happening. The locket didn't scorch my fingertips. The air didn't tremble. But as Boone's tune played louder, the wind chime rolled down the street. It blew through the trees, rattling the maple leaves. Then it blew down around us both, and pricked against the back of my neck. And I remembered something.

" 'Fair and Tender Ladies' was the Threadbares' favorite song. Remember when Rosie told us that? At your mom's shop? Must be one heck of a snicker of magic in that locket. . . ."

"Too bad we can't just open the dumb thing and look," Jonah said as he tried to pry open the locket. But it remained sealed shut. Tight-lipped.

"That locket's keeping a good secret," I said to Jonah. "I can feel it."

I watched Mama step back from the wall again, and sigh, and look over her perfectly imperfect painting. She was standing right there, right on Main Street. But when she looked toward the bridge that first brought us into town, I caught a familiar look in her eyes. A wandering look.

I had to figure out a way to break the Weatherly curse, I knew it. Or we might all be wandering forever.

Snip

Snip

  SN

  IP

I saw the words cut into pieces as Jewell Pickett slid her scissors across my bangs.

The wet tips of my hair spelled out more words on the floor:

Toggle

Hiccup

Cornucopia

"My brain's feeling crazy today," I sighed.

"My brain *always* feels crazy," Jewell laughed.

She tilted my face up and looked at my bangs to make sure they were even. Aunt Cleo had trimmed my bangs a few days ago, but she'd used her crafting scissors. Mama was not pleased with the outcome.

"*That* is so much better." Jewell nodded. "Your eyes are too pretty to keep covered up. There's a whole world of good to see that you might miss hiding behind your hair. And! This way you'll be able to look everybody in the eye when you duel."

"Yep." I gulped.

"Jonah says you're pretty nervous about tomorrow."

I looked through the window into Jewell's mechanic shop, where Jonah was sitting at a long table, helping Harriet Bond clean the tools. I didn't mind that he'd told his mom how nervous I was. Jewell Pickett would have figured me out anyway. Jonah'd warned me that she could massage the secrets right out of a person's scalp.

And sakes alive, was he right.

When Jewell washed my hair, every secret I knew came spilling out of my mouth. I told her about Stone Weatherly being my balloon-riding, globe-trotting, curse-bearing great-great-grandfather. I told her about how I was cursed to wander, cursed to fail, and most likely cursed to keep on riding around the country in a Pickled Jalapeño that smelled like Frito pies.

I told her that Mama was packing up to leave Midnight Gulch. I even told her the secret I hadn't told Jonah yet. "I heard Mama on the phone last night, talking about Seattle like it was some snazzy carnival."

Jewell told me everything would work out fine, and her words calmed me down, for about a minute and a half.

But now tears burned in my eyes all over again. Jewell put down her scissors and rested her hands on my shoulders.

Her fingernails were long and coral colored. Her perfume smelled like expensive candy.

"What's wrong, sweetie?" She said it in such a way that the words came spilling out of me again.

"Mama's got a wandering heart," I said. "She can't stay anyplace for long."

I thought back to that first night when Mama stared up at the lonely old moon, the way the light fell across her face. I thought the moon beamed because it was happy to see us. Now I knew the moon had recognized one of its own: bright, beautiful, lonesome.

Snip

Snip

    SN

    IP

Words fell loose around me:

Hunger

Safekeep

Refuge

"Maybe I'm meant to be like Florentine," I said. "Maybe I'm meant to keep drifting around to different places."

"OH!" Jonah's mother screeched. I grabbed my hair 'cause I was afraid she'd cut a big hunk out of the back, but my hair was okay.

"Jonah!" Jewell rapped her long fingernails against the window to the auto shop. "Come in here! I need to tell you and Felicity something extraordinary.

"Yesterday while y'all were painting the Gallery," Jewell said, holding the door open so Jonah could wheel inside, "Florentine came in for a trim. As soon as I started washing her hair, she started talking. . . ."

"We know Florentine's story," Jonah said.

"You don't know what I know!" Jewell grinned.

We both knew she was right. Neither one of us could give a proper shampoo.

Jewell motioned Jonah closer, then leaned in close so nobody else in the shop would hear.

"You'd already told me where Florentine came from. So I asked her how in the world she ended up here, in Midnight Gulch. I could see in her face that she didn't want to tell me, that she wanted to keep it a secret. She'd left that bag she's always toting along over in the waiting chair and she kept glancing at it, then back at me, real nervous-like. Finally, she sighed and told me exactly how she wound up here."

Jewell stood back and smiled proudly in the mirror. "She said that her great-grandmother was born and raised here in Midnight Gulch, but that she left town because she wasn't welcome here anymore. Florentine said her great-grandmother stole some burdens that did not belong to her . . . but she left a perfect memory in their place."

Jewell squirted a golf-ball-size dollop of pouf mousse into her hand and worked it through my hair. "Florentine figures if she can find the perfect memory, she'll be able to lay those burdens down.

"Now." Jewell propped her hands on her hips and looked back at Jonah. "You gonna ask me who that great-grandmother was?"

Yes, yes, yes. My heart pounded so loud I nearly said the word.

Jewell winked at me in the mirror. "You got it, kids. Florentine's great-granny was none other than Isabella Thistle."

✳ ◇ ✴ ✳ ◇ ✴ ✳ ◇ ✳

As soon as Jewell finished drying my hair, I shot up out of her chair and ran out of the salon. Jonah was faster than me in his wheelchair. He had to keep slowing down, waiting for me to catch up.

"Sorry," I said. "My legs are too short for running."

"It's no problem." Jonah smiled. "Your hair looks cool, Flea. Messy but in a spindiddly way."

"I don't want to talk about my hair," I said. "I can see every single thing around me and it's weird."

My hair felt good, though, feather-light and bouncy. I ran faster so I could feel it swoosh into my face.

Then I tripped over my own sneaker and decided the swooshing probably wasn't worth falling over.

"Is she there?" I yelled ahead.

He shook his head no.

"What if she already left town?" I said. "What if she's gone? She could have helped us, I bet. She's Isabella Thistle's kin. She'll know how to break that stupid curse."

I waited for Jonah to give his usual speech about Isabella's curse, but he didn't. Instead, he nodded and said, "Then we'll find her."

Even Jonah had to face the truth: Our time was almost up.

And goodness knows we tried; we searched every shop on Main Street, asked everybody we passed if they'd seen her. We called out her name. We searched. We waited. And hoped. We never found her. And nobody knew where she went. By the time night dropped its starry curtain over the mountains, Florentine still hadn't turned up anywhere. My family was still cursed. As soon as the Duel was over, we'd wander away again.

"I should ground you for getting home so late and not call-ing first," Mama scolded as she set a glass of milk down in front of me.

"I was trying to find Florentine. I had something I wanted to show her."

Plus, I had a curse that I wanted her to undo or fix or whatever a person does to make a curse worthless. My mis-sion failed. Nobody had seen Florentine and no wind-chime wind alerted me to her whereabouts. Now it was too late. The Duel was happening tomorrow. The Gallery was almost finished. We'd be gone before the week was over; I could feel it.

Mama sat down at the table across from me, clutching a warm mug of tea. She looked so pretty with paint in her hair.

"Gallery's looking good," I said.

Mama grinned, just barely — her smile resting like a crescent moon behind the rim of her mug. "Something's still missing. I can't quite figure out what —"

"Take all the time you need!" I squealed.

Mama sighed. Her eyes glossed over in a far-off, far-away stare.

"That Gallery," Cleo said around her cigarette, "looks more beautiful than it has *ever* looked. I'll bet it didn't look that good back when Stone Weatherly painted it."

"I hope everybody's pleased with it." Mama nodded. "It was nice of them to let me be part of something so special."

Was.

Them.

Those are distance words. Mama was already past-tensing, already reminiscing about a place we hadn't even left yet. I settled back in my seat and asked the question we were all afraid to ask. But there was no point holding back any longer. "How soon are we leaving once you get done?"

Cleo glanced up from her quilt. Boone looked over the couch at us. Frannie Jo was about to snap the last piece into a puzzle, but she stopped and looked at Mama, too. Mama didn't look at us. She looked at the door. She'd already packed up some grocery bags and laundry baskets full of our stuff.

"Day after tomorrow." Mama sipped her tea. "I told them we'd be there by next week."

One more day.

That's all I had left in Midnight Gulch. Twenty-four measly hours.

Cleo looked back down at her quilt, but I could see her lip trembling. Boone looked straight ahead again and Frannie Jo picked up her puzzle, piece by piece, and put it back in the box. Her little blue suitcase was propped by the door, too, ready for a new beginning, as Mama liked to say.

But I was sick of always beginning. I just wanted to be.

"June Bug." Mama's voice broke the silence. "Do you want me to help you with the rest of your poems for the Duel?"

I shook my head. "I think I need to do that part on my own. Thanks, though."

"Are you still feeling good about it?" Mama reached to touch the fringe of my brand-new bangs.

Before I could answer, we all heard the music. Not wind-chime music. Banjo music. And it wasn't coming from Boone. The banjo music was coming from outside in the parking lot.

"What in the . . . ?" Cleo asked.

Boone was already opening the door onto Cleo's tiny patio, the one Mama never let us step on because she was afraid it would crumble.

"That's Day Grissom!" Boone yelled.

"Oh, *no*," Cleo groaned.

"Cleopatra Glorietta Harness!" Day yelled at the top of his lungs. "I wrote a song for you, and I'm about to play it. Right here. Right now."

"Somebody shut that man up before the police come!" Cleo threw down her quilt pieces. "Or before every dog in Midnight Gulch starts howling." She stomped out onto the patio and yelled, "Or before everybody in this complex realizes some drunk old idiot is singing in the parking lot!"

"Hey there, Cleo!" Day hollered from down below.

We all ran for the patio and crammed out onto the little porch beside my aunt. She groaned, pulled the cigarette out of her mouth, and stared down at my gnarly-bearded bus driver.

Day Grissom cleared his throat and sang:

"Well, the stars don't shine
And the moon don't glow,
That I don't think about a girl I know.
Cleo-pa-tra . . . Cleo-pa-tra . . .
I love her pretty blue eyes
And her sweet ol' smile
And she loves me, too,
But she's the queen of de-Nile. . . ."

"Day *Grissom*." She hissed through clenched teeth. And then she shouted out a string of unsavory words that caused Boone to laugh and Mama to clamp her hands down over Frannie Jo's ears. "Get outta my parking lot!"

"Then you get outta my heart!" Day yelled back. He clutched his banjo across his chest the same way I'd seen Boone do, like that plunky instrument might keep his heart safe from harm.

254

"What's that s'posed to mean?" Cleo asked.

"I only mean that . . ." Day shuffled nervously back and forth. "I came to tell you . . ."

"Spit it out, you old geezer," Cleo said.

"I came to tell you" — Day stood up straight and looked right up at the balcony — "that I'm sorry."

That shut Cleo up. Whatever she was about to shout back got stuck in her mouth. She took a long draw on her cigarette instead.

"You should have told me that twenty years ago," Cleo said in a curl of smoke.

Patch it

Mend it

Stitch it back together

"You're right," Day said.

"And I ain't the same girl I was twenty years ago," Cleo said. "And you definitely ain't the same man. Look at how you've let yourself go! Showing up here looking like some Cracker Barrel Santa Claus."

Cleo was trying to talk mean, but she didn't sound very convincing. Day Grissom could tell it, too. "I should have married you, Cleo Harness. I'd marry you right now if you'd have me."

"The way we fought?" Cleo laughed. "Mercy! I'd have pushed you off the bridge by now if we were married. That's a fact!"

"If I was married to you," Day hollered back, "I would have jumped off that bridge by now. Shoot, I'd let you push

255

me." He grinned big and goofy up at the balcony again. "I'd *fall* for you, Cleopatra. Get it?"

"What I *got*," Cleo said, "is age and insight."

"Hindsight," Mama whispered.

"Hindsight, hind end, whatever!" Cleo smashed out her cigarette on the rail. "We're too old, Day. We've made too many mistakes now."

"I still love you," Day said. "The way I figure it, that should cover every single mistake from here on out."

Cleo let out a ragged breath. She wiped the sweat off her forehead.

"Maybe you should come down and hear what I have to say? And if you don't like what I'm saying, you can mosey back up to that apartment and I'll never bother you again."

"You might as well go down, Cleo," Mama said. "He's a persistent man."

"Don't I know it," Cleo sneered. Day Grissom howled out another song as we shut the patio door and crowded back into the living room. Cleo mumbled unsavory words as she slid on her flip-flops and stomped to the door. She flung the door open. Instead of walking out, she shut the door and sighed.

She checked her reflection in the mirror. Her hand was shaking as she fluffed her hair. "I ain't the same girl I was," Cleo mumbled. "I ain't pretty like I was back then. He's forgot. But he'll remember when he sees me up close."

"You definitely aren't pretty like you were back then," Boone said. He put his arm around Cleo and kissed her cheek. "You're beautiful now. A person has to work hard to be your kind of beautiful, Cleo."

"Don't be stupid, Boone." Cleo waved him off, but I could see her real answer shining in her eyes. Boone's words meant the world to her. Better yet, I could see in her eyes that she knew Boone's words were true.

"I mean it," Boone said. "Don't make this too easy for Day Grissom."

Cleo nodded, her lip trembling again. Then she sighed, held her chin up high, and stomped out the door.

* ◇ ✳ * ◇ ✳ * ◇ *

I wrote to the sound of the banjo's plink and the clock's ticktock.

I thought Cleo's wall clock was spindiddly when I first saw it, but now it only made me sad. The clock sounded like a fake heartbeat, every *tick-tick-tick* a steady reminder that my time was almost up.

I heard Boone and Mama talking about Aunt Cleo, and Frannie Jo talking to Biscuit, and the weatherman talking about seasons changing. The whole world seemed to be yammering away while I tried to work. Only the midnight moon stayed silent as it peeked through Cleo's window, checking on my progress. The bone-white light shimmered over my words and made me feel like I held the finest magic, words worth spinning, stories worth telling.

"Okay!" I hollered. "I'm ready to practice!"

I ran to the center of Cleo's living room. Boone muted the newsman, then he and Mama and Frannie Jo and Biscuit all crammed close together on the couch, watching me. I clutched my blue book tight as I read my first poem, but the words didn't feel right. I barely got through two full stanzas before I was tongue-tied. "Boone?" I said, glancing up.

"You're doing great!" He nodded back.

"I wasn't in need of affirmation," I sighed. "I was wondering . . . if you'd play your banjo while I talk? Maybe the music will get my words where they need to go."

Boone pulled his banjo up into his lap and strummed softly. And I dueled once, then twice, then a third time. The first time was a mess. The second time was less messy but still clunky.

But the third time? The third time was spindiddly, if I do say so myself.

* ◇ ☀ * ◇ ☀ * ◇ *

I slammed the refrigerator door shut when I heard Cleo's key turn in the lock. I thought about trying to duck down, real sneaky, so she wouldn't see me in the kitchen. But then I thought about how she'd probably get after me with her broom, so I said, "I'm here, Cleo."

Cleo startled. She leaned down and stared into the dark, looking for me. "Felicity? You still awake?"

I opened the refrigerator door again so she could see my face. "I was hungry," I said.

"At midnight?" Cleo walked over to the kitchen and propped her hand on the door. "What are you hungry for at midnight?"

"Ice cream." I smiled.

Cleo nodded. "That's my girl. Hand me a carton, too. You finish your Duel stuff?"

"Yep," I said. I passed Cleo a pint of Chocolate Chip Pork Rind. "You marrying Day Grissom?"

"Ha," Cleo clucked. She shuffled out of the kitchen. "You go to sleep now. You gotta be top-notch for the Duel tomorrow. I got a big surprise for you in the morning." I could hear a smile in Cleo's voice when she turned back and said, "I sure am proud of you, no matter how it turns out. I don't want you to ever forget how proud I am of you, no matter where you wander off to."

"I never will," I promised.

Cleo walked on down the hall to her bedroom. I heard Boone yell *OOOF!* when Cleo accidentally kicked him. But then I heard Cleo chuckle and realized it probably wasn't an accident at all. After that, the whole apartment got quiet again.

I opened the freezer and took out the pint of Blackberry Sunrise.

SWEET
    AMENDS

If there was something in that ice cream that would help me break Isabella's curse . . . I needed to face it. Mama was packed and ready to roll. Even if we left town, I wanted to be able to look back and say that I tried.

The Beedle was for sure right about one thing: There was one memory I'd tried so hard to forget. Maybe I could never truly fix Mama's sadness. But I could do something about mine. And Oliver said that memories can heal you, if you let them. So I grabbed a spoon and snuck back to the craft room. Maybe if I could be brave enough to remember, I would be brave enough for anything.

The lonesome light of the full moon came down through the window as I pulled the red ribbon loose. I popped open the lid.

"Here goes nothing," I said. I scooped out a bite.

The ice cream melted, sweet and creamy against my tongue.

We lived in Virginia and I was riding the school bus home. I was so little my shoes didn't touch the floor. When the bus pulled up to my driveway, I saw Roger Pickle's car about to back out. But he pulled back in when he saw the bus slowing down.

I took another bite and shut my eyes tight.

"Dad!" I scampered down the big bus steps and jumped onto the gravel. Roger Pickle got out of his car and stood up tall. He wore jeans and a flannel shirt. He had red hair, like mine, and a red beard that matched his hair exactly. He sighed when he saw me coming toward him. The way he

looked at me stopped me as hard as if somebody'd rammed into me.

"Dad?" I stopped. "What are you crying for?"

"Allergies." He smiled. He reached out his arms for me. "I'm going to work early. Come hug my neck."

I gripped the spoon so tight my fingers ached. The ice cream tasted different now, so sour that it nearly locked my jaws. Biscuit stood up and stretched and climbed up in my lap. She rested her fuzzy face against my broken heart.

"Thanks, buddy." I kissed her fuzzy, stinky head. "I knew I'd hate this stupid ice cream."

I jumped up into Roger Pickle's arms and pressed a kiss against his neck. "Love you," I said. I rested my face against his strong shoulder. His worn-out shirt was soft against my face.

His face was wet with tears when I pulled back. He kissed me softly on the tip of my nose. "Love you," he said.

And then he let me down and I ran off and didn't look back. "See you tonight!" I waved behind me. I ran inside and wrote ten brand-new words, all different colors, on a blank sheet of paper. I gave them legs and I gave them eyes. I gave each word a heart of its own. And when it was time for Roger Pickle to come home, I sat outside on the front steps and held the words in my hand and I waited. I waited until after the sun set. I waited even after the stars came out and I was shivering. I fell asleep right there, on the steps, waiting. It was Mama who carried me back inside.

I wiped the snot off my face and tucked one of Cleo's flashlights against my neck. I opened my blue book and started writing.

"What's *factalactus* mean?" Mama's voice was soft, but it still made me jump. The flashlight clunked into my lap. I scrambled to turn it off before she could see what I'd written.

"I didn't hear you come in," I said, working to get the tears out of my voice. "Did you need something?"

"I just came in to check on you." Mama reached and tucked my hair behind my ear. Then she reached for the flashlight in my lap. *Click.* She held the light up over my pages again. "What's a *factalactus*?"

I'd rested my hands down on the open pages of the blue book, fingertips touching. When Mama shone the light, my hands made a heart shape. "*Factalactus* is a word I saw squished down in the ice-cream carton, glowing in the dark. I don't think it's a real word, so I gave it my own definition. A *factalactus* is a truth that hurts a little bit, that prickles and stings, like you tried to shake hands with a cactus flower. But just because it hurts doesn't make it less true."

Mama nodded. "I see."

I hoped she didn't read the examples I'd written down.

Factalactus: Roger Pickle cut out on us five years ago and most likely won't come back.

Factalactus: The last words I remember saying to Roger Pickle were "I love you."

Factalactus: Saying "I love you" doesn't make people stick around.

"Hold this flashlight for me," Mama said as she reached across me for the pale purple carton of Blackberry Sunrise.

"I wouldn't eat that if I were you," I sighed. "It'll just make you remember things."

"I know what it does, Felicity." I heard a kind smile in Mama's voice. "I make gallons of this stuff every night at work, remember?"

Mama squared around until she was sitting in front of me, holding the Blackberry Sunrise in her lap. "What's the opposite of a *factalactus*, you guess? What do you call a truth that feels so good, it's like you hugged the summer sunshine?"

I stared down at my shadow-heart hands. "*Facto . . . fabulous?*"

Mama nodded. "I like that."

She scooped a spoonful of ice cream into her mouth. I held my breath and waited. The only thing worse than me having a bad memory was watching Mama have one. I wanted her first bite to be sweet, not sour.

"Factofabulous." Mama gulped. "The time we stopped in North Carolina, and flew butterfly kites in the park. We ran beside each other until our legs ached. And then we all flopped down in the grass, but the wind still held our kites up high. Those butterflies looked like they were glued to the springtime blue. And you kept catching poems for your little sister. As soon as you finished one, she'd ask you for another. You never got tired of it. I loved that day."

I scooted closer, until my knees were touching Mama's knees. "I loved that day, too." I smiled. I was glad her Blackberry memory was sweet.

"Factofabulous," Mama said as she ate another spoonful.

I shook my head. "Don't press your luck, Mama. It might not give you two good memories in a row. . . ."

"Factofabulous." Mama said the word like she was casting a magic spell over me. "When we camped inside the Pickled Jalapeño and stared up at Spiderberg. I painted new castles and rivers and woods. And you made up stories about the people who lived there."

"Ruled there," I whispered. "We were the Queens of Spiderberg."

Mama angled her spoon down into the carton to scrape out another bite, but I locked my hand around her wrist.

I glanced at that rotten ice cream, then up into my mama's face. I didn't need the flashlight now. The moonlight had reached through the window and found us. The moonlight always reaches for her. "The ice cream . . . how do you make it do that? How do you keep getting good memories from it?"

"It takes some practice." Mama set the carton back down on the floor. "But even if I taste something sour, even if the bad memory comes first, I choose to replace it with a good one instead."

"You just choose?"

Mama nodded. "It's as simple and difficult as that. Sad memories don't just come in ice cream, you know. Everything you touch, everything you smell, everything you taste, every picture you see — all of that has the potential to call up a sad memory. You can't choose what comes up first. But you can choose to replace it with something good. I choose to think on the good parts."

I leaned close so I could talk with less than a whisper. "I was remembering when he left. I'm not mad that he left me. But I'm mad that he left Frannie Jo. She's little and weird and she needs people. I'm mad that he left you. I knew I'd think of him when I tasted the ice cream; I knew I would."

"It's fine to be mad at people for a little while. Being mad doesn't mean you don't love somebody."

"Is Roger Pickle the reason you stopped painting for so long?" I asked.

"One of the reasons," Mama sighed. "Someday you might get rejected. Someday you might go through a rough spell. Someday the world might press down so hard on you that you don't see your words anymore."

"But you're painting again," I reminded her.

"Thanks to you." She tapped my nose with her finger. "You kept loving me and I kept loving you. And we can get through anything."

Mama held the ice cream out to me again. "Give it a try," she said. "Even if the sad memory comes first, choose to remember something good."

I closed my eyes. I thought about my family. I reached for the ice cream. I took my first brave bite. Pure sweetness.

"*Factofabulous.*" I smiled. "The day Boone wore fairy wings at Snapdragon Pond." We both laughed. "You showed me the tall trees. We climbed as high as heaven . . ."

* ◇ ☀ * ◇ ☀ * ◇ *

It was late by the time I finally crawled into bed. I curled up on my side. Biscuit snuggled against my back. I was just about to close my eyes when Frannie Jo rolled over and touched her forehead to mine.

"I have a factofabulous," she whispered.

"Frannie," I whispered back. "You shouldn't eavesdrop."

"Okay. Do you want me to tell my factofabulous or not?"

I smiled. "Tell me."

Frannie grinned and rolled onto her back again. "Do you remember when you were talking at the school assembly last year and you accidentally said 'Great Kentucky Arm Fartists'?"

I groaned. Leave it to Frannie Jo to drag up that awful memory the night before the Duel. "Of course I remember. Wait . . . that's not your factofabulous, is it?"

"Hush and let me tell you," Frannie sighed. "This is what happened. I was in the lunchroom, and Ronnie Barnhill saw you walk down the hall."

266

"That kid was mean," I said.

"Shhh," Frannie cautioned. "Ronnie started making fart noises at you. So when he stood up to take his tray, I pulled my peanut butter sandwich apart and left the goo half faceup on his seat. And he sat down on it. And I never got in trouble for it, because people thought I was too little and sweet to do anything so mean."

Frannie giggled so hard the mattress shook. "That was a fun day."

I guess I should have been mature enough to tell Frannie Jo that picking on people was never right, no matter how big or mean or little or sweet they are. But I'd have that conversation with her another time. I leaned over and planted a quick kiss on Frannie Jo's blond hair. "Thanks for taking such good care of me."

She rolled into me and tucked her little face under my chin. "You take better care of me. Felicity?"

"Yeah?"

"You don't need that bird on your wrist to do good tomorrow. You're factofabulous already."

Factofabulous: My Blackberry dreams that night were the sweetest.

My aunt Cleo says that only fools run away from what they fear. Fear always finds you no matter what, she says. And it growls louder and grows bigger, the longer you run away from it. That's one reason I decided to run to Stoneberry Elementary on the morning of the Duel, instead of hitching a ride in the Pickled Jalapeño. I thought running at my fears might make me feel brave, and it did. A little bit. The other reason I decided to run was because I wanted to tell Jonah about my Blackberry memory.

And I wanted to tell him about my own sweet amends.

Here's what I didn't take into consideration: Stoneberry School is farther away from Cleo's apartment than I realized.

Also, running a long distance was making me sweat.

I slowed to a jog when I saw Jonah waiting for me on the sidewalk in front of the school. His hair was its usual every-which-way mess, but his button-down blue shirt didn't have a wrinkle to be seen. He was tugging at his red necktie as I came up beside him.

"Pumpernickel!" I called out.

"Flea!" He grinned. "You picked a good day to be late. . . ."

"You thought I changed my mind, didn't you?" We raced for the front-end auditorium together. "You thought I'd ditch you."

"I knew you'd come," Jonah said.

"No point in backing out now —"

But then I saw the Stoneberry parking lot, which was so full that folks were parking their cars on the playground and all up and down the sides of the street.

"Wow," I heaved. I wiped the sweat off my lip. I wiped my sweaty bangs away from my forehead. "Do I stink like sweat?" I asked Jonah.

"You smell normal." He laughed. "You look fine. You look pretty."

I was so nervous that I didn't even get embarrassed over his compliment. Cleo's surprise was a new dress she'd made for me. The dress was pink, which didn't thrill me at first. But she said if I wore my sneakers with it, I'd make the dress look punk pink. And that sounded kind of awesome. My shoes squish-popped all the way to the auditorium doors. Miss Divinity Lawson had strung a banner over the entryway that read:

MAGIC HAPPENS HERE

As soon as I walked through the door, I knew it was true. Because it seemed like everybody in town had turned out for the Duel. Divinity Lawson was setting up flower

269

arrangements on the corner of the stage. Ponder and Oliver, who were in charge of refreshments, had set up an entire dessert booth in the back of the building. Jewell Pickett worked the room, socializing with her customers. Virgil Duncan sat in the front row, holding what appeared to be a very large remote control with a small, revolving satellite. Elvis Phillips was sharing a bag of popcorn with Charlie Sue. The thought of leaving them in less than a day made my chest hurt.

"You okay, Felicity?" Jonah said to me.

I nodded, afraid my words would come out too gravelly if I tried to talk. We pushed our way through the noisy crowd and down the aisle toward the stage. The gargantuan stage.

I swallowed hard. The stage was so high that every last person in this auditorium would see me when I dueled. Toast was already up there, preparing his work station. It'd be hard to win against gourmet grilled cheese made from a clothes iron, but winning had never been my big goal. Toast saw me staring and waved. I waved back, and then he pointed to the design on his blue T-shirt: a llama in a space helmet.

"The space llama's his trademark," Jonah reminded me. Then his voice gentled as he said, "Are you about to puke?"

"It's possible." I nodded.

"Maybe concentrate on your bird instead of that stage," Jonah said. "That's still your good luck charm, right?"

"It *was*," I sighed. "Hope flew the coop a few days ago."

Jonah stopped wheeling so suddenly that I crashed into the back of his wheelchair.

"Where'd the bird go?" Jonah looked stricken. "You were banking on the bird!"

"I know!" I fanned the heat away from my face. I wished for enough magic to make the air conditioner work. "I sent the bird to your dad."

Jonah's voice softened. ". . . You did what?"

"It doesn't matter. I'll be fine without the b-b-b-b . . ." My words were failing me already. And my face was already red and my heartbeat was already pounding in my ears. This time my heart didn't sound like it was saying *yes*. It sounded like it was saying *RUN*.

More people herded into the auditorium and pressed in around us so close that I felt even smaller than I was, too small, like a bug nobody sees before they accidentally squish it.

"Maybe I shouldn't d-d-d . . ."

Jonah Pickett reached out and took my hand. He pulled his red pen from his pocket and clicked it, and then he pushed the tip of it to my wrist, exactly where hope was before it flew off.

"You don't need the bird," Jonah said. And he made a list from my wrist to my elbow:

Splendiferous
Spindiddly
Wonder
Enchanting

Curious
Stalwart
Plumb Pretty
Plumb Awesome
= Felicity

"There's a bunch more I want to write." Jonah looked up at me. "But I'm running out of room."

"Now who's the word collector?" I smiled.

"There's one word I'm keeping for myself," Jonah said. "*Wonderstruck*. That's how I feel whenever I'm around you. No other word fits."

Wonderstruck

. . . was full of lightning bolts. I saw it flickering somewhere close to the ceiling, but I imagined it zapping down the middle of my heart, too, cutting it in two pieces. One piece might fold into a paper airplane. The other would become an origami bird. And they'd both zoom around the room until they collided.

Wonderstruck: My heart would crash against itself and fizzle in a flicker.

"I think you're wonder-striking, too," I said to Jonah. "I think you see people way better than they are."

"I see people exactly as they are."

How would I ever say good-bye to the best friend I'd ever had? How could I leave when our adventures were just getting started?

Tick-tock, everything I loved was slipping away from me.

I had to duel in approximately five seconds.

I had to leave town in less than twenty-four hours.

All because of that stupid curse . . .

"I tried to solve the riddle," Jonah said sadly, as if he could read my mind. "After we looked for Florentine, I went home and tried to figure it out. I still don't know what it means."

"So now you believe in the curse?" I asked.

"Maybe a little bit," he admitted. "But I believe in you more. You'll do great today."

Part of me wanted to crawl off like a spider word and hide under the chairs, far away from all that crazy. Part of me wanted to throw my arms around Jonah's neck and hug him tight.

What I did instead was lean down and kiss Jonah's cheek, fast as a flutter. The kiss POPPED against his cheek. A bottle-rocket kiss. Then I ran for the front row and sat down and stared straight ahead. I was too embarrassed to look at the reaction on his face.

Impulsive. I was too much of that.

Ridiculous. I was plenty of that, too.

Opportunist. I smiled.

The bottle-rocket kiss had as much magic in it as anything I'd ever seen.

I might have kept on thinking about it if I hadn't heard somebody holler, "Find us some seats together, Day! Make yourself useful!" followed by a wheeze and a cough.

I cranked around in my chair to see two Harnesses, two Pickles, and one Grissom lumbering down the aisle, Aunt Cleo leading the way. She'd tied her leopard-print bathrobe

273

around her red dress. The man following her was Day Grissom; I knew by the way she kept talking to him, but he didn't look anything like the Day Grissom I knew. Day had shaved off his gnarly beard and cut his hair. He looked sharp, no holes in his jeans, shirt tucked in. He looked mighty handsome, as far as old people are concerned.

"Excuse me," Day said to the Smith family on the middle aisle. "Are those seats down there taken?"

But then Cleo pushed him out of the way and said, "Make room, y'all! Scoot!"

Uncle Boone filed in behind Aunt Cleo, carrying his banjo around his back. He wore faded jeans, but he'd pulled a snazzy blazer on over his old T-shirt. And he'd traded his cowboy boots for a pair of Converse. Boone looked different from the first day he wandered into Midnight Gulch, but I'd never seen him look more like himself. Miss Lawson had asked me for Boone's contact information a few days ago. She said she was hoping he'd consider playing at the end of the Duel. Truly, I think Miss Divinity Lawson just wanted Boone's phone number. I was happy to oblige regardless.

The Pickles came last. Mama carried Frannie Jo, of course. She still had paint splatters on her arms and had braided a feather into her hair.

I watched my whole family, all except Roger Pickle, lodge themselves in the middle row, where they could see me and cheer for me when I took the stage.

I could duel if they were with me. I could do anything if they were with me. My fears were monster big. But their love for me was bigger. Fear seems like all the world when it takes hold of me; it's all I dream about, think about, and see. But it was love taking hold of me right then. And love is the whole universe — so wide I can't even see the edges of it.

Love is wild and wonderful.

Love is blue skies and stardust.

I reached for my blue book so I could collect those sentences.

. . . And then I realized I didn't bring my blue book. Which meant that I didn't bring my poems.

Cold sweat trickled down the side of my face. I squeezed my eyes shut and tried to remember the poems I'd written last night. Nothing. I opened my eyes and looked at the gym floor, hoping for a few words, any words. But I only saw letters, as scattered and sparkly as stars in a kaleidoscope.

My locket warmed up against my chest. At exactly the same time, Toast Terry plopped down in the seat beside me and said, "What's wrong, Pickle?"

But I couldn't answer him. First, I was afraid I'd upchuck if I opened my mouth to say anything, on account of my frazzled nerves.

But second, and most important, I couldn't focus on Toast long enough to answer. All I could see was the guitar he was holding. "Is that . . ."

"Ramblin' Rose's guitar," his voice crackled happily. "Miss Lawson asked her to bring it, said maybe she could play sometime today. But Miss Rose says she just got acrylics and doesn't want to mess them up, so she asked me if I'd play it instead. Can you believe it? Ramblin' Rose asked me to play her guitar! This guitar is better than grilled cheese sandwiches."

Miss Divinity Lawson stepped to the podium and tapped the microphone. It squealed as she said, "Welcome to the Stoneberry Duel! I have a few announcements to make and then we'll get started. . . ."

The guitar.

The banjo.

The locket.

My sweet amends.

They were all connected. I was connected to all of them.

"Did you forget to eat breakfast?" Toast asked. "You look pale."

As I concentrated on Ramblin' Rose's guitar, words slid down the taut strings and curled around the frets:

September

Sorrow

Surrender

Mistake

Memory

THREADBARE

I swallowed hard against the sudden, burning tingle in the back of my throat. "Toast, do you realize this is the first time in a hundred years that both of the Brothers Threadbares' instruments have been in the same room?"

"Awesome!"

"Felicity Pickle?" Miss Divinity Lawson said. Her voice echoed across the auditorium. "C'mon up. You can start us off."

"My name is Felicity Juniper Pickle." The microphone squealed so loud that I shrugged away. "I came to say that . . . I came to tell . . . I came to read my . . ."

How could I have forgotten the blue book? I stepped back from the microphone and breathed in deep, until my lungs felt like birthday balloons. I glanced toward the middle row and made eye contact with my mama. She looked so sad for me that I looked at Boone instead. As soon as our eyes met, he shot up out of his seat, still holding his banjo tight. He ran down the aisle toward me.

His Converse stomped out such pretty words:

Violet

Star singer

Moonlight

Primrose

Miss Divinity Lawson nearly fell out of her chair when Boone walked past her.

Boone came to stand right at the edge of the stage. He looked up at me with a smile on his face and said softly, "I'll play for you, like I did when you practiced. I'll strum a song and help you get the words where they need to go."

"That'd be spindiddly," I whispered back.

Boone nodded, pressed his fingertips against the neck of the banjo, and started strumming.

QUIT

The word chugged along the back of the room, leading a long, silent train of more words.

GIVE UP

MOVE ON

WANDER

But I concentrated on Boone's music. Because the music was bright, and happy, and it reminded me of a songbird. I looked at the words Jonah'd scrawled on my arm. He believed I was those things.

I looked at Mama. And I smiled.

I'm okay, I mouthed.

She nodded.

And then, for the first time in the history of my word-collecting existence, words appeared over Mama's hair:

Love you

"Love you," I whispered.

And my fear simmered down, just barely.

I concentrated on the rest of my crazy family — Uncle Boone, Aunt Cleo, Frannie Jo, and Biscuit. And Roger Pickle, too, wherever he was. And as I thought about them, the love I felt crowded out all the fear in me. There was no room for fear after that. Frannie Jo gave me a thumbs-up like I was doing a great job, even though I hadn't even started. Day Grissom draped his arm around Cleo's shoulders and they both leaned in closer, watching me without blinking. Boone was jamming close to the stage, proud to be standing beside me.

There was no magic in the world more powerful than that kind of love.

And suddenly I knew what Isabella Thistle's memory meant:

If you're brave enough to love, and forgive, and call up the factofabulous memories . . . there's no curse in the world that has any power over you.

"Love you." I believed the words; they tasted sweet on my tongue. I savored them. I said them.

No windows were open in the Stoneberry auditorium, but suddenly the wind-chime wind was there, rolling softly down the aisles. I felt it blow against my face. The hair on my arms tingled. The locket warmed against my skin.

And a glittery rope of letters appeared over my family:
C H O R D S
Chords
Chords align. Of course, I realized, Isabella's curse had to do with music. . . .

I leaned down and whispered to Boone, "Do you remember how to play the song 'Fair and Tender Ladies'?"

"Sure I remember." Boone nodded.

"When I finish talking," I breathed, "will you play that song in time with Toast's guitar?"

Boone nodded again. I hopped off the stage, breathless with excitement, and ran toward Toast Terry. Miss Lawson reached out to stop me, but I assured her that I had no plans to run away. I whispered my same plan to Toast, and he said, "Sure, I'll play the song. Just tell me when."

I ran back up on the stage and pulled the crackly microphone toward me.

"Once upon a time," I said, because every story should have such a spindiddly beginning. "Here on this hillside, here in this place where I'm talking, two magicians met up and made a mess of things. People say that when they left town, they took all the magic with them. There's still a snicker of magic left, but that's not much, not compared to what it was before. There's more sorrow, now, than joy. People leave here, and never come back. They don't want to stay here. They don't want to end up here, because this doesn't feel like home anymore."

Boone kept playing. He winked at me as I took another deep breath.

"Some people say the Threadbare magic had to do with music," I said. "And maybe it did, a little bit. And some people say it had to do with luck — they knew how to make an opportunity work out exactly right. And maybe that had something to do with it, too.

"But their best magic didn't have to do with any of that, not really. Because once the Threadbares parted ways, their magic wouldn't work at all. It was plumb useless. And in the end, I don't think they even cared about the magic. They didn't figure out until it was too late, they should have made amends. Instead of being so hateful, instead of dooming each other to wander off alone . . . they should have said the words that mattered most of all. I think their words were more powerful than any magic trick they ever did."

I pushed my hair away from my face and carried on boldly. "By the time the first Duel came around, I think the Brothers Threadbare had forgotten all about who they really were. Because, really, they were just farmers, just Stone and Berry. They wore shabby-looking suits and they played the kind of music that set hearts to spinning. Firstly, most importantly, they were family. And if they had it to do over, I don't think they would have abandoned each other out here on the hillside. I think they would have said, '*Sorry* for what I did to you.' And 'I choose to *remember the good*.' And they would have said, 'I love you.' Maybe if you say those words, maybe if you believe them, no curse in the world has any power over you."

I breathed deep, smiling at the feeling of boldness rising up in me. "I've collected whole constellations of words. But these words are my favorite: *Mama, Cleo, Boone, Frannie, Roger,* and *Biscuit*. I wouldn't know anything about love if it weren't for them. No matter what happens, or what I do, or how far apart we are, I know they love me. And if you say 'I love you,' and you mean it, then love makes up for a whole lifetime of mistakes. That's some kind of magic." I smiled.

I stepped back from the microphone. Boone played faster on his banjo, and people applauded. Mom was clapping so hard that the wind from her hands was blowing her hair back from her face. Cleo waved at me and I waved back. And then she pulled back her bathrobe and I saw Biscuit hiding inside. My dog gave me a big smile, too. Frannie Jo was bouncing happily in her seat.

And Jonah Pickett . . . well. He wasn't clapping. But he was looking at me like I'd handed him a forty-gallon carton of Dr. Zook's. Some things are better than applause.

Of course, none of them realized I wasn't exactly done yet.

"Play the song now," I said to Boone. And then I nodded toward Toast Terry. Toast nodded back to me and stood up from his seat. He tucked his pick between his teeth as he situated the guitar. Then he locked his hand around the fret board and strummed a first note, sad and pretty.

For the first time in over one hundred years, the instruments belonging to the Brothers Threadbare played in perfect unison.

"Chords align," I whispered. "And all's made right."

"What in tarnation!" Day Grissom hollered out. He stood up and ran out in the aisle, shaking his pant leg.

"He's got the Spirit!" hollered Elvis Phillips.

"He's got chiggers!" yelled Harriet Bond.

Day kicked again and I realized what was happening: His shadow was pulling apart from his body. Day's shadow was standing upright now, tall as Day, and I watched as the shadow leaned down and grabbed Day's ankle and pushed itself on off. That shadow ran back down the aisle and pulled Aunt Cleo's shadow off of her.

"Hey now!" Cleo hollered out.

And their shadows lit out down the aisle, dancing and spinning and jumping up and down. And they weren't the only ones.

People screeched and screamed as their shadows jumped up off the floor and spun across the walls of the auditorium. Shadows danced down the aisles and across the stage; one passed right through me. It felt as sweet and peaceful as the springtime wind.

Boone was so busy playing his banjo, eyes shut tight, fingers fluttering across the strings, that he didn't see his shadow take leave. Boone's shadow ran for Divinity Lawson, who was sitting in her chair with her mouth open wide and her eyes open wider, glancing from side to side around the room without moving her pretty head.

Boone's shadow bowed low and reached out its hand. Divinity Lawson's shadow reached its hand out, too; it looked as if the shadow hand reached right out of her heart, in fact. And they slow-danced together, even though the music was fast.

Elvis Phillips was teaching his shadow some new moves. Ponder Waller was chasing her shadow around, yelling, "Get back here!"

"Well, I never!" Rosie Walker slapped her hands down on her lap and looked around. "Scoot back, y'all. I ain't letting my shadow have all the fun!" And she stood up and spun around and I knew then why she was a country music *star*. Some people are born starry. Some people shine so bright you can't help but sit back and stare. Some people can't help but shine.

Frannie Jo was dancing in a circle with her shadow. Biscuit was chasing hers around the room.

And my shadow was standing still beside me. Shadow-me kept her head bowed, her shadow-sneakers turned in toward each other.

"You should dance, too . . ." I whispered.

My shadow made its way down the steps, down the aisle to where Jonah Pickett was sitting. I watched our shadows dance together for a time, not slow-dancing the way Boone and Divinity's shadows were doing. We pumped our arms up and down and we spun in circles, dizzy, wild, wonderful circles. My shadow's hair was flinging wild around its shoulders. Jonah's shadow played an air guitar.

I'd done it. Surely, I'd done it. Amends were made. Chords aligned.

. . . But as I glanced frantically around the auditorium, I didn't see Mama anywhere. If Mama wasn't in the room when it happened, would it matter if I'd broken the curse?

. . . And why wouldn't Mama be in the room?

I jumped off the stage and took off in a run, but some-body grabbed my arm and pulled me out of the aisle just before Elvis Phillips, who happened to be chasing his seri-ously speedy shadow, ran smack into me.

"Felicity!" Jonah yelled over the commotion. He loos-ened his grip on my arm. "What'd you do?"

"Chords," I gasped. "Musical chords. That's what Isabella Thistle meant. She wanted the Threadbares to apologize to each other and play again someday. That's it! I think we broke her curse. But I've got to find Mama to make sure —"

Suddenly, Jonah grabbed my arm again. "The locket . . ." His face paled. "Felicity, the locket is open."

My hand trembled as I reached to check the pendant. In all the commotion, I never heard it pop. I never even felt it click. "It must have opened when the chords aligned . . ." I said as I pulled it over my head.

I opened the locket wide, until it looked like a golden moth snuggled into the palm of my hand. Jonah wrapped his hand around my wrist and leaned in closer so we could both see what was inside.

The outside of Berry Weatherly's locket still looked like a simple, solid piece of metal. But the inside looked like a window to another world. Through the locket, we saw a field at twilight; the sun had set, but the stars weren't out yet. There were mountains in the distance. Leaves fluttered in a wind I couldn't feel.

Suddenly, a woman ran onto the field. She wore a yellow flower tucked behind her ear. The wind rippled against her long skirt and blew her dark hair down over her face. She crossed her arms over her chest and spun around, looking for someone.

And then a tall, lanky man in a brown suit walked up behind her. He tapped her shoulder and she spun around and flung her arms around his neck.

I could tell by his build and by the dark hair falling around his face that he was one of the Weatherly brothers. But which one, I wondered? Isabella Thistle had loved them both.

The couple in the locket danced around in the tall grasses while fireflies lit up the air around them. The scene faded for a moment, and then played again, from the beginning.

"This is Isabella Thistle's perfect memory," I whispered.

Jonah nodded. "We've got to find Florentine."

I agreed. But first, I had to find Mama. I scanned the room, looking for the faces of the people I loved the most. Frannie was teaching her shadow how to do cartwheels now. Cleo was chasing her shadow around the room, stomping at it. Day Grissom didn't seem to care where his shadow was. He laughed happily as he pushed a stepladder over to the entryway of the auditorium. He climbed to the top, pulled a fat black marker out of his pocket, and added one wonderful word to Divinity Lawson's banner:

MAGIC *STILL* HAPPENS HERE

Jonah and I pushed our way through the dancing crowd until I found my aunt Cleo. I grabbed her arm and said the two words I hoped I'd never have to say: "Mama's gone."

"Maybe you should let me drive, Cleo," Day Grissom said to my aunt as she swerved the Jalapeño out onto the main road. We were all packed in tight: Cleo, Day, Frannie, Boone, Jonah, Toast, and me. It was Jonah's idea to bring the musicians along with us, just in case Mama'd left before the curse was broken.

Mama left. She really left. "What if she's gone?" I asked as Cleo came to a screeching halt at Midnight Gulch's only stoplight.

"We'll find her," Cleo said, clutching the steering wheel.

"I don't have my suitcase!" Frannie rubbed her eyes. "I forgot to bring it."

"You won't need it," Cleo said. But she wouldn't look back at us.

Day Grissom said, "Cleo . . . let me drive."

"Day!" Cleo hollered. "How long does this infernal red light last?"

"I'm gonna be carsick," Toast groaned.

Jonah raised his hand. "We might need Le Barfbucket!"

"Why are you raising your hand?" I asked. "We're not in class."

Boone popped open the way-back window with his elbow so Toast could get some fresh air. "Holly walked, so she can't be too far off, right, Cleo?"

"Trade seats with me," Day said. "I get nervous when you drive."

"Everybody HUSH!" Cleo scolded. "'Specially you, Day Grissom. If you don't like my driving, you can walk."

"THERE!" Frannie yelled as the Jalapeño squealed its way onto Main Street. Mama was painting the Gallery.

"That's what I figured," Cleo said. The Jalapeño bumped up on the sidewalk near Abigail Honeycutt's bench. Cleo pushed her door open at the same time Day Grissom reached down to shift the gear into park, because Aunt Cleo had forgotten. As usual.

"Let me go see her first," I said. "I'll make sure everything's okay."

I scampered across the street, yelling her name. "Mama!"

When she spun around I noticed three things:

First, I noticed that she'd been crying. Her eyes looked red and glassy. Long, inky rivers of mascara rolled down her face. But she looked pretty that way; she looked painted that way.

Second, I noticed she was holding one of her old paintbrushes. She'd been doing detail work.

And third . . . even through her tears, I noticed, she was smiling.

I flew at her. I latched my arms tight around her waist and she wrapped her arms around my shoulders.

"Did you see the shadows?" My throat burned the way it always does when I'm trying not to cry. "Did you hear the music at the end? The chords aligned and the curse is over. Did you —"

"Shhhh," Mama cooed against my hair. "I don't know what shadows you're talking about. . . ."

I was about to holler across the street to Boone and Toast and tell them to fire up the music! But then Mama tilted my face up so I was looking at her, so she was looking right into my eyes. She said, "I heard *you*. As soon as I heard you start talking, I figured out how to fix the Gallery. I figured out how to fix . . . lots of things. Let me finish this, Felicity, and then . . ."

"And then . . ." I whispered.

"And then we'll talk," she promised. "But first I need to fix this. Alone —"

"I'll keep you company," Cleo said, shuffling up the sidewalk. "Day and Boone said they'd take the kids for ice cream. I'll stay here with you."

Mama finally let go of me and turned back to the Gallery. "I'll be here a while."

Cleo nodded. "That's fine. I got my soap operas set to record. Go on, Felicity. I'll come get y'all when she's ready to unveil the masterpiece."

I was just about to argue when I caught the flicker of a

yellow ribbon out of the corner of my eye. I glanced across the road to Abigail Honeycutt's bench.

"Florentine!"

I must have looked half crazy as I ran across the street, because Florentine raised one eyebrow. "I don't know what's got into you." She nodded across the street. "Don't know what's got into your mama, either. But I can see already that your mother ain't talented. She is gifted. There's a difference. You see? By the time she's done, that wall's gonna be something special."

"Don't I know it," I said. "And speaking of special things . . ." I took the locket off my neck. I could hear it chiming, even as I closed my hand around it. "Jewell Pickett told me about your people. Did you know we had some history in common?"

"Yeah, I figured it out." Florentine nodded. "I figure everybody's got history in common if you go back far enough. A curse ain't such a great thing to have in common, though, so I didn't bring it up."

"We're not cursed anymore," I said. "Jewell told us Isabella took something that didn't belong to her and left a perfect memory in its place. She says that's what you came here looking for. I don't think you have to look any further. I think this is Isabella Thistle's perfect memory."

I'd never seen Florentine's eyes shine like they did when I dropped that cold locket into her hand. Florentine locked her fingers around it. And I locked my hand around her hand. The locket made her finger bones cold.

"The story's too long to tell right now," I said quickly. "But the music made it open."

"How 'bout that . . ." Florentine's voice crackled.

"When you open that locket, you'll see something spindiddly."

Florentine lifted her fingers, one at a time, and stared down at her reflection in the locket. I figured she'd want to be alone when she saw Isabella's memory for the first time, so I stood and began to make my way back toward the Jalapeño. My chest felt funny without the locket pressed against it. It was just a pendant, just a tacky little snicker of magic that weighed next to nothing, but it was strange not carrying it. That reminded me.

"Florentine," I turned and said. "Why don't you let me get rid of those burdens for you? If you're ready to put them down, I mean."

At first, I thought Florentine might just keep the burdens with her. She'd been packing them around for so long, I knew it'd be hard to let them go. But then, very slowly, she shrugged off the strap around her shoulder and nodded to me. When I reached for the bag, her bony fingers clutched my wrist.

"Let me take them," I whispered. "Enjoy your perfect memory."

The Pickled Jalapeño was full of happy chatter as Day drove us toward the Dreamery Creamery. He turned on the radio and turned up the volume of a Bob Dylan song about a tambourine man. Boone and Toast both sang along and plucked their instruments. Frannie Jo dozed against my side. On my other side sat Jonah, nervously wringing his hands. "Go ahead," he whispered. "Open the bag."

"What if I set those burdens loose in the van?" I whispered back. "That's worse than spiders. Who knows what kind of magic she's got packed up in here?"

Jonah shrugged. "Only one way to find out."

I pulled back the flap and held the bag as far away from me as I could. Slowly, I reached down inside. "It's probably gonna bite my hand off. . . ."

"Is it magic you feel?" Jonah asked.

"No," I said. I pushed the bag open wide to make sure I wasn't imagining things. "It's just . . . old jars." Two old jars, to be exact. Jars as dark as midnight on the inside.

I handed one to Jonah. I wiped the dust off the other one and tried to open it, but the lid wouldn't budge. I held it so close to my face that my eyelashes fluttered against the glass. But all I could see was murky, dusty nothing.

"Nothing rattling around in it," Jonah said. He held the jar up to his ear. "No sound of any kind."

I turned the jar around, carefully examining it. That's when I noticed a yellowed note taped, and retaped, to the front of the jar. The words on the paper were scrawled so small and so fine that I had to lean in close again to read them. "This jar's got a riddle on it, Jonah."

"Mine does, too!" Jonah said. "And look! It's the same as yours!"

I snuck and took to do some good,
To make a way
For peace to find
Its silent, shadowed simple way
Back to the place it left behind.
O restless dreamer, don't despair.
There is still magic in the air.

"Felicity," Jonah whispered. "Look who wrote the riddle. . . ."

My heart fluttered hummingbird fast when I saw the handwriting underneath:

I. Thistle
September 15, 1910

"I don't know what you've got planned this early, Felicity Pickle." Aunt Cleo drew on her cigarette. She wheezed a puff of smoke. "But I've been awake nearly twenty-four hours, so this better be worth it. Else I'll be in a bad mood all day long."

The sky was still dark when my family piled in the Pickled Jalapeño again. Cleo still had curlers dangling from her hair. Mama sat in the front seat. She didn't put up much fuss over Cleo driving. Mama had been so quiet all morning. I knew she was probably just tired from working on the Gallery all night. But she seemed almost peaceful, too. Or maybe I just wanted her to seem peaceful. We still hadn't had a chance to talk about the Threadbare curse, or the dancing shadows. The plastic grocery bags full of our worldly possessions were still packed up all bulgy and full, propped beside Aunt Cleo's door. But we'd already done our packing before the Duel. So maybe Mama just hadn't had time to unpack. That's what I hoped.

I wished I could see some words close to Mama and maybe I could get a hint of what she was thinking about. But I couldn't see a thing. Frannie Jo called dibs on the second seat so she could keep on sleeping. Biscuit had the same thing in mind, apparently. Boone and I sat in the way-back with his banjo.

Boone yawned and put his arm around the back of the seat. He said, "Care to divulge what this little road trip is all about?"

"Not yet." I shook my head. "You'll see when we get there. And when I tell you, you play 'Fair and Tender Ladies' again. Got it?"

"Got it." Boone ruffled his hand through his shaggy blond hair. "But just so you know, no song I play's going to sound good this early. Why couldn't we play later? After dark?"

"Because I couldn't wait till then," I said. The base of the sky was turning orange and pale pink. I figure that was the sun's way of yawning and stretching before it puts its hands on the hills and pushes on up into the sky.

Mama rolled down her window so we could hear the sounds of a mountain morning: wind and birdsong and the *per-clunk*, *per-clunk* of the Pickled Jalapeño.

"The Pickled Jalapeño's heart is beating fast this morning." Frannie Jo said, yawning. "Felicity must be taking us somewhere good."

"I wish Felicity would have waited till sunset," said Boone.

"Amen," Cleo coughed.

"Not me," Mama sighed. "I'd rather go with the sunrise. And I would have dragged everybody out of bed this early, anyway, if Felicity hadn't done it. I can't wait for you to see the Gallery."

Boone scratched his scruffy jaw. "You figured out what it was missing?"

Mama nodded. "I did. I absolutely did." I couldn't see much of her face; it was turned toward the dip-dyed sky. But I could tell by the sound of her voice that she was smiling. *Sunrise* is a good word to smile over.

"I don't like how stories always end with folks riding off into a sunset," Mama said. "I've never cared for that. I'd rather ride all the way to the end and see that there's a sunrise still waiting for me. Morning in my eyes, stars at my back."

When Cleo swerved the Jalapeño onto Main Street, the wind carried all sorts of smells through the open windows: The smell of autumn and cool wind and rain. The smell of coffee brewing in somebody's kitchen. Bacon frying on somebody's stove. I never thought there'd be much to see or hear or smell before the sun came up, but I was wrong. I liked watching Midnight Gulch come awake.

Songbirds swooped through the trees. Lights flickered on in the little square windows of the houses we passed. Somebody was probably taking a shower and somebody was slapping SNOOZE on their alarm clock and somebody was making a to-do list for the day.

I had one more thing to do. The curse was broken already. But Florentine's burdens were in my arms now. I wanted to lay them down for good, put them someplace where nobody could pick them back up. I can't see much good in carrying regrets around like keepsakes. That's why I didn't just chuck the jars into Cleo's recycle bin. Florentine laid the burdens down. I planned to turn them loose, for good.

I clutched Florentine's bag tight against my side. Mama must have heard the jars clink, because she turned around and her forehead wrinkled.

"Why'd you bring that?" she asked. "What'd she keep in that satchel anyhow?"

"You'll see," I said.

Mama shook her blond hair away from her face. "I don't know if I wanna see. . . ."

Aunt Cleo sneezed. Then she cussed.

"Cleo!" Mama yelled.

But Cleo hollered, "Felicity!"

"Ma'am?"

She glared at me in the rearview mirror. The skin around her eyes was extra creased and puffy. "Why you bringing them nasty old jars out to the Gallery?"

"That's what I just asked!" Mama said. "Felicity says we'll see!"

"Oh, mercy," Cleo sighed. "Please tell me those jars don't have anything to do with us."

"I don't think so," I said. "Not really. This is more of a symbolic observance."

298

"A *what*?"

"I think it's probably a snicker of magic."

"I knew I shouldn't have got outta bed for this." Cleo cranked the steering wheel and parked us on Second Street, near the Gallery.

Midnight Gulch was still quiet when we climbed out of the van. The sun was rising, reflecting off the puddles in the road. The whole world looked golden that morning, as if there were a big light inside of Midnight Gulch that nobody could turn out, not even the night.

Good magic, I thought. And as I thought it, three words fell down from the sky, parachute shaped:

Magic

BELIEVE

THREADBARE

"This is going to be a good day," I whispered.

"What are the Picketts doing here?" Mama waved.

Jonah and his mom were waiting at Abigail Honeycutt's bench.

"I don't know what these two are up to," Jewell said. "I'm almost afraid to find out."

"Not me!" Ramblin' Rose came clomping down the sidewalk, her pajamas tucked into her cowboy boots. "I trust these two with all my heart. I sure do."

"Felicity." Mama looked down at me with the sort of stare insinuating I might be in trouble. "Why did you get Miss Walker out of bed so early? You better have a good reason."

"I do!" I said. I slung Florentine's traveling bag down onto the sidewalk. "Trust me."

"Whoa . . ." Florentine said as she walked up behind us. I thought she might be wondering what in the world I was doing with her magical jars. But Florentine wasn't looking at me, she was looking at the Gallery.

I hadn't even looked at Mama's painting yet. But what I saw was even more wonderful than I'd imagined it to be. I knew Mama was painting a landscape of Midnight Gulch, the mountains, the river, the tall pine trees that stood all across town. But I didn't know she was painting the people. People I knew, and people I'd never seen, filled up all the land space.

"Look at those faces," Florentine sighed, stepping closer to the wall. She pointed to the painted likeness of Ramblin' Rose — red dress and cowboy boots and silver hair falling in curlicues around her face. Rosie's smile was spot-on perfect.

"She even painted the roses on Rose's boots!" Jonah laughed. "And there's Oliver, and Elvis . . . and Team Pickett!"

Cleo snorted. "There's Charlie Sue Hancock. Ha!" She nudged me with her elbow. "Bet that's the only picture Charlie Sue's ever shown up in."

"And there's you," I said to Florentine. Mama had painted Florentine sitting under a tall apple tree, reading a book. "She didn't paint your burdens."

"She knows I put those down for good." Florentine

glanced down at her traveling bag. "Why are *you* carrying 'em around?"

Before I could explain, Boone rested his hand on my shoulder. "Did you see how she painted us, Felicity?"

He pointed to the corner of the building. And there we were. All of us.

"Holly Beth!" Cleo said as she stomped over toward our likenesses. "You gave me a different hairstyle!"

Had she ever. Mama had given Cleo a cooler hairdo than I'd ever seen my aunt actually wear — but she'd captured everything else perfectly: the blue in Cleo's eyes, the kindness in her face. Cleo had a hedgehog quilt wrapped around her shoulders.

Boone was beside Cleo, playing his banjo with his head tilted back. She'd painted him singing. She'd painted him exactly right, all the way down to his cowboy boots.

Frannie Jo was tight against Mama's leg, her eyes big and blue and full of trust and a little bit of mischief, too. *Factofabulous* Frannie Jo.

Mama painted herself exactly right, too — slender and small, with messy, paint-streaked hair. She had the beginning of a smile on her face. Mama was good at seeing herself exactly the way she was: no more, no less.

And then she'd painted me. I'm kneeled down on the ground, hugging Biscuit close to me, and Biscuit and me both have smiles on our faces. My red hair is falling all around my shoulders. My freckles are extra sparkly.

"I figured out what was missing from Midnight Gulch," Mama said softly as she walked up beside me. "Us."

I looked up into her face, squinting against the morning sun. The light spilled down over her shoulders. She squeezed my hand, and I squeezed her hand back and I decided to remember that moment, forever and always. Because that's when I realized that it's possible to have a happy ending, even if the ending isn't what you imagined. I still missed Roger Pickle. I was still hurt that he hadn't come back to us. But I didn't feel like my family was in pieces anymore. We might never look like a normal family, but I didn't mind. *Normal* was never one of my favorite words anyway. I glanced up at the painted faces of all the people I'd come to know, and wanted to know. Home isn't just a house or a city or a place; home is what happens when you're brave enough to love people.

"Hey!" Boone shielded his eyes from the light as he looked toward the painted sky. "You painted the Threadbare balloon! Spindiddly detail, Holly."

"That reminds me," I said as I stepped back from Mama and slung Florentine's bag off my shoulders. "I've got an idea, and it's going to sound silly, but you need to trust me."

Jonah was by my side in a flash. "I trust you."

"You're the only one." I smiled. I pulled one of Florentine's jars out of the bag and passed it to the Beedle. "Wait till I tell you before you open it."

And then I stood up tall and yelled, "Everybody stand over here in a line, facing the Gallery."

"Felicity," Mama sighed. "What on earth . . ."

"Boone," I said. "And Miss Walker . . . you two play that song together. 'Fair and Tender Ladies.' Boone, you can sing the words, too, if you want."

Rosie Walker nodded to Boone. "You start us off, young man."

Boone pulled the banjo across his heart. He strummed the tune alone for the first few bars, but then Miss Rosie joined in with her guitar.

"Nothing's happening," Jonah whispered.

"Give it a second," I said.

The wind-chime wind rolled down Main Street, whipping through my hair. The jar in my hand began to rattle.

"Now?" Jonah asked.

"Almost . . ." I said.

"Felicity!" Cleo hollered. "Do not open that infernal jar! Who knows what diseases and dirt and critters might come spilling out!"

Boone sang out the first lyric, loud and clear and beautiful.

"Now try," I said to Jonah. The lids on both our jars twisted as easy as if we'd just put them on.

We got them open at the same time and held them out. Sure enough, two tall shadows spilled out onto the pavement.

"Oh, this can't be good . . ." Cleo said. Everybody else was too dumbstruck to say much of anything.

The long and shapeless shadows stretched out farther, and farther, until they were on the Gallery wall. Then the shadows settled into the shapes of two men, both lanky and tall.

"Hey-yo," said Oliver Weatherly, who'd come to stand behind all of us. "If that don't beat all . . ."

As we watched the Gallery, the two shadows wandered around in the painting as though they were looking for something. Or someone. Finally, the shadows spun around and faced each other. They didn't move for a time. And then one shadow opened up his arms. And the other shadow ran into those arms and held on tight.

I suppose there's no way of knowing which shadow belonged to which brother. There's no way to tell which shadow reached first. I guess it doesn't matter who reached first, though. What matters is that one of them reached out. What matters is that the other one held on.

We watched as the shadows climbed into the painted tree, then jumped up into the hot air balloon my mama had painted.

Boone played the music faster; the music sounded happy now, even though the words were still sad.

Bittersweet, a ribbon of a word, came drifting off the edge of Rosie's guitar.

As Boone and Rosie played, the painted balloon sailed back and forth across the wall.

The shadows waved at us. We all waved back.

And then the balloon disappeared off the wall completely. We watched its shadow slide across the pavement, all the way down Main Street. And then it was gone.

We all stared at the sky so long that we startled when Cleo said, "Mercy! Something else is moving up there!"

"That's Felicity's tattoo," Frannie said matter-of-factly.

"Felicity's *what?*" Mama yelled.

Oliver laughed out loud. "I'll be! There's my bird roosting on your wall. Hope's coming down, y'all!"

But Oliver was wrong. Instead of coming down, hope pulled up in a big Greyhound bus. And when the air brake puffed and the bus pulled out again, a tall man in a camouflage uniform was standing on the pavement, a thick duffel slung around his back.

Jonah gasped, "Dad?"

Jewell looked at her son first, then she looked back across the street. Then all three of them were moving toward each other, meeting in the middle. I heard the sound of three hearts colliding: a sob, then a ripple of happy laughter, then a whispered *hallelujah*.

The shadows of all three of them, holding on to each other, stretched out on the sidewalk. If I was a shadow catcher like Isabella Thistle, I'd have stolen those shadows, just so the Picketts would always remember that day. Just so we all would.

I caught a sudden movement in the corner of my eye and turned in time to see Florentine running toward the bus. "Hold on!" she yelled.

The bus lurched to a stop right at the edge of Second Street.

"Homeward bound!" Florentine yelled, waving her hands in the air.

"You're leaving?" I yelled, running up behind her. Florentine motioned to the bus driver to give her a minute. Then she smiled down at me and slung one skinny arm around my shoulders.

"I got some things to make right myself." She reached for the golden locket around her neck.

I smiled up at her. "You're off to find Waylon?"

"I reckon I am."

"You don't have to wander anymore, either," I told her. "Wherever you go, you can settle down if you want."

Florentine nodded, like she was considering my words. "I'm going to find Waylon. That's the first thing I'll do. But the truth is — I don't feel cursed to wander, Felicity. I feel blessed to wander, as long as I got somebody I love wandering with me. You might feel that someday, maybe. But I don't blame you for wanting to be here, either. We all need a place to start out. Might as well start out at home, right?" She smiled and shook her head as she glanced over at Jonah's family. "Tell that Honeybee I said good-bye."

Florentine boarded the same bus that had just brought Jonah's dad into town. She waved good-bye from the window and I waved back. It's so weird how life is so full of moving around — people coming and going, people passing by each other all day long. You never know which person's going to steal your heart. You never know which place is going to settle your soul. All you can do is look. And hope. And believe.

Oliver Weatherly invited us all to his house for Charlie Sue's chocolate pancakes and a side of Blackberry Sunrise.

"Can we go home after that?" I asked Mama.

And she leaned down and kissed the top of my head and said the most wonderful words: "We are home, Felicity."

It was the sweetest day.

EPILOGUE

In the days after the Duel, Midnight Gulch became a famous place. Oliver Weatherly paid for a fancy new sign:

MIDNIGHT GULCH, TENNESSEE
a magical place to call home

Mama became the director of the new community arts center. Then she helped Aunt Cleo launch her quilting business. Mama even did up the business cards:

Cleopatra Glorietta Harness Grissom
Patch it. Mend it. Stitch it back together.

Hedgehog quilts are back in demand, so Cleo's a busy woman. Mama rented us an apartment across from Aunt Cleo's so we could run over and pester her whenever we wanted.

Since the shadow incident in the auditorium, tourists have flocked to Midnight Gulch again to hear the story of the Brothers Threadbare. Day Grissom converted an old bus to shuttle tourists to all the pertinent historic locations. The last stop on the tour is always the Gallery.

Some days, the painted balloon is there. Sometimes the balloon is big, up close. And sometimes the balloon is tiny, hovering up in the corner. Sometimes there is no balloon at all.

"They repaint it every night when the tourists leave," somebody says.

"It's a trick," somebody else says with a shrug.

"It's a phony."

"Those are just stories."

But my favorite response is this: "Why can't my town be this way?"

Because I'm convinced Midnight Gulch can't be the only magical town in the world. I bet there's a snicker of magic on every street, in every old building, every broken heart, every word of a story. Maybe it's hidden away and you need to look harder for it. Or maybe the magic is right there, right in front of you, and all you have to do is believe.

* ◇ 　* ◇ 　* ◇ *

Miss Divinity Lawson is humming a song while she grades our spelling tests. She decided to teach class outside today, because she wanted us to feel the October sunshine against our skin. The wind is cool now and the leaves are red and yellow and rust colored.

We're scattered around in a circle on the playground, molding clay planets while Miss Lawson works. She's whistling a tune that I recognize; it's the song Boone sings in front of the Gallery every Wednesday afternoon. The two of them are spending more time together these days. I owe the Beedle for that. The Beedle helped me get those two together.

I can't even count all the good things that have happened to me in Midnight Gulch thanks to that do-good-pumpernickel-Beedle-best-friend of mine. Jonah is sitting beside me. He finished his planet a long time ago. The pages of his newspaper are fluttering in the autumn wind.

Miss Lawson starts tapping her foot. With every *click-de-click*, I see new words rise up off the dusty ground:
Sunshine dress
Spinning
Lilies
Blooming
Hands hold
Hearts fold
The words all float up toward the sky. I decide to capture them all, every last one of them. I put down the clay planet I've been shaping and I pick up my blue book to catch a poem.

Today I'll wear a dress made of sunlight,
I'll spin like the lilies,

I'll bloom like the stars.
Hands hold,
Hearts fold,
Under my thumbprint sky.

I pick my planet back up off the ground. I write *hope* across the clay sea.

"Felicity," Jonah breathes.

I look up, but Jonah's not looking at me. He's looking straight ahead and his eyes are wide like somebody yelled *Surprise! Happy Birthday!* But it's not Jonah's birthday and nobody is hollering anything. Nobody's talking at all. They're all looking in the same direction — out toward the tall-grass fields rolling into the mountains, the place where Midnight Gulch rolls on into forever.

"Do you see it?" Jonah whispers.

I look just in time to see it coming: the shadow of a hot air balloon drifting slowly down the mountains, over the hills, and across the field where we're sitting. No matter how often we see the shadow, we tremble when it passes over. We will never stop looking for it.

Yes, my heart sings out. *Yes. Yes. Yes!*

The end
Swan song
Finale
Done

ACKNOWLEDGMENTS

My amazing agent, Suzie Townsend, is smart, passionate, and a dream advocate. She's capable of magic, and I'm so blessed to be working with her. I'm also indebted to the rest of the talented team at New Leaf Literary: Joanna Volpe, Kathleen Ortiz, Pouya Shahbazian, Danielle Barthel, and Jaida Temperly.

One of my favorite Blackberry Sunrise memories will always be the day my lovely editor, Mallory Kass, first called to chat about this book. She always understood the heart of this story, and helped me realize its full potential. I'm bowled over by her talent, patience, kindness, and enthusiasm.

I'm grateful to everyone at Scholastic who added their own snicker of magic to this journey, particularly Lori Benton, Tracy van Straaten, Bess Braswell, Lizette Serrano, Sheila Marie Everett, Nina Goffi, Starr Baer, and David Levithan. Seeing a Scholastic tattoo on my book's spine still seems too wonderful to be real. Working with all of you is a dream come true.

Like Felicity Pickle, I've had some A+ teachers who've exposed me to great books and encouraged me to write. I'm particularly grateful to John Watson, Pat Sexton, Anna Hull, Gary Sexton, Bev Olert, Doug Renalds, Sheridan Barker, Ellen Millsaps, Jennifer Hall, and, most especially, Susan Underwood.

Sarah Wylie read this story in its early stages, squealed over Jonah Pickett, and cheered me on. She's absurdly talented and kind, and her feedback meant the world to me. The wicked-talented Jenny B. Jones also bravely read an early version of this story. I don't know what I'd do without her advice, insight, and encouragement. I'm also grateful to Sarah Keith, Melanie Garrett, and Hannah Jones, who frequently take it upon themselves to drag me out of my house for fresh air, concerts, cheese fries, and/or cupcakes. I have the most splendiferous friends in the world.

The word *love* doesn't seem heavy enough to describe how I feel about my family. They're a haven for my wandering heart. My grandparents — Orangie, John, Virgil, and Jean — were my safe place and my favorite storytellers. They left me with a heart full of sweet memories. Gene and Harriet Bond, whom I love like grandparents, have cheered me on through this and countless other crazy endeavors. My mom, Elaine, is my first reader, and best friend. My dad, Jim, is my biggest cheerleader and my anchor. Bridgett and Ed have the most marvelous back porch for making up stories (and they don't seem to mind when I drink all their coffee). Andy and Erin Asbury are the most spindiddly people in the world. They make every day magical, and I love being their aunt. My brother, Chase, is lion-hearted, fearless, and fun. I want to be just like him when I grow up. My dog, Biscuit, snuggled beside me through every revision. Above all, I'm grateful to God for always turning my heart toward hope.

And even though I'm quite certain they'll never see this, I would be remiss not to thank my favorite band, The Avett Brothers, whose magical, marvelous music kickstarted this whole adventure for me. And it has been the sweetest adventure.

Factofabulous: Some dreams really do come true.

NICKEL FIERCE VIOLET PUMPERNIC
BELIEVE
Everlasting Kalamazoo Mag
ULOUS Popsicle BE
Everlasting SNICKERDOODLE
Dragonfly HOPE Wonder
Secret Apple Fritter KALEIDOSCOPE Zippity
Crunch HOPE
LENDIFEROUS FACTOFABULOUS HICC
VIOLET Enchanting Plumb Ado
Sunrise WHIMSY FIERCE
Dragonfly SNICKERDOODLE HOPE
ROUS BITTERSWEET VIOLET
CCUP Secret
Magical Plumb Adorable SPINDIDD
Crunch I
BELIEVE Wonder Rebel
OODLE STONEBERRY Everlasting SPLEN
Secret I LOVE YOU Magnolia Apple Fritt
HOPE Enchanting SERENDIPITY
bel HICCUP SPINDI

PUMPERNICKEL

KEEPER

KALEIDOSCOPE

P

Magical

Magnolia

BELIEVE

Rebel

Kalamazoo

FAC

RDOODLE STONEBERRY

WHIMSY

Plumb

E

Zippity

I LOVE YOU

Magnolia

KALEIDOS

HOPE

Enchanting

Wonder

Zip

SERENDIPITY

LOUS HICCUP

SPINDIDDLY

Plumb Ad

Adorable

BISCUIT

Apple Fritter

Secret

SPLE

nous

WHIMSY

Zippity

Everlasti

Crunch

UMPERNICKEL

Magnolia

FIERCE VIOLET

RY HOPE I LOVE YOU

Enchanting

Popsi

Wonder

Kalamazoo

BITTERSWEET SNI

ALEIDOSCOPE WHIMSY

Magical

Wonder

ty

BELIEVE

Crunch

SNICKERDOODLE

KALEIDO

YOU

Enchanting

Secret

Plumb Adora